Naked Vengeance

Praise for Sophia Rae's *Naked Vengeance*

"You will not be disappointed in this book NAKED VENGEANCE is a great suspense thriller."

~ *Billie Jo, Romance Junkies*

"Naked Vengeance is a skillfully crafted mystery, that forces the reader to the end in record time."

~ *Christine, Simply Romance Reviews*

Naked Vengeance

Sophia Rae

A Samhain Publishing, Ltd. publication.

Samhain Publishing, Ltd.
577 Mulberry Street, Suite 1520
Macon, GA 31201
www.samhainpublishing.com

Naked Vengeance
Copyright © 2009 by Sophia Rae
Print ISBN: 978-1-60504-110-0
Digital ISBN: 1-59998-909-3

Editing by Eve Joyce
Cover by Scott Carpenter

This book is a work of fiction. The names, characters, places, and incidents are products of the writer's imagination or have been used fictitiously and are not to be construed as real. Any resemblance to persons, living or dead, actual events, locale or organizations is entirely coincidental.

All Rights Are Reserved. No part of this book may be used or reproduced in any manner whatsoever without written permission, except in the case of brief quotations embodied in critical articles and reviews.

First Samhain Publishing, Ltd. electronic publication: April 2008
First Samhain Publishing, Ltd. print publication: February 2009

Dedication

To Lora Leigh. Thanks for all the encouragement and friendship. I always look forward to our dinner dates. Love ya!

Acknowledgements

To the dancers and costume designers who offered advice and input on a world I knew nothing about. Thanks for sharing some of your secrets, ladies!

Chapter One

She knew he watched her. Watched the way she worked the stage, the pole and the audience. If he came for her tonight, she'd be ready—to kill or to die.

No matter the outcome, the revenge would be sweet.

Her scantily clad body slithered through the velvety red curtain as the seductive beat of the music picked up its rhythm. The policeman's jacket she wore hugged her every curve, stopping just under the swell of her ass.

As she stepped out into the lights, she kept her cop's hat pulled down to shade her face. The men didn't care what her face looked like, only her body. And with her rigorous two-hour workout each day, she had a hell of a body.

With legs spread wide, she allowed her hips to pump back and forth to the music's sensual beat. One hand remained on the bill of her hat while the other worked the buttons of her jacket, one by one by one.

"Yeah, take it off, honey!"

Her hands were a little shakier than she would've liked, but she kept telling herself this was just like any other night on the stage. The unwelcome nerves and humiliation were a small price to pay for vengeance.

Between the colored lights blinding her and the choking atmosphere of cigarette smoke, she couldn't make out any particular face. Was he sitting close to the stage? In the back by the bar? At a table in the corner nursing a drink?

Regardless of where he was, he was no doubt plotting and calculating his next move.

Just as the music hit its climactic point, she ripped off her jacket to reveal a sheer black demi bra and matching thong. Hoots and hollers roared in her ears, and she only prayed all her hard work and sacrifices would pay off.

She had to admit, though, a small piece deep down inside her actually got into this routine. The power of knowing she had control over the room, over the men, made the adrenaline rush through her veins.

As the music soared, she wrapped a leg around the tall, silver pole and rolled her body against the cool steel. At this moment in time, every man in the room fantasized about her.

How could she not enjoy the attention? What woman, if she was totally honest, wouldn't want to be desired?

With her long, toned leg still wrapped around the pole, she arched her back, giving the paying customers a view of her perky, well-rounded chest. She unwrapped herself and eased her way around the edge of the stage on her hands and knees to allow the sweaty dollar bills to be stuffed into her G-string. Old men, young men, fat or skinny—they all loved a woman wearing scraps of sheer material while crawling around within inches of their grasp.

Money clung to her damp body as she slinked back off stage just the way she'd come in, whistles and shouts following her. Behind the curtain, the other girls gave her a pat on the back and told her she'd performed another great routine…for a newbie.

The newbie, who'd danced as Corporal Nastee, had done another dance without a flaw. As she accepted a short, silky black robe from a fellow stripper, she pulled the cash out and counted it. Seventy-three dollars for a two-minute routine. Not bad.

She made her way down the short concrete hall toward the back of the club. Girls rushed behind the scenes as they pulled on leather and silk, teased their hair, shimmered their cleavage with powder, and mastered a seductive walk on four-inch stilettos. Now seated at her own dressing table, she proceeded to remove the pound of make-up she'd applied only twenty minutes before.

Focused on wiping off the layers of thick black mascara and charcoal liner, she ignored the man who'd stepped inside the dressing room from the back alley. A man who'd turned the other ladies' heads as soon as he stepped through the "Employees Only" door. A man who looked like he had a mission to accomplish. A man who had his eye on her.

"Eve."

If a heart could actually stop beating, Eve believed hers did for a split second at the sound of her name coming from the total stranger's mouth.

Her eyes shifted and locked onto her mirror, but she didn't turn to answer. She hoped whoever it was would go away—any slip-up now could be detrimental...or deadly.

"My name ain't Eve, but you can call me anything you want, darlin'," a sexy blonde clad in only gold body glitter said as she draped a bare arm over the stranger's shoulders.

He pried himself loose without taking his eyes off Eve. She sat perfectly still at her table, praying he would just leave if she didn't respond. She didn't know who this man was, but he looked downright dangerous. Had someone figured her out? Could this be the cold-blooded killer she'd hunted for so long?

Tall, at least six-three, with inky hair and mesmerizing coal-like eyes beneath black brows. Being a warm-blooded woman, it would be impossible not to notice him.

The breadth of his shoulders filled out his basic black T-shirt to the limit and well-worn jeans hugged his long legs. No doubt the man could be intoxicating and if he didn't leave soon, she had a feeling there'd be a fight amongst the women.

"You need to come with me."

It wasn't a request. He hadn't budged an inch since he stepped inside the door; not even his eyes had shifted around to take in all the nearly naked women strutting about. This man was on a mission.

"I'm sorry, honey, I don't do private parties," she answered in her sweetest fake-Southern voice.

The instant he took a step toward her, her heart picked up its pace. But before she could decide whether to run or stay, fate took over and filled the room with darkness.

Screams erupted from the women just before total chaos filled the dressing area at the sound of gunshots. A large, rough hand wrapped around Eve's biceps, pulled her up from her stool and dragged her to the back of the room. He pushed her ahead of him, using his body as a shield while he ushered her out the building.

"Let go of me!" She doubted he could hear her over the screaming.

Eve nearly fell down the small, concrete step just outside the back door. The dim overhead alley light allowed her to see once again.

"Take your hand off me," she spit out.

Without releasing her, he spun her around to face him. "That's a nice way to say thanks to someone who just saved your life."

Eve tugged her arm free and stepped back, barely managing to stay upright on the uneven pavement in her stilettos. "Who are you?"

"A friend."

Eve laughed as she rubbed her arms up and down the silky robe. "Well, friend, why don't you go back in there and tell your other *friends* to stop shooting?"

"They aren't my friends."

"Really? Well, everything was fine and dandy until you showed up. I still have another dance to do. Maybe you should try entering the front door like all the other men. But I suggest taking that shoulder holster off and leaving it and your gun in your car. You'll scare the other women, not to mention make those big, burly bouncers as mad as pit bulls."

Now that she stood so close to him, she could make out his face. And what a face he had. Even with the piss-poor light, she could see the man had strong lines with a square jaw and thin lips—no doubt due to anger. Dark eyes surrounded by darker lashes, with a small scar running through his right brow. From this angle, a shadow cast over a portion of his face, making him all the more mysterious.

Even with her neck-breaking high heels on, he still had a good five inches on her, so he loomed over her with ease. If he thought he could intimidate her, he had another thing coming. With the mood she had been in lately, he'd be better off getting the hell out of her way.

"I've been hired to protect you."

Eve ignored the prickle on the back of her neck. "By who?"

The intriguing stranger showed no emotion. "The person wants to remain anonymous."

Could this all be a ploy? Did this man really know her true identity and her plans? She sincerely doubted it, seeing as how she'd been so careful not to tell anybody at all her whereabouts and she'd used only her real first name, making up her last.

On the other hand, what if he worked for the man she'd been waiting for? What if this dangerous stranger could lead her to the killer?

Eve eyed him as the questions and possibilities whirled in her head. "Why should I believe you when I don't even know you?"

"It's up to you whether you want to believe me or not," he said with a cockiness to his slow Southern drawl. "I've been paid to do a job and I intend to do it."

Eve's chin came up in defiance. "Well, you can do what you want, but I have to get back inside before I get fired."

Eve turned, teetering on one heel, but before she could move away from the irksome yet captivating stranger, a shot sounded through the alley. The deafening pop had her looking back over her shoulder at her "protector".

The stranger grabbed her arm and hauled her behind an overloaded dumpster. "Stay down. I'm about to save your ass again, honey."

He pulled a Glock from the leather shoulder holster and fired around the metal garbage bin. Seeing as how she was unarmed, Eve kept her head down, her arms up by her face. She would not die in the back of some dingy alley beside a rank dumpster with a man who looked like a god, acted like Rambo and could very well just be the devil in disguise. She had a job to do and she intended to see it through to the end—just as soon as she got out of this little predicament. Allowing this stranger, who might or might not be on her side, to take control of this situation was all she could do, considering she was half-dressed and without her own gun.

"That should do it." He shoved his gun back into his holster.

"Did you kill him?"

He extended his hand, reaching for her. "Nah, just nicked him. Amateur wouldn't have hit us if we stood right in front of him. You're safe now."

Eve ignored his outstretched hand and rolled her eyes at his stand-behind-me-little-lady attitude. Damn, she hated being protected, especially by a stranger.

She came to her feet now that the fight seemed to be over. The deep V in her robe had fallen open and before she could cinch it back together, she caught him taking a good, long look at her breasts, still only covered by the sheer black bra.

"I already told you once, I don't do private parties. I don't do peep shows either."

He shrugged. "I don't do strippers, so we're on the same page. But that doesn't mean I'm not a man. If you go around exposed like that, I can't help but look."

"Gosh, what was I thinking coming out here in only a robe? I forgot to grab my jeans and T-shirt before you so rudely pulled me from my dressing area."

He laughed and ran a hand down his face. "Are you really that stupid? I saved you. What don't you understand about that?"

Fury bubbled up through her and before she knew it, her fist connected with the side of his smooth face. He jerked back as his hand came up to rub the red spot she'd made.

He straightened himself and grinned. "You pack an impressive punch, but I was looking for something a little along the lines of gratitude."

Eve wouldn't rub her hand. She refused to give him the satisfaction of knowing how much it hurt when she connected with his stone-like jaw.

"Gratitude?"

"Do you have to repeat everything I say?"

Eve clenched her fists to keep from hitting him again. "You've said so many idiotic things, I'm just making sure I get it all right."

"I don't lie, sweetheart. Everything I say is the truth."

Eve didn't like the shudder that rippled through her when the word sweetheart slipped through his kissable lips.

Naked Vengeance

Whoa! Did she just think his lips were kissable? More like smackable. Why would her mind betray her like that? She didn't have time for sexual encounters or shenanigans in a back alley with this man. Her mission didn't involve getting sidetracked even for a second. If he worked for the enemy, he was trying his damnedest to keep her out in this ratty alley.

"You've got a pretty eye," he said, eyes roaming over her face.

"Eye?"

"Yeah." He motioned to her right eye. "The one without all that crap piled on it."

"I was in the middle of taking it off to redo it when you barged in." Eve let out a sigh and glanced down the alley. "Look, I'm going back inside."

"You're going to go back in there after all that happened? Not too smart, are you?"

Eve didn't appreciate the way he assumed to know her or her intelligence level. "All my stuff is inside. I need to see what's going on." Eve shrugged. "Maybe with all the commotion, I'll have the rest of the night off."

"I'll wait around to make sure you get home okay."

She resisted the urge to growl. "Actually, it's not okay, but I can hardly stop you."

Eve stalked toward the club door on her skinny heels, not giving a damn that with each step her silky robe shifted in the back. She didn't care what this so called bodyguard thought of her, so it didn't matter that his last impression would be her derrière.

෴

What did she think she was doing? Nick's mind veered off track at the sight of her sweet little ass as it peeked out from underneath the scrap of material she called a robe. His hands ached to grab hold of that firm flesh she teased him with.

The sight of that curvy, seductive woman had been enough to make him forget, momentarily, the last time he'd been in this alley. The scene played over and over in his head. Blood, sirens, mists of rain on his face. And the cries. He'd never forget how they echoed through the dark, damp night. Cries that still came, only this time in his dreams.

By the time his mind jerked back to reality and the job, she had disappeared back into the club. There wasn't a doubt in his mind the club would close for the night due to the shots fired. Also, swarming cops kind of put a damper on the whole ambience of watching a strip show while getting liquored up.

Out of habit, he checked his back again to make sure no surprises lurked in the shadows before heading to his car, which he'd conveniently parked beside Eve's red Jeep Wrangler. His black BMW M3 chirped as he used the keyless remote. He slid in behind the wheel to wait for Eve.

Some might consider him flashy for his pick of vehicles—well, okay, maybe he was flashy. Many people put money into their homes or lavish vacations, but not Nick. Cars all the way, baby.

He'd bought it after the last op, when he'd decided to retire. Only a bodyguard in the business needed an incognito vehicle. That left him out.

Until now.

Beside him, Eve's profile lay in a plain brown manila envelope, a stark contrast to the sleek black leather seats. The useless information wouldn't help him on his mission, as it contained only her name, her previous address and an old phone number. No family listed or significant others. No list of who might want her harmed or for what reason. That would've been too easy.

Going in on a job blind didn't sit well with Nick, a job he didn't even want to begin with. The last time he'd been hired to protect someone...

Fortunately, for his sanity, he had to push that op out of mind in order to focus on this one. Not the past. At the moment his job revolved around Eve Morgan, or whatever alias she used these days. Period. The feisty redhead obviously didn't believe him and didn't want his help, but that wasn't going to be an option. He'd promised a friend and he never went back on a promise.

In no time at all, Eve emerged from the front of the club.

For a second, he didn't recognize her, but the untamed mass of curly hair tipped him off. She'd exchanged her sexy robe for a pair of faded cut-off jean shorts and a red tank top. Nick had a feeling if the woman wore a burlap sack she'd still be sexy as hell.

When her eyes locked onto his through the windshield, Nick simply lifted a hand and waved. She returned the gesture with a one-fingered wave. Nick chuckled as she took off in her Jeep, leaving him to follow behind.

Fifteen minutes later she parked parallel in front of a two-story apartment building. He pulled in behind her and killed the engine. It didn't surprise him that she didn't even look at him as she got out of her car and disappeared inside.

After he locked her worthless profile in his glove box, Nick pulled the gun from his shoulder holster to check his ammo. He'd fired off some rounds back in the alley, but hadn't emptied the clip. He also didn't figure he'd need it anymore this evening, but he wouldn't take any chances until he found out what, or who, he was up against.

Nick walked up the concrete stairs to the front door of Eve's building. He should've known—he needed to be rung in. Yeah, like she'd do that.

He leaned against the chiseled stone entryway and thought back to the picture she made sitting at her make-up table. All that long, curly red hair tousled from her routine, a heart-shaped face with eyes the color of the Caribbean ocean, perfectly shaped cupid mouth. She all but screamed sex and innocence rolled into one erotic package. He'd definitely gotten an eyeful as he waited to get her attention.

Much to Nick's surprise—and his initial reaction—she seemed to have good sense about her. She'd been skeptical when he told her he'd been hired to protect her and shot him a disbelieving look when he wouldn't give up the name. Either she really didn't know why she needed protection or she was a good actress.

Nick pushed off the stone and thanked his lucky stars when a couple emerged from the building. Finally, he could get inside and concentrate on something other than his raging hormones.

"Man, am I glad to see you guys."

The young couple exchanged a look. A look that said, "Do we know him?"

"The wife locked me out and won't ring me up," Nick continued. "I've been standing here for nearly a half hour. Thanks a lot."

Without another word, Nick stepped inside and walked toward the elevator like he'd done it a dozen times in the past. As suspected, her name wasn't listed on the directory, but he'd seen a light on the second floor come on just after she'd entered the building. He hated assuming anything, but he figured the apartment in the far left of the building was hers.

He raced back to the elevator, put a hand on the door and held it open just wide enough to slide in. When the doors opened on the second floor, he took a quick glance to make sure no one saw him. He found Eve's apartment, number 215, at the end of the wide, carpeted hallway.

Should he knock? Just barge in? She wouldn't be happy to see him regardless, so he opted to knock in an attempt to show her he did have manners. Well, some.

The first knock went unanswered.

He knocked a second time.

Again, no answer.

Concern grew and he took all of ten seconds to pick the lock. He shook his head in disgust. Taking the previous year off had made him rusty.

The short, high-pitched scream catapulted Nick's adrenaline. He pulled his gun from his shoulder holster and threw open the door only to find her living room empty. His grasp on the downward-facing gun tightened as he took light, quiet steps farther into her apartment.

To the left of him was a small galley kitchen; to the right, a short hallway. That scream had come from this apartment. Did someone have Eve in her bedroom? Nobody had entered the building while he'd waited outside... That could only mean the intruder had already been in the apartment. Waiting.

Muted footsteps fell on the beige carpet as he crept toward the hall. He followed her floral scent, trying to ignore the sinful things it did to his senses. It only reminded him of the last time he'd gotten side-tracked on a job by a gorgeous woman. That mishap had cost a man his life.

Just as he started to grab for the doorknob, the door flew open and Eve stood before him. Because she wore only a skimpy, white towel, iridescent water droplets on her bare shoulders and anger in her eyes, Nick relaxed.

"What the hell are you doing sneaking around my apartment?" Eve glared. "Did you come in to shoot me?"

"No, I was out in the hall. I knocked twice, but you didn't answer. I started to worry, so I picked your lock, but then you screamed so I drew my gun."

As he holstered his Glock, Nick had a hard time keeping his eyes on hers and not on her damp porcelain skin. One lucky drop of water rolled down her neck, disappearing into the valley between her breasts. Why couldn't he have been called in to protect a sixty-year-old man?

"You *picked* my lock?"

Eve shoved past him to examine her front door, which still stood wide open. She slammed it and whirled back around. With one hand, she held the top of her towel together as she brought up her other hand to point at him.

"You had no right to let yourself in." Pure rage dripped from her voice. "Just because someone supposedly paid you to keep an eye on me doesn't give you permission to invade my privacy, and it sure as hell doesn't give you free rein to snoop around my apartment."

Nick remained in the hall, tucking his thumbs through his belt loops. "What was I supposed to think when you didn't answer my knock and then screamed as if you were hurt?"

Eve's eyes practically shot daggers toward him. "I *was* hurt."

Nick followed his gaze down to the top of her thigh, where she lifted the white towel just enough to expose a purple bruise already forming on her flawless skin.

"What did you do?"

"I slipped and fell," she snapped as she covered her wound back up. "Now, since you're here, uninvited, I want to know who the hell is paying you to break into my apartment. If you don't tell me right now, I'll call the cops and have you arrested for trespassing."

With a shrug, Nick moved into her living room. "I've already told you I can't reveal the person who wants to keep you safe and I've already explained to you why I broke in, so if you want to call the cops, go right ahead."

Eve growled when Nick plopped himself on her couch and smiled. He could practically see the smoke streaming out her ears as she seethed. For some reason, Nick found himself actually enjoying this op. It would be best to make her hate him. The last thing he needed was a woman this sexy and feisty to feel the same sexual attraction he did. So far so good.

"You're not staying." Eve moved to the door. "Take your overactive imagination and your big, manly gun and get out."

Nick remained on the couch even though she'd opened the door, obviously waiting for him to leave. For nearly a whole minute they stared. He had to give her credit; the look he gave her had most men backing down, but not Eve. She held her ground, kept her pointy chin in the air and narrowed her emerald eyes into slits.

"You better shut that door before your neighbors see you," he finally said.

Eve slammed the door for a second time in the span of ten minutes. When she stalked over to where he sat, Nick could see the rapid pulse at the base of her throat. For ridiculous reasons, it pleased him to see the erratic beat just under her pale skin.

Her bare thigh brushed the hand he had dangling over the arm of the sofa. Before his better judgment could take over, he jerked, muttering a curse as he pulled his hand back to safer ground. Now with his fists firmly clenched in his lap, Nick took a moment to push aside the thought of her silken skin and the way she felt against his rough fingers.

Even though his mind had toyed with the idea of touching her, kissing her, having wild, crazy, monkey sex with her, he knew all of those fantasies were not only impossible, but out of the fucking question. Protecting her—from who knew what— had to be the first and only priority in his life right now, a fact he had to keep reminding his pubescent brain and dick.

"If you're trying to piss me off, you've succeeded."

"I wasn't trying," Nick said honestly. "Pissing people off

must come naturally."

"Look, if you want to stay here, I'm going to need more information. Let's start with who sent you." Eve held up a hand to hold him off. "And I don't want to hear the crap about anonymity. This is my life and I want to know what the hell is going on."

"We've been through this several times before. Why do you think I'll suddenly give up the name?"

A slow, sultry smile spread across Eve's full, unpainted lips. She leaned down, loosening her towel just enough to give him a peek of the tops of her pale breasts.

"Because if you don't," she began, "I'll go in my bedroom and get *my* gun. I'm still a little rusty. I'd hate to hit an important part of your anatomy."

Before he could even think his actions through, Nick grabbed hold of Eve's arm and pulled her over the side of the couch and onto his lap. Her towel fell open, her eyes widening in both shock and anger.

When Eve reached to pull her towel back together, Nick grabbed her wrist. "I don't take too kindly to threats."

Eve jerked from his grasp and covered herself. "I don't take kindly to being manhandled. Let me up."

This was wrong. He knew it was wrong but, God help him, he had no control over his body or emotions right now. With the slightest touch, he trailed his fingers up her slender arm, over the curve of her shoulder, down the imaginary line to her chest. In that second her cat-like eyes had gone from angry to aroused, and he had no doubt she could feel his matching response just under her delicate bottom.

When his fingers stopped just above the towel, Eve's breath caught. She might want him to keep exploring, but Nick knew she couldn't want it nearly as much as he did.

Damn it! Now what? He'd started this perverted game and it had backfired. Why wasn't she clawing his eyes out or grabbing him by the balls until he let her go? Why didn't she scream and yell?

Because she couldn't deny this instant attraction either. An attraction he'd hoped had only been one-sided.

"Oh."

The plea drifted from her lips. Only moments ago her voice had been filled with rage, now it sounded almost...willing.

Shit. Shit. Shit.

With all the gentleness he could afford, Nick positioned her towel and eased her off his lap. He came to his feet and stepped off to the side. Distance had to become his new best friend.

From the corner of his eye he could see the hurt and confusion on her face as he stalked to the window—not an easy feat with constricted jeans. Even though he kept his back to her, her uneven breathing echoed in the silent room.

Nick rubbed his fingers against the side of his jeans trying to rid himself of the tingling. Would he ever get that sensation out of his mind? The feel of her off his fingertips? They'd touched for maybe a total of sixty seconds, yet he knew he would feel her for a long time to come.

He had to call Grady. Someone else had to take over, because if his hormones got any more out of control, they could both be in more danger then either bargained for—not just from the unknown perpetrator, but from each other.

"Get out."

Nick cringed at the raspy, yet wounded tone of her voice. "I'm not going anywhere."

"Like hell you aren't," Eve declared. "After that little stunt, you think you're worthy of the check someone's giving you to protect me? So far the only person I've seen that I need protection from is you."

How could he argue with the truth? Even Nick had no idea who or what threatened Eve, but it was damn well time he found out.

When he turned to face her, any passion that had filled her eyes seconds ago had long since gone. Good, her distance would make his job easier until he could get someone else here.

"I think for the time being, until I know more, you should call off from the club," Nick said, trying to get this unbelievable situation under control.

Eve laughed, brushing strands of now-dried crimson curls over her shoulder. "I'm pretty sure I won't be taking any orders from you. You jerked me from my dressing table, I almost got shot, I have no idea who you are or what you really want. You broke into my home and all but felt me up. What would you do if you were me?"

Since her anger seemed to be accelerating, for very valid reasons, Nick took a step back. "Look, it took me a long time to find you. I'm here for your protection. I don't think you know how dangerous that club can be."

"I don't know how dangerous *you* can be," she countered. "I don't even know your damn name."

Nick held his hands up in defense. "My name is Nick Shaffer. As I said before, a mutual friend sent me but I can't say who. He said you were a loner and wouldn't like me hanging around."

"Well, that part's right," she muttered.

"I just want to make sure you're okay while you're working at the club. It can get a little hairy down there sometimes. I figure you can't have too much protection."

Eve crossed her arms over the towel as she eyed him with suspicion. Nick swallowed hard at the innocent gesture that pushed her breasts up, all but spilling over the top of the terrycloth. Her creamy skin still had a pink tint, indicating her water had been too hot.

As far as information went, he couldn't offer very much because he hardly had any facts himself. He knew she wanted answers; so did he, but he had to trust Grady. The head of the FBI wouldn't ask this of him if Eve weren't in real, immediate danger.

Eve let out a laugh. "What are you? A bodyguard?"

"If that's what you want to call it. I just don't want you to be worried."

"Why would I be?"

Nick sank back against the soft leather. "You see, that's what I've been trying to figure out. You didn't scream when the shots started. You didn't even look scared. And you don't seem too concerned that a total stranger has been in your home for a half hour now. Want to tell me why you're so laid back?"

The change came immediately. Eve's eyes darkened, her shoulders straightened, lips thinned. "My father was a cop. I got used to violence and I learned how to take care of myself at an early age. It takes quite a bit to scare me."

Nick nearly shuddered at the tone of her voice and the way she spoke of her father in past tense. He didn't push anymore; he didn't care. Grady could have someone else to replace him within twenty-four hours. Hopefully.

"Tell this *friend* of ours," she went on, "that I do not need a bodyguard. I knew the consequences when I took the job at The Excalibur. I'm still fairly new to this town, but I know where I work is in a bad area. Drugs exchange hands in the club nearly every night. All the other girls warned me about who to steer clear of and who will pay top dollar for a lap dance. So thanks for the help, but the only danger I'm in is having my ass squeezed too tight."

Eve sighed. "I have no idea why I just shared all that with you. Must be all the excitement of the evening that has my mind scrambled."

Could this woman be for real? If she wanted to think the gunshots had to do with drugs, then so be it. She didn't need to know that club was a front for something much more sinister than stripping.

But he knew, all too well. He'd been to that club once before. Memories of that night forced their way back into his head. Nick steeled himself against the guilt and focused on Eve.

"I'll pass your message along to our friend, but I doubt he'll back down. He seemed awfully concerned about you." Nick made his way to the door. "If it's any consolation, I'm not too thrilled about this either. I don't like to baby-sit."

"That's good then, since I'm too old for a baby-sitter."

"Well, that may be, but I'll be calling my friend to see if he can put someone else on this job. I don't think we're very compatible."

Eve rolled her eyes. "Gee, you think?"

"If I can't get someone by tomorrow night, I'll be at the club myself."

"How did you know when I work again?"

With his hand on the doorknob, his tone became dead serious. "I know all I need to know about you at the moment."

"I have one more question." When Nick cocked his head to the side, she stepped forward. "Are you a cop?"

"No."

Eve drew her brows together as if she didn't believe him. "You smell like a cop."

Nick leaned forward, took a whiff inches from her neck and stepped back. "You smell like trouble."

He shut the door behind him. Eve went over and flicked the deadbolt as she rested her forehead against the door, her heart still pounding from Nick's nearness.

Who was this Nick Shaffer? She'd seen the cockiness in his face, heard the arrogance in his voice. Maybe he was nothing to worry about, just a typical man with an over-inflated ego. A quick run of his name through the database would tell her everything she needed to know.

Well, *she* couldn't run his name, but she could have someone at the Bureau run him. Thanks to her suspension, her freedom was somewhat limited—okay, very limited, but maybe Grady would do it for her. Granted he had been the one who'd suspended her, but he'd only done it for her own good. She couldn't fault him; had she been in his shoes, she'd have done the same.

Eve pushed away from the door, pulled her towel off and strode naked back down the short hallway to her room. She had to remain in control of this situation, no matter how this Nick character affected her. Good looks and a cocky personality were nothing she hadn't dealt with before. God knew in her line of work, she'd been surrounded by Alpha males each and every day.

But who had put a bodyguard on her? If Nick was telling the truth, who could this "mutual friend" be? No one knew about her stripping at The Excalibur. Hell, no one knew she was in South Carolina, for that matter. She hadn't opened a checking account in her name or used a credit card. Everything she bought had been from the cash she received from the club.

Including her weekly "paycheck", which was just more under-the-table cash. God, if she weren't undercover she could have that place busted for countless crimes. Fortunately, she'd made up her last name when she'd hired in. Knowing the shady business didn't actually run background checks, she figured she'd be safe.

Eve hung her towel in the bathroom right next to the silky robe she'd worn home from the club. Without bothering with pajamas, she slipped beneath the crisp, cool sheets and pulled them up to her waist. The full moon beamed straight into her bedroom window, casting a pale glow about the room. She watched the blades of the white ceiling fan spin against the darkened ceiling until her eyes went crossed.

As the cool air slid over her bare skin, she wondered how she could finish her job and get Nick out of the picture. She couldn't risk someone blowing her cover. She'd come too far, sacrificed too much to be discovered now.

She'd broken her own rule earlier—never let your defenses down. Boy, had she ever. The second she'd tumbled into his lap, the walls had come crashing down. Goosebumps popped up along her skin as she recalled the way his fingertips had glided over her. She'd never been touched in such a delicate, sensual way. Fortunately, Nick had come to his senses and pushed her away...even though her body had felt neglected.

Eve refused to let herself dwell on Nick and why he'd entered her life. So he knew her name, so what. Obviously he didn't know much else or he would've been more aggressive. Maybe she'd let him stick around. For all she knew he could be working for the other side. This whole "mutual friend" crap could be a strategy to see how much information she knew. If that was the case, she needed to keep her eye on him. That shouldn't be too difficult, just as long as he kept his hands off her.

Eve smiled into the darkness. It would be a shame, she thought. A dangerously sexy man like that working for the enemy... Well, if he did, she'd have to kill him.

Chapter Two

Allison Myers knew she would be sold. She also knew, if she couldn't escape, she wouldn't be the first to be sold under this monster's practiced hands—or the last.

In only two weeks a new girl would be locked into this exact suite, wearing these exact clothes, and this impressive room would more than likely be exciting to the new girl at first. Adorned with exotic house plants, lush white carpet, a rich mahogany king-sized bed draped with gold sheers, and a Jacuzzi tub tucked into the far corner, it was a room any woman would love to call home.

For two months Allison had been treated as a high-class whore. She'd been kept longer than any other girl before her, but only because she gave Roman everything he wanted. *Everything.* As long as he remained happy, Allison remained close to home.

So what the hell had happened?

By the end of next week she'd be sold to the highest bidder, unless she could somehow get out of this living hell. To be shot to death during her escape attempt would be better than sticking around being used and sold to the man with the most cash as a sex slave.

Allison rubbed her bare arms as a chill ran over her. She laid her forehead against the cool glass of the French doors and looked out onto the estate.

Crystal-clear water filled the oversized swimming pool, stone walkways led from the main house to small white guest cottages, flowers of all kinds sprinkled over the grounds in a vast array of colors: orange, pink, yellow, red, purple. On the outside, the immaculate landscaping looked like a fairy tale, but like the owner, looks were definitely deceiving.

More than once she'd tried the French doors and windows in her room only to find them sealed tight. In two months she hadn't smelled fresh air, felt sunshine on her face, swatted at bumbling bees or caressed the silky petal of a rose. She focused her sights on the rose garden nestled in by the pool, trailing her fingertips over the glass as if she could actually feel the velvety flower.

Allison lived in a state of numbness. She had to, in order to have survived this long without breaking.

The guards outside her door began talking again, Allison stilled her breathing when she heard her name. They were discussing her "rack".

Could she possibly use one of them to help her? Roman's employees were loyal, but Allison wondered how that loyalty would hold up against seduction. The guards were young and hopefully easily distracted. If she had to use her body to gain freedom, she would.

∞

Eve nearly jumped out of her skin when she opened her front door for her morning jog.

There, in the hallway of her apartment building, Nick Shaffer proceeded to do push-ups—with no shirt. God, did those muscles have to look so...muscular?

"Mornin'," he said as he continued pumping his body up and down.

Eve tried to form a sentence, but she could only stare at the way his back and arms flexed then relaxed, a sheen of sweat covering the upper half of his tanned body. When he came to his feet and stood before her, Eve made herself lock her eyes on his face. But damn it, that's where the cocky smile lived. That flirty, arrogant smile had filled her dreams and kept her restless for most of the night. Did the man have to be so appealing? Worse, did he have to know it?

"Do I have to call the police to get you to leave me alone?"

Naked Vengeance

Eve demanded as she placed her hands on her hips. Her sneakered foot tapped impatiently without sound on the carpet.

Nick popped his neck and crossed his arms over his massive chest. "Do what you want, but they won't make me leave once I explain to them I'm a hired bodyguard. Besides, you don't own the building, so this isn't your property."

Eve let out a very unladylike growl as she brushed past him on her way to the elevator. She had no doubt he'd follow her, but that didn't mean she had to acknowledge him. Nor did she have to acknowledge the way her body reacted to seeing him again.

When she stepped onto the elevator, she punched the L. Shoving his gun into the waistband of his jeans, Nick settled in beside her as the doors closed. Just as soon as they started going down, he reached over and hit the Emergency button. A shrill alarm sounded for only a second before silence enveloped them.

The car jerked to a halt, causing Eve to fall back into the corner and grip the rail. "What are you doing?"

Nick put an arm on either side of her, caging her against the wall. "We need to talk."

Eve tried not to inhale his masculine scent. She really, really tried. Even though he'd slept in a hallway all night and done who knew how many push-ups, the man still smelled of sin. His coal-like eyes seemed to look straight into her mind as they roamed over her face. She wasn't tempted. She *wasn't*. Not at all.

Okay, maybe a little. But if he'd put a damn shirt on she'd be fine. Maybe.

God, she couldn't even lie to *herself* anymore.

"Then you can talk while I jog. If you can keep up," she added with a smile.

She hadn't known it possible, but he leaned in closer. He moistened his lips as a grin split across his face to reveal perfect white teeth. Eve swallowed. Why did she let him get to her?

"You just don't get it, do you? I'm here to protect you. I'm not really sure from what yet, but my source has never led me on a wild-goose chase, so I have to believe he's right this time."

29

Eve rolled her eyes. "I have no idea what you're talking about. Who would want to harm me? I'm just a dancer who lives in an apartment alone. I have no family, no friends. So you can go back and tell...whoever that I'm safe and sound."

His eyes roamed over her face, pausing on her lips. "You do have one friend."

"*You?*"

He shook his head as his eyes glistened with something she couldn't describe, didn't want to. His gaze finally settled on her lips. "I don't want to be your friend."

"Then wh-who?" she croaked out. Why did her voice pick now to betray her? She couldn't sound strong if she spoke like an adolescent schoolgirl. She was an FBI agent for crying out loud, and even though she was suspended, it was damn well time she remembered that fact.

"The man who hired me. He said you two were very close."

Eve took her hands, rested them on Nick's bare chest and pushed him back. "Then he's lying. I don't get close to people, it's a waste of time."

Nick cocked his head. "Why is that?"

With a shrug, she hit the button to resume the elevator. "They all leave eventually, so what's the point?"

Before he could comment further, the elevator doors slid open and Eve stepped out. She bounded down the steps of her building and began her stretches on the sidewalk. As she leaned down to touch her toes, a pair of bare feet came into her line of vision.

"You're going to have a hard time running without shoes." The back of her hamstring burned from the stretch.

She ordered herself to stay focused. The elevator incident still had her shaky and a bit confused. Two emotions she couldn't afford to have.

"I'm not running and neither are you," he said.

Now she did come up to look at him. "Excuse me? Who do you think you are? You don't rule my life. I run every day and today will be no exception. Now get out of my way."

He put a hand on her bare arm. "Why don't you come back upstairs with me so we can talk?"

"We had a talk in the elevator, now get your hands off me."

Nick tightened his grip. "I want to know everything about you so I can see what I'm up against."

"This song and dance is getting a bit old, don't you think? I'm letting you out of this 'favor'. You're off the hook. So go back and tell this friend that I fired you."

Eve turned to start her morning workout, but got caught off guard when a strong arm snaked around her waist. Eve's back fell against a rock-hard male chest as he lifted her off the sidewalk.

"Put me down, you Neanderthal," she screamed, her feet and legs flying about. "I swear you'll be sorry."

Damn, she couldn't even get in a good elbow to his side or a foot to the groin. He had her, literally and figuratively. Now what? If only she had her gun.

Nick hauled her back up the stairs to her building, threatened her if she didn't get out her keys and unlock the door, then proceeded to take her back to her apartment. He didn't let her down until they were back inside her apartment. He grabbed his boots, socks, shirt and empty shoulder holster from the hallway before stepping inside to block the door.

"Damn woman made me forget my stuff," he mumbled.

"It's not my fault if you're incompetent."

"I'm not incompetent," he insisted. "I was preoccupied with chasing your ass downstairs."

Eve said nothing as she went over to the antique trunk in front of her couch, picked up the cordless phone and dialed.

"Yes, 911, I have a burglar."

Nick dropped his stuff, took two strides, grabbed the phone from her hand and held the receiver up to his ear. With his palm on her forehead, all she could do was swat at the air while he spoke with the dispatcher.

"Hello, I'm sorry. My wife is upset with me for not taking out the garbage. I'm so sorry this won't happen again... Yes, I know it is illegal to place a call to 911 when there's no emergency... You have my word this is the one and only time she will do this Yes, I'm taking out the trash now... Thank you."

Nick disconnected the call and slid the portable phone into

the back pocket of his jeans. "Are you done with your tantrum? Now we have to leave unless you want a cop showing up at your door to make sure I'm really *not* an intruder."

"Kiss my ass."

Nick quirked a brow. "I've thought about it."

Eve gave up and threw herself down on her cushy leather sofa. The man was impossible, not to mention infuriating. Had she mentioned sexy? If he didn't put a shirt on soon, Eve feared she'd start salivating.

"What? No snappy comeback?"

Eve eyed him as he took a seat beside her. "What do you want me to say? It's your problem if you like my ass so much."

Nick laughed, but the ring tones of her cell cut off anything he may have said. She pulled the phone from the pocket of her nylon shorts and rolled her eyes when Nick leaned down to read the screen.

"Private name and number."

"Thanks for screening my calls. I hope your friend is paying you well." Eve kept her eye on him as she answered.

"Hello."

"I saw you dance last night."

Eve's heart rate picked up. "Who is this?"

She felt Nick move to her side, but she concentrated on the caller. A man. He tried to disguise his voice, and if Eve were just an average civilian, she wouldn't have picked up on it.

"I wonder if you'll do it for me privately before the end."

The caller hung up, and Eve sank back into her sofa. The end. What did he mean by that? Obviously he thought he could threaten her now.

"Eve."

With the phone still up to her ear, she barely heard Nick calling her name.

"Eve. Who is it?"

"He...he hung up."

Nick pried the phone from her grasp and snapped it shut. "What did he say?" he asked impatiently.

Eve took a deep breath and turned. "Wrong number."

Naked Vengeance

"I can't help you if you won't tell me the truth."

Sitting up straighter, she cocked her head toward him. "I didn't ask for your help, remember?"

"Well too bad, sweetheart, you've got it. So don't try telling me that was the wrong number. Someone on the other end knew what buttons to push because you lost some of the color in your face."

Too restless to be still, Eve stood up and paced back and forth. When she stopped at the window overlooking the street below, she concentrated on a small, red Honda as it tried to parallel-park in a tiny space. She didn't have time to fill Rambo in on her suspicions. She had to think of her next move because obviously she was making someone nervous.

But the silence in the apartment deafened her. Nothing good would come from being alone with her thoughts and for the first time in a long time, she had no idea what to do next. And there was only one person to blame for that, and he stood breathing heavily behind her.

Did she call Grady and confess to what she'd been up to and ask for help? Even though she was an FBI agent, albeit suspended, she wasn't naïve enough to think she could do this without backup. At some point, she'd need help.

First and foremost, she had to get rid of Nick. She'd been sailing along nicely before he showed up. She was getting closer than she'd been in a year to catching a killer and a bodyguard would only spoil her plan. She found it a little odd she hadn't had a phone call like this one before Nick showed up.

Just a little trickle of fear rested in her; not for herself, though. She feared she'd never catch this person who'd murdered and gotten away with it. Rage filled her as she tried to focus on the caller. It could have been the killer, or it could have been one of his men. She didn't care; they would all pay in the end, and she had a feeling the end would be coming soon.

When a set of strong hands came to settle on her shoulders, Eve tensed. She stayed that way, afraid if she loosened up she'd like the feel of a man's touch too much. Or maybe it would just be *this* man's touch.

"Look, Nick," she said as she continued to watch the street below. "I don't have the energy to fight you right now. I have to

33

get to the club. And if a cop is really on the way to check on things, you need to go."

Nick's large, rough hands slid from her shoulders down her bare arms before he let go. "I'm not leaving until we settle this. And I don't want to fight with you, either. I'm only here to help. Can we start with the phone call?"

Eve turned to find Nick merely inches away. God she needed space. Between his dangerous looks and the sincerity in his voice, she came close to caving in. If only she could trust him. If only she knew what side he worked on, maybe she could...

What was she saying? Trust no one. Isn't that what her father had always said?

If only he'd taken his own advice, perhaps he'd still be alive.

Nick's close proximity had her breathing and heart rate a little unsteady. For all she knew, he could be the man who shot her father. She had to get away before hormones overrode her common sense. Nothing could take precedence over avenging her father's death.

"Stop it!" Eve yelled as she shrugged him off.

Nick stepped back with his palms up. "What?"

"You're trying to be nice to get me to open up. It won't work. I have to leave now, which means you have to leave. I don't want you to follow me or to be at the club when I work tonight. Got it? I'm done with this conversation and I'm done with you."

Nick's eyes hardened as he nodded. "Fine, I wasn't too thrilled about taking this job anyway. You want to get into trouble, by all means go right ahead. Maybe before it's too late you'll realize you need someone to protect you. I hope your friend is still interested in saving you."

Nick turned, grabbed up his belongings and walked out the door without looking back. If she didn't want him, there was nothing he could do about it. One death on his hands would be more than enough to last his lifetime.

Nick waited until he sat in his car before he pulled out his cell. He dialed the familiar number and waited for an answer.

"Grady Prescott, please."

Grady wouldn't be happy. Well, Nick had done the legwork and found Eve; hopefully Grady could take it from here. Although it hadn't taken much time or effort to find her once Grady gave him an idea of where to look.

"Prescott."

"Grady, it's Nick."

"Did you find her?"

Leave it to Grady to cut right to the point.

Nick started the car and cranked the air up full blast. "Oh, I found her," he said as he adjusted the vents. "She's worse than you described."

Grady let out a low chuckle. "I was afraid you'd turn me down if you knew what a pistol she was."

Now it was Nick's turn to laugh at the understatement. "You know me better than that. I'd never turn you down, but I'd like to know how it is you know a stripper in South Carolina so well."

"She's stripping? God have mercy. She just doesn't know when to use her head." Grady let out a frustrated sigh. "If she's taking her clothes off, she must think she's onto something. Damn it, I should've guessed she'd do something like this. You can't let her out of your sight. I need your word, Nick."

Grady sounded almost desperate at keeping this vixen under guard. Looked like he'd be sticking around after all. Dammit.

Nick sighed. "Fine, but I need to know exactly what is going on."

"What did she tell you?"

A quick glance in his rearview mirror showed nothing suspicious. "She didn't say anything. She's definitely hiding something. I just don't know what a stripper could have to hide that could be so life-threatening. Just from our short conversations, I know she's only been in this area a few months and she's worked at the club since then. The miniscule file you gave me didn't tell me a thing. I don't like working a job without all the facts and key players."

Nick heard Grady mutter under his breath. Silence followed and Nick wondered if Grady was going to give him any more information.

"I've known Eve for about six years," Grady offered. "She's a good kid, but she doesn't know when to back off trouble. Basically, she's been trying to find who killed her father."

"You're kidding. Why is she stripping? Does she need money to hire a P.I.?"

"No, she's doing it on her own," Grady stated.

"Does she even have a clue who she's after?"

"She says she does, but she won't tell me anything. That's the reason I called you in for the job. You are the best person to protect her."

"You know what happened last time you thought that?" Nick asked.

"It wasn't your fault, Nick."

"That's what the shrink said, too." He rubbed a hand down his face. "Okay, finish your story about Eve and I'll decide if I'm going to stick around."

"You're not going to like it."

"I haven't liked anything up to this point anyway, so shoot."

"Eve's father was killed last year," Grady began in a slow, cautious manner. "He was one of the finest detectives in Charleston, South Carolina."

Nick's fingers went lax; he nearly dropped the phone. There had to be a mistake, he thought. Fate couldn't be this cruel.

"You see why I need you to protect her?" Grady asked after a period of silence.

Nick ran a hand through his thick hair. "Roger was Eve's *father*? You want me to protect the daughter of the man I let die? A man who died where she is now working? Are you out of your fucking mind? What do you think she'll say when she finds out I worked with her father on the bust that got him killed? I don't like this, Grady."

"No, I'm sure you don't. Eve is even more of a hothead than her old man was. She won't stop until the killer is dead." Grady paused. "Or until she is."

Nick found himself stuck between the proverbial rock and the hard place. "I'll get back with you."

Naked Vengeance

He ended the call and rested his head against the seat. In the year since Roger's death, Nick hadn't taken another job and now he'd come full circle and smack in the middle of The Excalibur's illegal actions once again.

Now he had no choice but to keep an eye on Eve. He wouldn't let her see him, though. He could remain in the background and still watch out for her. If he saw anything suspicious, he'd call Grady and have him send someone else. That was all he could do.

ஐ

Eve's night at the club had gone much better than the last. Hank, the manager, didn't blame her for leaving when the chaos erupted the evening before, much to Eve's relief. Running from the action went against everything she stood for, but in order to stay in character, she had to play the role perfectly if she wanted to put an end to this case once and for all.

After she dressed in her faded jeans and white tank, Eve grabbed her bag from her dressing table and headed out the door of the club. She'd made over two hundred dollars in her G-string tonight and found out that the gunshots fired last night were the result of an angry man who hadn't received the particular dancer he'd asked for in the VIP room. Such a classy clientele they brought in.

Now the poor bastard probably sat cozied up to Bubba in the county jail, Eve thought as she crossed the dimly lit parking lot.

Just as she dug out her car keys, she spotted a small note tucked under her windshield wiper. Using the keyless entry, she unlocked the car, grabbed the note and settled in behind the wheel. She tossed her bag on the passenger seat and flicked on the interior light to read.

Tick, tock, tick, tock...
It's only a matter of time now, Eve.

Without hesitation, she grabbed her bag and jumped from

the car. Eve's legs ate up the pavement, taking her as far from her car as possible. With her apartment only a five-minute drive, she didn't stop running until she reached the steps to her building.

Eve rested a hand on the concrete banister as she caught her breath, dug into her tote bag for her cell and glanced around to see if there was anything suspicious. She didn't know if anybody had actually planted a bomb in her car or if the note was just supposed to be a mind game, but obviously, she had someone running scared. Good, they'd better be. She refused to believe in coincidence. This wasn't just some random stalker or psycho fan from the gentlemen's club. No, this person knew something about her father's death and the missing women from The Excalibur.

After the dispatcher had taken all the information, she assured Eve that someone would go take a look at the car and call her if they had any further questions. Although Eve wasn't surprised with the lack of concern in the dispatcher's voice, she had to admit she thought the police might take a potential threat more seriously.

Keeping an eye out, Eve climbed the steps to her building. Not a soul around. Of course not, she thought as she checked her watch. At three in the morning, normal people were sleeping.

Even though she'd been up since early this morning—well, yesterday morning—once Eve let herself into her apartment, she couldn't sleep. The adrenaline flowed well now. She didn't know the local police enough to trust them, so Grady would have to be informed. She had no one else.

Maybe tomorrow night she would talk to the other girls about her note and the call. Word would get out she brushed it off as a pervert who was too afraid to talk to her in person. She had to draw this bastard out in the open. This ongoing nightmare had to end.

The case her father had been working on when he died had to do with strip clubs, particularly The Excalibur and the illegal goings-on behind the scenes. The manager seemed to be taken with her in the short time she'd been there. Now she just had to give him a little extra attention and perhaps she could find out more.

The three missing women had to be found and brought home...sooner rather than later.

When Eve's cell beeped, indicating she had new messages, she rooted around in her bottomless pit of a bag until her fingers grasped the phone. She toed off her tennis shoes where she stood in the in the entryway, hung her bag on the wooden peg by the door and flipped her phone open as she made her way to her bedroom.

She entered her password and tucked the phone between her ear and shoulder as she slid her jeans off, leaving them in a wad on the beige carpet. The laundry fairy still hadn't shown up, she thought as she stepped over mounds of dirty clothes.

There were only two messages, the first from Grady. "Just checking in," he said in his deep, caring voice. "I know you won't tell me where you are, but call me when you get a chance just to let me know you're okay."

Eve shook her head as she erased the message. Grady might be a tough-as-nails FBI leader, but the man still had a soft spot. He truly cared about his agents...even the ones on suspension.

The second message came just as she hit the bathroom light. She held the phone out just long enough to jerk her tank over her head and unsnap her bra. The familiar male voice that came through the phone paralyzed her.

"I saw you dance tonight. Maybe if you dance for me privately, I won't get rid of you as quick as the others. Think about it, Eve. Think about me."

Even though her nerves were on edge, Eve didn't erase this message. She snapped her phone shut and finished taking off her bra and underwear.

So now he wanted to play. Well, she was up for a good fight. A whole year of pent-up anger and revenge just waited to be unleashed. From now on, unless she was stripping on stage, that bag would not leave her side. She needed to keep her gun close by at all times.

When she looked down at her hands braced on the marble vanity, she cursed at the way they shook. It would be a rookie mistake to go into this without fear, though. The inevitability of the unknown would keep her sharp and cautious. This had to be done without mistakes and at precisely the right time.

With her clothes still in a careless pile on her bathroom floor, she shut off the light and stood by the window to look out onto the starless night, keeping her cell clutched in her hand. She'd already checked her Glock, put the clip in and set it beside the phone. Once she'd been suspended, she'd had to turn in her badge and gun. Thank God she had her father's old Glock as a backup. Even though she could get another with no problem, she wanted to use his gun in order to stay focused. The vengeance in the end would be all the more sweet.

Shouldn't be too much longer, she thought. And finally, once she put this whole ordeal behind her, she could get her job back. Her dad would be proud of her when she finished the case he'd started on.

If only he were still alive to see it.

Eve took a deep breath and sighed when her eyes began to burn. What did tears accomplish? Nothing. One tear always led to a hundred others. Right now she needed to concentrate. She didn't figure the person who placed the threatening note in her car wanted to kill her. No, they were too smart and they liked playing games. They just wanted to scare her. Well, Eve Morgan wasn't easily scared. People who weren't afraid to die tended to not scare easily.

She just wished she could figure out exactly where Nick Shaffer fit into all of this.

No matter how she tried, his dark eyes kept interrupting her thoughts. The sight of his face when she'd refused his help that final time filled her mind. He'd looked both relieved and concerned. She didn't know why he'd accepted the job when he obviously didn't want to be with her any more than she wanted to be with him.

But, she knew to keep her enemies close and for now, Nick Shaffer was an enemy.

She still hadn't had a chance to ask someone to run his name. First thing in the morning, she'd return Grady's call and see if he'd do this favor for her. Right now, though, she needed to call Grady and come clean as to what she was up to and beg him for some back-up. He wouldn't be happy.

Eve jerked around when the loose floorboard under the

carpet by the front door squeaked. She damned the intruder as she grabbed the gun from her nightstand. Now was not the time to piss her off.

Whoever broke in would have to die, she vowed. Between little sleep, the threatening calls, a potential bomb note, and working at that damn club, Eve had had about all she could take. And if this person wanted a piece of her, well bring it on. She wanted nothing more than to come face to face with this monster who'd controlled her life for a year.

With her gun in one hand, she reached for her doorknob with the other. Slowly she opened the door and crouched down, holding her weapon with both hands, arms extended straight out. With light steps, she tiptoed down the short, narrow hallway.

When she heard a sigh come from the other side of the wall, she jumped around the corner with her gun aimed high, her stance wide.

"Nick!"

On her sofa, with booted feet propped up on the trunk, hands folded across his flat abdomen...with that naughty smile on his face, sat Nick Shaffer.

"Well, well," he said as his eyes roamed over her bare body. "I hope you don't greet all your company in the buff brandishing a gun, but hey, if you're into kinky stuff..."

Eve lowered her gun. "Throw me that afghan, asshole, and keep your eyes on the ceiling."

Nick laughed as he reached behind him to grab the throw. He did toss her the afghan, but his dark eyes remained on her. Well, on her chest. Typical man.

"May I ask why are you breaking into my apartment? Again?"

Eve tucked the blanket under her arms and pulled it tight. She did not, however, set down her weapon. She had to keep the upper hand here.

"You know, I can see through those little holes. If you don't want to expose anything, you'll need to cover up with something other than yarn."

Eve narrowed her eyes, refusing to be baited. "What do you want?"

He ignored her and nodded to her gun. "Is that thing registered?"

She gritted her teeth and told a teeny lie. "Of course." Her father'd had it registered when he'd been alive.

"I wanted to know if you were ready for my help now."

"And why would I choose now to give in?"

His eyes hardened as he met her gaze. "Because your car just exploded right outside the club."

She tried to look surprised, and in all honesty she was a little. Maybe the killer had had enough of her as well.

"Don't have anything to say?" he asked.

"What do you want me to say?"

When Nick stood, Eve nearly dropped her gun. It must be lack of sleep and the evening's events, she thought. It had to be. No way would she, under normal circumstances, think this brute of a man held any sexual appeal. This stripping gig had boggled up her thought process. All her thoughts lately had gravitated towards sex—a subject she did not want to associate with Nick.

Sex had never been on her mind before. She didn't even like sex. Okay, maybe she would like it if she ever tried it. But any relationship, sexual or otherwise, could not exist between her and Nick. Too bad.

With his hands on his narrow hips, he tilted his head and gave her his signature cocky smile. The one that said, "I know what you're thinking." The way she'd been staring, he probably did.

Eve righted herself and tilted her chin. "Lock the door behind you when you leave."

"Would you just be an adult for two seconds and talk about this?" he demanded. "Your car exploded only minutes ago, for crying out loud, and the beat cop checking it out was sent to the hospital with minor burns. Don't you want to know why?"

Guilt seeped through her. She didn't want innocent people getting hurt, whether they were law enforcement or not.

"Not particularly. I wanted a new car anyway." Damn she hated sounding like a spoiled brat, but she wanted him gone.

Nick ran a frustrated hand down his face and stepped

towards her. "The bomb squad was called in."

Eve rolled her eyes, cocked her head and attempted to look bored. "And..."

"Someone put a bomb under the passenger seat, Eve. You could've been killed." When she only continued to stare, he took her by the shoulders and shook her. "Do you hear me? Dead. You could be dead now."

Eve didn't know if the shiver that crept up her spine came from his truthful words or the fact his strong hands covered her bare shoulders. She felt so small, so fragile under his large, rough palms. She'd never thought of herself as small or fragile before and now that she had, she didn't care for it. And she certainly didn't care for the way her body reacted to him standing so close to her.

His fresh, masculine scent filled her senses. She couldn't escape his touch, his scent, his face. Those dark eyes roamed over her face, down to her lips.

Heat rushed through her. Dampness formed between her legs, and Eve had to cross her arms over her chest so he wouldn't see her nipples poking through the afghan.

"I'm fine, Nick." Eve looked into his deep brown eyes. There was that look again. Concern. "I really don't need your help. If what you said is true, that we have a mutual friend, then he'll understand when you go tell him I declined your protection."

"Tell me who would want to kill you," he demanded.

"If I knew, then I wouldn't be in this little predicament, would I?"

Nick pushed off her shoulders and paced her small living room. His whole body seemed tense. His hands clenched and relaxed over and over as he walked back and forth.

Eve didn't know what was worse, being up close and personal with him or watching him from the backside.

"Look, Nick," she began when the silence and her carnal thoughts got to her. "I've only had about three hours of sleep and I'm exhausted. I have to work tonight, so if you want to stay here and pace, by all means. I can't keep my eyes open another minute. So unless you want to be up front with me about who sent you, I'm done with this charade."

"Doesn't any of this get to you?" He turned to look her in

the eye. "Would you just use your head for one damn minute and think? Obviously someone wants you harmed or worse. Fortunately for you, you have someone else who is willing to hire me to protect you. Why won't you put your pride aside and let me help?"

"How do I know you're not the one who's trying to harm me?" She tightened her grip on the afghan. "I don't know you, so why do you expect me to just jump behind you and let you take over my life? I won't tell you again. I don't want you here or in any other aspect of my life. I can handle this on my own. I'm sure the cops are working on what happened. They should be here soon to talk to me about my car, anyway, so if I need protection, I'll call them."

Eve turned with every intention of never seeing Nick again, but his words stopped her cold.

"Grady sent me."

Chapter Three

Ever so slowly, she looked over her shoulder, one brow lifted in question. He watched her emotions go from surprised to downright pissed.

Uh-oh, maybe he shouldn't have dropped that bombshell.

"He what?" she asked, coming to stand within inches of him.

Nick eyed the gun she still held. "Why don't you put that down and we'll talk."

Fury filled her eyes. "Talk. Now."

"All I'll tell you is Grady is worried about you, he said you disappeared without a word. He called me about a week ago to see if I could find you and if I did, to keep an eye on you. He cares, Eve."

"Keep an eye on me?" She laughed. "Well, isn't that just lovely. What else did he say?"

"He figured you'd be heading this way from Virginia. He said you wanted to find who killed your father and you might get into some trouble."

Guilt consumed Nick when the mention of her father put a lost look in Eve's eyes. Damn it. He hated this. She deserved to know the truth, but if he came completely clean, she'd never let him protect her. He might have failed Eve's father, but he damn well wouldn't fail her.

"How do you know him, anyway?" Nick asked.

"What did he tell you?" she countered.

Nick shrugged. "He said you were special to him and that he'd known you for six years. Are you guys related or something?"

A sad smile formed from Eve's full lips. "Or something."

"Maybe you should call him and see what he says about me sticking around," Nick suggested.

Eve spun on her heel and went in the direction of what he assumed to be her bedroom. When the door slammed, it wasn't long before he heard her muffled voice through the thin wall.

Poor Grady. He didn't want to be in that man's shoes right now. Nick went back to the couch and resumed his position with his feet on the old trunk, his hands on his stomach.

Unwanted doubts filled his head. What if he couldn't protect Eve? The more she put up a fight, the more difficult it would be to protect her. Hopefully Grady would talk some sense into her, make her realize what was at stake here. Her life.

Nick rested his head on the back of the cool leather sofa. Eve didn't even compare to any other woman he'd ever known. With a body made for the stage she strutted on, a kick ass attitude and just a touch of softness about her, any man would be damn lucky to get with her.

Nick chuckled at his next thought—Eve would make a great cop. She didn't take shit from anybody and insisted on having all the facts before she reacted to any situation. But he had to agree with Grady...The woman had a hot temper.

Moments later she came back into the living room, only now she had on a pair of cut-off denim shorts and a white tank. No bra. The thin white material pulled against her well-rounded tits, basically the same way his jeans were pulling against his dick.

"Grady and I have come to an understanding," she announced as she plopped down on the other end of the couch. "You can stick around, but I call the shots."

Nick laughed. Hard. "Oh, that's great. You? So I'm just supposed to follow you around like a...a..."

"Bodyguard?" Eve finished with a grin. "Isn't that what you are? You were hired to guard my body, were you not?"

Nick couldn't help when his eyes wondered over that said body. She'd pulled her knees up to her chest and crossed her feet—red toenail polish always did something to him. With her arms wrapped around her shins, she looked so...dainty. Nick nearly laughed at that realization. Dainty and Eve did not belong in the same sentence. Feisty, stubborn, cautious... Yeah, those words fit her.

"I will protect you, but you have to fill me in on what you know regarding your father's death. When and how did it happen? Do you have any leads? Who was handling the investigation?"

Eve extended her legs, her very toned legs, and sighed. He nearly sighed himself when her feet, with perfectly polished red toenails, came to rest on his lap. He should be thankful she trusted him now, but all that ran through his mind was her naked body when he'd first arrived.

Focus, he told himself. He had to listen to her story and act as if he knew nothing of her father or his death.

"My father was murdered a little over a year ago," she began. "He was a cop in Charleston. We hadn't been close for a while."

Nick looked away when her voice trembled. A crying woman always did him in and made him feel useless. He really didn't want to put his arms around her and offer comfort... That would only lead to disaster.

When Eve cleared her throat, Nick looked back up. Not a tear in sight. He shouldn't be surprised. This woman wanted people to think she was made of steel. He knew better.

"I've lived in Virginia since I was five and my parents parted ways. They were never married, they just lived together. Since then I had only seen my dad maybe a half-dozen times. We weren't close, but I loved him because he was my dad.

"To make a long story short, when I found out about his death from Grady, I went crazy. For months I let guilt and the 'what-ifs' plague my mind, then I was so focused on harassing the Charleston PD that I lost my job. When the cops he'd worked with his whole career weren't moving fast enough for me, I decided to move down here and start looking myself.

"I knew he'd been working on a case where prostitution was said to have been going on in the back of some gentlemen's club. Some of the women just vanished and were never heard from. I was told The Excalibur was the club my father was closing in on the night he was killed."

Nick listened to her talk. She sounded as if she'd rehearsed her words. They had no emotion, no depth. Her eyes never wavered from his and her body remained tense.

In an effort to get her to relax, Nick began rubbing her feet, a gesture he doubted she even noticed. She kept talking in that monotone voice, relaying facts he already knew. But he nodded his head now and again as if he were hearing all the facts for the first time.

"I was told he fired his weapon as he got shot," she continued. "He died before the ambulance could get to him. All I know now is that the case remains unsolved and those women are still missing."

Eve's body slid down a little more into the cushy sofa as she relaxed, her lids growing heavy. "The last conversation I had with my father wasn't pleasant. It was five years before his death. I wasted five years because I allowed my pride and his pride to get in the way. That's why I'm here. I need to know who did this."

Eve's head lay on the arm of the sofa, leaving her long, creamy neck exposed. Nick could practically see himself running his tongue in a path up to her mouth. But just because he could envision it, didn't mean it would happen.

Before he knew it, her breathing had slowed. Her breasts rose and fell softly under the cotton tank; her hand fell freely to the side. He let his hands rest on her feet while he listened to her calm breath.

The woman had spunk. She'd moved from everything she knew and taken a job stripping simply to find the person who killed her father and lay her guilty conscience to rest. She risked her life in a world she knew nothing about. Nick couldn't help but admire her, even though he feared all that spunk would get both of them into some sticky situations before all was said and done.

The shrill ring of the telephone startled Eve from her sleep. She looked down at him and jerked her feet off his lap, out from under his hands almost like she didn't know how she'd gotten into that position.

Because she'd left one of the phones in her bedroom, she ran to the small galley kitchen for the other cordless and grabbed it off the charger on the third ring.

"Hello?"

Nick followed her, intending to remain in the background, but when her face turned stone-like, he wrenched the phone from her and held it up to his ear.

"Too bad about the car, Eve. Maybe I'll see you dance tonight. Don't forget, you owe me a private show."

"Who is this?" Nick asked a second too late. The caller had hung up.

Nick slammed the cordless on the tile countertop and looked down at Eve. Her eyes remained cold as she continued to stare at the phone.

"Eve. Eve," Nick said again to get her attention. "What did he tell you?"

"He said, 'It's almost time.'"

Nick drew his brows together. "Time for what?"

Eve shook her head. "I don't know. He has to be watching me because he knows where I work and live."

Nick figured that out himself seeing as how the caller knew she danced. "Is this like the call you got the other day when you told me it was the wrong number?"

"This voice didn't sound the same."

He didn't like the sound of that. "Any other calls?"

Her silence answered his question.

"I need to know it all, Eve," he said, losing his patience.

"I had a note on my car when I got off work. It said something about time being almost up and it implied a bomb." She lifted a shoulder. "Then he left a message on my cell phone. I called the cops as soon as I saw the note and got away from my car."

"I want to see the note and listen to the message."

"Well, the note exploded with my car, but I did save the message on my phone."

Nick followed her to her bedroom where she grabbed the cell off the small table by her unmade bed. If he weren't so preoccupied he might have taken a moment to make some smart-ass comment about her lack of organization. He did remain in the doorway, though, for fear of tripping over what looked like all of her dirty laundry since she'd moved here.

She walked on shirts, shorts and who knew what else as she came back to him and extended her phone.

"Press three," she said.

Nick listened to the call and got angry all over again. He snapped her phone shut and strode back to the living room.

"Is something wrong?" Eve asked, following close behind him.

"You have to come with me," he said matter of factly as he rounded on her. "It's not up for discussion. I don't want to hear your mouth. You're not staying here."

"Excuse me?" Her hands came up to her hips, her brows lifted as if she dared him to repeat it.

"You heard me. You have two minutes to pack whatever clothes you want."

"I'm not packing anything."

Nick lifted a shoulder. "Fine, then come as you are. I don't care."

When he reached down to take her by the arm, she stepped back. "I'm not going anywhere until you tell me what has got you so riled up."

"Do you really need to ask? It's not safe for you here. That bastard implied you would be taken like those other women. Would you even have told me about that call or the note if I hadn't pressed?"

"No," she said, tilting her chin defiantly. "I've told you I don't need watching over. The only reason you're sticking around is because Grady insists."

"Yeah, well, why don't I call him and see what he says about your safety, being alone in your apartment."

Nick pulled out his cell and began to dial, or so he made her think. He had no intention of calling Grady over her tantrum. The day he couldn't handle a snotty, stubborn, independent woman was the day he retired. Well, technically he'd retired, but still.

"You are so childish," she vented, "acting like a big brother, tattling to Daddy when things don't go your way. You are free to walk away at any time, Nick. I don't want you here. I've been

Naked Vengeance

doing just fine on my own."

She'd provoked him one too many times with that smart mouth of hers. In one move he had her petite, curvy body wrapped in his arms and tucked against him. He had the pleasure of seeing her eyes widen in surprise, then narrow when she knew his intent.

"Don't you d—"

His mouth came down hard and fast. For a second, she fought him, pushing against his chest. But when he slipped his tongue into her mouth, he took it as a good sign when she didn't bite him.

The rough, one-sided kiss only lasted for only a moment before Eve gave into the inevitable...and his little plan to intimidate her turned into a hot, smoldering kiss.

Those long, slender arms came up around his neck, her fingers threading through his hair as she pulled him closer. Her firm, yet lush body rubbed against his, making his jeans fit a little tighter than he liked. His hands took on a mind of their own as they made their way up her cotton tank. Silky skin warmed under his fingertips. Her body shivered beneath his hands as he roamed up her sides, finding the softest spot on a woman's body, just on the underside of her breast.

He swallowed her moan as he stroked her with the pads of his thumbs. Her gentle lips continued to explore his as she changed the angle and the intensity of the kiss.

Control of the situation slid right from Nick's hands when the slow, easy manner in which she took his mouth made him nervous. No way would he let passion and lust guide him again.

Nick pulled his hands out of her shirt and stepped back, knowing he'd be sorry for his next comment. "Did that feel brotherly to you, *Sis*?"

Eve's swollen, wet lips thinned right before she took her hands and gave him a shove. "You bastard. How dare you kiss me like that? Why don't you go ahead and call Grady? While you're at it, tell him you can't keep your fucking hands off me."

"Said the girl who rubbed her tits all over my body."

Nick made the biggest mistake by looking down where his hands had been only seconds ago. Her nipples remained stiff. Would this be a bad time to ask her to always wear a white tank and no bra? Probably.

"Watch those wandering eyes, Nick," she warned. "I'll come with you, only because I'm not sure who blew up my car and it's stupid of me to think I'd be safe here. But if you pull a stunt like that again, I'll make sure Grady knows what kind of man he hired."

While she could still move on wobbly legs, Eve went to her room to grab some clothes. She shut her door and leaned against it just in time. Her whole body trembled and she had to admit to herself, that kiss was more than she could handle at the moment.

Being pulled up against that hard male body would feed her dreams for a long time. There had been so much heat and power behind that kiss, even more power in the arms that held her so close.

Now that she had a moment alone, Eve gave in and smiled when she thought how good it felt to be ravished. Granted, he'd only done it out of arrogance to try to gain the upper hand, but the way he'd kissed her couldn't have been fake. The man had acted like he would have taken her right there on her living room floor had she not slowed it down and taken control.

Eve grinned. So that had been the problem. He'd pushed her away when she tried to dominate the kiss. It scared him to let a woman take over his emotions. She'd file that bit of information away for another time.

With her lips tingly and her stomach still in knots, Eve threw her stuff together in a small suitcase. She hoped they weren't going to an airport, seeing as how her father's gun nestled right between her thongs and a new leather bustier she'd just gotten for work.

Once her nerves were under control, Eve went back to the living room. Nick snapped his cell shut and put it back in the pocket of his jeans as she entered.

"I called Grady and informed him of the situation," Nick said as he reached down to take her luggage.

Purely out of defiance, Eve shifted the bag to the other hand and walked past him. She had no doubt the "situation" he spoke of had nothing to do with the I-want-my-hands-all-over-your-body kiss.

"Where are we going?" she asked as she grabbed her small bag off the hook by the door. Nick held out her cell phone and she slipped it into the outside pocket.

"A hotel for now," he stated, then grinned like the devil. "We're sharing a room."

"Oh, no." Eve stepped away from the door and shook her head. "I'm not going to share a bed with you."

Nick sighed. "I'll get us a room with double beds, so don't go throwing one of your tantrums now."

"There's no reason we can't get separate rooms. They can be adjoining, if that would make you feel better."

"No. This is not up for discussion."

Eve kept her fierce glare on Nick as his jaw muscle constricted. His hand reached out to grab her suitcase. Before she could say anything, he hoisted her up and over his shoulder in a fireman's lift. Too stunned to scream, all she could do was watch his denim-clad ass as he carried her out the door. Her shoulder bag banged against his side and for a split second, Eve contemplated grabbing his gun from his shoulder holster and shooting him in the ass.

"Put me down," she demanded as he hauled her onto the elevator. "People will see us."

He said nothing, just continued to carry her out of her apartment building. He crossed the street and went to the passenger side of a sporty black BMW that chirped when he unlocked it. Without any effort, he deposited her in the front seat. When he closed her door, she settled back and set her bag in her lap.

Eve knew she needed to get out of her apartment, on that they were in agreement. She would not, however, let Nick know that, deep down, the bomb had shaken her more than she liked to admit. And, since she was being honest with herself, she felt safer with him than without him.

If Grady sent him, that could only mean one thing. Nick Shaffer had to be the best at what he did.

Nick climbed in behind the wheel, after depositing her suitcase in the trunk, and drove off. Eve waited for him to speak, but he just kept his eyes on the road, except for the occasional look to his rearview mirror.

"Go ahead and tell me what a jerk you think I am," he finally said.

Eve wound her fingers through the thin strap of her bag. "I don't need to if you're already aware of the fact."

"You need to call the club and tell them you're taking a few days off."

"No."

Eve almost smiled when his hands tightened on the steering wheel. Good, at least she wasn't the only one frustrated with this situation. Normally she wasn't so difficult to get along with, but something about this man made her want to go against his every demand. Perhaps it was because as much as she despised him, she wanted to kiss him even more. Stupid female hormones.

"You are not stripping there," Nick said through clenched teeth. "Use some common sense. How can you find your father's killer if you're dead?"

"It's bad enough I left my apartment. I need to be at the club. I won't let them scare me off."

Nick exploded. "If you had any sense about you, you would be scared. Do you know what could happen to you? You could become the next victim to disappear from the club. Is that what you want?"

Eve fisted her hands around the leather strap so she couldn't haul off and hit him. If he thought he could frighten her into succumbing to him and letting him take over, he was insane. She would not let this pushy man tell her what to do. Somehow he'd come in and taken over her life and for some asinine reason she'd allowed it.

"Look," he said in a calmer, yet still irritated voice. "We need to work together here. First of all, we have to be completely honest. I really don't mean to be so hard on you, but it comes with the job. If you want to stay alive and figure out who killed your dad, then I will have to remain the asshole you think I am."

Eve nodded. "Fine. I can do honesty, so long as you can. Do you have it in you to be up front with me at all times?"

"I'm dying to pull this car over, pull you onto my lap and bury myself in you until you're out of my system. How's that for honesty?"

Eve refused to look over. She felt his glare on her for a second before he turned his eyes back to the road. She didn't know what scared her more, his bluntness or the idea he might actually pull the car over and...and...

"What, no snappy comeback?" he taunted.

"If you think I'm coming with you so you can 'bury yourself in me' as you so eloquently put it, you'd better think again."

"The least you could do is offer a lap dance for my troubles," he muttered.

Eve ignored him and his immature comments. Anything from her would only add fuel to the fire he seemed to have going on in his pants. It couldn't compare to the raging inferno she had going on herself.

This sexual tension and banter had to stop. For a year, she hadn't allowed anything to come between her and her father's killer—not even her job with the FBI. So why did she now allow all of her priorities to get jumbled?

Nick drove for about forty minutes before pulling into a hotel lot, just in front of the main entrance. Eve sat in the car while he ran in to check on the availability of rooms.

If this were some bad movie, the hotel would only have one room left with a single bed. Wouldn't that just top off her day?

"We're in luck," Nick said as he climbed back in the car. "There's a room around back with two double beds."

"How lovely."

"Don't pout, darling. We're on our honeymoon."

Eve looked over at Nick, who had an actual smile on his face. "Excuse me?"

"Well, I told the front desk we were on our honeymoon and we didn't want to be disturbed for any reason. She eyed me funny when I had the request for two beds, but I told her you snored."

Eve rolled her eyes. "You think pretending to be honeymooners will divert the baddies?"

Nick parked the car and turned to face her. "Look, until we know what we're dealing with, I'll do whatever I can to keep you safe. If that means playing your husband, then I will and you'll go right along with it. Got it?"

Eve stared into his intense eyes. With his face only inches from hers, she couldn't help but remember the way he'd kissed her, held her, touched her. The start of a five o'clock shadow covered his jaw line and chin. Funny, she thought, it hadn't scratched her earlier.

Now, though, she ached to run her fingers along his face. To feel that rough, ruggedness under her skin. Or better yet, along her inner thigh.

"Eve," Nick said. "Do you understand me?"

"I'm the dutiful wife." She smiled sweetly. "Got it, babycakes."

She couldn't be sure, but Eve thought she saw a smile spread across Nick's face as he got out of the car.

Without wasting any time, they gathered their luggage and found their room. The summer heat proved to be unbearable. Eve sighed with relief when they stepped over the threshold and into the air conditioned room.

"I don't know," Eve stated from the doorway. "I'd always imagined my wedding night in a little fancier place than this."

Thick beige paper lined the walls, gaudy floral prints clung to the bedspreads, and a simple cherry desk sat tucked into one corner with a matching cherry television stand across from the first bed. The tacky striped curtains were pulled shut, blocking out the late afternoon sun. Eve dropped her suitcase on the second bed and went to let some light in.

"No," Nick said without turning around.

"This place is dark and smelly. I want some light and air in here."

In two strides, Nick grabbed her hands and jerked them from the curtains. "I said no. We don't want people to see in."

Eve knew she shouldn't open the curtains for precisely that reason, but she'd kept her eyes on the rearview mirror and she knew nobody had followed them. Still, it probably wasn't a good idea. Damn him for being right—again.

"Fine," she muttered.

Nick went back to his suitcase. He pulled out a Glock, checked the clip, and set it on the nightstand between the two

Naked Vengeance

beds. Eve only saw two colors in his bag, blue denim and black.

"Fancy wardrobe you got there."

When Nick said nothing, Eve walked over and flopped, belly down, onto her bed. The shabby comforter reeked of smoke. Eve pillowed her arms under her head and looked toward the wall, where a large, flower garden print hung cockeyed on the stained wallpaper.

Now what? Should she come clean and just tell Nick she was FBI? Maybe then he wouldn't treat her like a distressed damsel. Of course, he also would hightail it out of there and leave her to face this monster alone. She really hated that Grady knew her well enough to know she needed help. She also figured he had to know she would never admit that to anybody.

When Eve's eyes started to burn due to lack of sleep, she let her lids fall. Even through the smoky scent and crabby company, she allowed her body to relax. Nothing could be done right now and if she didn't take care of herself, she wouldn't be able to face whatever came next.

"You hungry?"

Nick's low, smooth voice jarred her from her thoughts as she teetered on the brink of sleep. Eve rolled over to face him, only to find him standing at the edge of her bed. He loomed down at her with his hands on his hips, lips thinned, jaw muscle tight. The signature black tee stretched across his well-defined chest and shoulders. For a second, Eve wondered what would happen if she patted the bed in an invitation. Would she have the courage to follow through? Would he even be interested?

Yes to both, she thought, without any vanity on her part.

"Eve?"

"Sorry, what?"

"I'm going to get us something to eat. What do you want?"

Eve laughed at her previous thoughts. When she swung her legs to the side, Nick took a step back until he bumped into his own bed. He continued to glare as she came to her feet.

"Where are you going?"

"There's a McDonald's about a block away."

Eve wrinkled her nose. "I don't really like hamburgers."

"Then get chicken nuggets," Nick suggested as he ran a hand over his face.

"I don't think it's really chicken in those things."

"Are you for real?"

Eve jerked back in shock at his raised tone. "Excuse me?"

"Either you're hungry or you're not. I'm leaving in thirty seconds with or without your order."

"Fine, get me a fish sandwich. Plain. No fries and a diet."

"Great," he muttered as he stalked towards the door. "Deadbolt this door behind me and don't open it for anybody but me. Got it?"

With a salute, Eve grinned. "Yes, master."

Nick slammed the door behind him. Did he think she was an idiot? Like she'd let Joe Blow inside if he knocked. Did Nick really think she had no common sense? Obviously.

With a few minutes to herself, Eve thought now would be a good time to grab a shower. Once she'd stripped and adjusted the temperature of the water, she stepped under the pelting spray.

The hotel soap she used didn't smell too bad, she thought as she rinsed the suds from her skin. A jasmine scent. After a quick lather of complimentary shampoo, Eve rinsed her hair as well.

Just as she stepped out of the shower and wrapped a towel around her body, she heard her cell phone ring. Still dripping wet, with her hair clinging to her damp shoulders, Eve stepped out of the bathroom and grabbed the phone from her shoulder bag she'd left by the door.

Probably Nick, she mused. Eve shook her head as she pictured him at the McDonald's counter, her order forgotten.

"Hello," she answered as she walked to her suitcase to dig out some clothes.

"You ran from me."

Eve's hand froze on the zipper of her luggage. "Who is this?"

"Your biggest fan."

"Really? Why do you say I ran from you?"

"You're not home right now."

Chills crept over her bare skin. "How do you know that?"

An eerie laugh came through the receiver. "I know everything about you. I even know when you'll die."

※

Nick juggled the plastic bag and two large drinks. He couldn't dig out the key card so he kicked the door, by way of knocking, with his dingy boot.

"Open up. It's me," he yelled.

After a few seconds, he kicked the door harder. "Eve, unlock the door."

Nothing. A trickle of fear tingled down his rigid spine.

Just as he started to bust in the door, the deadbolt clicked and the door opened a crack. He nudged his way inside, kicking it closed behind him.

Eve crossed the room with her back to him. Her bare back. She wore only a thin, short white hotel towel. A mass of wet fiery red curls hung past her shoulders. God, why did she look so damn good and...virginal in a white towel?

"I got you two fish sandwiches in case you get hungry later. I don't want us going back out if it's not necessary."

Nick sat the bag of food on his bed and the cups full of diet soda on the night stand. When he looked back around, her back still faced him, her head bent and her shoulders sagging.

"Eve."

After a moment, she turned around. Her face had lost all color, now matching the towel. Dark circles lined her eyes. With one white-knuckled hand, she clutched her towel together and held onto her cell.

Protective instincts kicked in on high alert.

"You got a call."

Eve nodded.

"What did he say?"

"He knows I'm not home." Eve went over to rummage

through the bag for her sandwich. "He said I ran from him."

"Did he say anything else?"

Nick watched her hand squeeze the paper around her food. Good, she used her fear to fuel her anger. That would keep her sharp and more alert. It would also keep him from consoling her, because God knew if he had to hold her right now...

He really wished she'd put some clothes on.

"He said he was my biggest fan and that he knew everything about me." Her emerald eyes came up to his. "Including when I'm going to die."

Nick muttered a curse and sat on the edge of her bed. "How long did he talk?"

Eve shrugged a slender, naked shoulder. "Maybe thirty seconds or a little less."

"I'll still see if I can get a trace on all your incoming calls."

"I doubt it," Eve said as she unwrapped her fish sandwich. "It said 'Unavailable' on the caller ID."

"He didn't indicate that he knew where you went or that you were with me?"

"No, so I'd say he doesn't know, or he would've bragged about it."

Nick nodded in agreement.

"Aren't you going to eat?" Eve asked with a mouth full of food.

"Yeah, I'm just taking a minute to think." Nick rubbed his forehead and sighed. "You need to call the club and tell them you quit."

Eve raised one perfectly shaped brow. "I beg your pardon?"

"You heard me."

"I'm not quitting. Don't even suggest it. If I'm making someone this nervous, then I have to be close."

"That's precisely why you're not going back. You're getting too close and whoever this person is won't back down. He's already killed before and who knows where those missing girls are. I can take over from here."

Nick hated the lost look that came over Eve's face, but she had to understand her life hinged on their every move. This wasn't a game.

"You can't go back," he said in a softer tone.

"I have to," she insisted. "You can sit in the back of the club and watch everything. I just need to get more information. The owner is really starting to like me and I think with a little more time, he'll trust me."

Nick shook his head. "I don't like it. I don't like you being in the forefront like this. There has to be another option. Just let me think for a minute."

"It's the only way and we both know it. Unless you can grow breasts and learn to work a pole, I'm the answer."

Nick hated when she made sense. Hated it even more he had to go along with this insane plan if he ever wanted to gain closure on this case that had haunted him for nearly a year.

"If I see any sign of trouble, I'm jerking you out of there," he finally said as he dug into the paper bag for his own sandwich.

"If there's trouble, then I need to be there. How can I get inside his inner circle if I run all the time?"

"I'm not going to argue. I will let you work, but if anyone so much as breathes wrong, you're out of there. I can go back after I get you to safety."

"I don't need you to rescue me," Eve clarified as she tossed her sandwich aside and came to her feet. "I was doing just fine on my own. This whole plan of you protecting me is stupid and unnecessary."

"For your information, I don't like trying to guard a spoiled brat who always thinks she can get her way."

Eve glared down at him. "Since we've established we don't like each other, why don't you take me back to my apartment so I can resume my life?"

"What life? You've given it up. What the hell are you going to do if you find out who killed your father?"

Eve ignored his question. Nick wasn't quite sure he really wanted to know the answer.

Nick stood up, coming within inches of her, and smiled. "Whether you like it or not, I'm going to help you. I'm going to do what I think is best. No risk is worth your life."

Eve stared up at him like she wanted to argue, but how

could she argue with the truth? He made a vow to himself—he would not let Eve get hurt. No matter what he had to do to prevent it.

Eve stared up at him with those deep green eyes, unpainted face and a look of trust. Damn it, why did she have to put herself out there? Couldn't she just let the authorities handle the investigation? How the hell would he ever live if something happened to her?

Nick had a sinking feeling. Eve Morgan had inched her way under his skin and in no time at all had become much more than a job.

ಸಿ

The edge of the bar bit into Nick's back as he nursed the same stale beer he'd had since he arrived. Three hours ago.

Eve had danced twice now. And both times, he'd nearly busted out of his Levi's. Damn, that woman could move. All the women were popular with the audience tonight, but something about Eve stood out. She had a way of making a man think she only danced for him. The eye contact, the slithering across the stage, the sinful grin she would pass out to no specific man. Oh yeah, teasing came naturally to her and he'd become just as pathetic as all the other men in this smoke-filled room.

With only one more routine to go for the night, Nick couldn't complain. There hadn't been anything out of the ordinary so far, but that didn't mean he'd let his guard down.

His eyes roamed from table to table. Same old, same old. Just men drinking, cursing, and enjoying a damn good show as far as he was concerned. And smoking, he added. They all seemed to smoke. He didn't need to light up a cigarette—he'd inhaled at least three whole packs second-hand.

"Her name is Eve, but she's never volunteered her last name. She's pretty private."

Nick's ears perked up at the male voice behind him. He remained still while two men discussed "the hottest dancer they'd had in a while". Nick sipped on his warm beer, patiently waiting for a name of some kind.

"She may be a good candidate," one said.

"We'd get a pretty penny from her, no doubt," the other stated. "The boss likes her, and you know how much money he gets from those high-class men for a woman that looks like that."

"She has one more set to do, then I'll bring her back to the office to talk. I'll set up an appointment."

Nick didn't like this. Not one bit. But before he could go in the back and drag her out of the smoke-filled pit, she popped back up onstage. This time she wore a starched white nurse's uniform that started just above her nipples and ended right below her sweet, round bottom. White garters peeked out from beneath the costume. Thigh-highs accentuated her long, toned legs. Spiked white heels marched down the stage as she started the routine.

Nick needed a good shot of whiskey to set him straight. Unfortunately, he needed to stay sober.

When Eve's hand went to the top of her uniform, her eyes darted over to his. She licked her sinful red lips as she drew the zipper down over her perky breasts. The costume fell to the stage, leaving Eve in a sheer white bra and thong that matched her garter and hose.

A virginal stripper—any man's fantasy.

Nick tried to look around the club for anything suspicious, but his eyes kept betraying him when they focused back on Eve. Damn her for taunting him. He saw her naughty grin after she'd shed her outfit. She was paying him back for that kiss he'd instigated.

Maybe he should instigate another if he got a show like this.

Nick's erotic fantasy came to an abrupt halt when a short, pot-bellied man moved along the outer wall, heading toward the dressing rooms. Eve had described the shady-looking manager well enough. Nice comb-over, Nick thought as the man disappeared behind the stage.

Nick waited and sure enough, after Eve finished dancing, she appeared moments later following the man back to the office.

A silky red robe covered her white lingerie. Nick only stared at her as she passed. That's right, he thought, don't look at me now. She wasn't stupid. She had to know he didn't like this.

Once Eve and...what was his name? Hank. Yes, Hank. Once they were out of sight, Nick took one last disgusting swig of his warm beer and tossed some bills onto the bar.

With all eyes on the stage as another stripper worked the audience, Nick moved away from the chaos of the bar. He stood against the wall by the office within hearing range, but kept his eyes on the stage so he didn't look suspicious.

"Eve, I'd like to talk to you about something," Hank said.

"Am I in trouble?"

Nick rolled his eyes at the innocence in her tone. Trouble wasn't the word for it. Once she'd stepped into that office, she'd upgraded herself from trouble to deep shit.

"Not at all," Hank assured her. "In fact, you're doing so well, I have a little side job you may be interested in."

"Like two jobs?"

Lay off the stupid act, Eve, you're going into overload. Nick hated standing by waiting for something to happen. At this point they didn't even know if this operation still existed. It had been two months since the last dancer went missing. Right before Eve started dancing.

If these guys had a clue what Eve was up to, they would kill her. He had no doubt. Why had he agreed to this?

"The money is great," Hank explained. "You would still work here, but you would also work with an associate of mine. He runs an upscale business. We like to call it an escort service."

"I don't know, Hank," Eve replied.

Good girl, Nick cheered in his head. Don't jump right for it, get more information.

"I work here nearly every night. When would your associate need me?"

"We'll work something out," Hank promised her in a condescending voice. "Would you like me to schedule a meeting with him?"

"Um...sure. Has he been in here to see me dance?"

"Nearly every night. His assistant just left, actually."

Nick wanted Eve out of there. She'd found out enough for one night. If she pushed too hard, they might get skeptical.

"So what's the name of this guy I might work for?"

Damn the woman, she just had to ask one more question. But now that she had, Nick couldn't wait to hear it.

"Roman Burke."

Fuck.

Nick fell back against the wall, his knees barely holding him upright. Somewhere in the distance music blared and men cheered while a tall, slender woman jerked off her Jane of the Jungle outfit. Smoke filtered over the colored lights. Impatient men yelled their orders to the bartender. Nick stood frozen, unable to do anything but concentrate on breathing.

All the while, Eve stood inside some dingy, smelly office making a date with the devil.

Nick should know. Roman Burke was his stepbrother.

Chapter Four

Keys jingled against the door and Allison had to file away her plan of action and focus on Roman. He always came at this time of the day to check on her. She'd never met a more predictable man. The sex he came for at eleven in the morning, three in the afternoon, and midnight always made her physically ill. Unfortunately, he would allow some of his workers to "enjoy" her as well.

"Darling." His rich, baritone voice erupted from behind her. "I hear you didn't eat your breakfast."

Allison pasted on her most convincing smile, turned and stepped toward him. Should she tell him she'd lost her appetite once she found out she was being sold? In the matter of minutes, her life had gone from shitty to shittier.

"I'm sorry. I guess I was still full from that lovely dinner you had your chef prepare for me last night."

When Roman Burke smiled, he didn't look like the devil. Unfortunately, Allison intimately knew the monster that lurked behind that charming grin.

Roman Burke enchanted women. He made his way through life by becoming the master manipulator and before you knew it, he'd spun you into his web of cruel sexual acts. She'd been wound so tight, so long ago, she feared she'd never break free.

With a gentle hand, he cupped her chin and looked into her eyes. "You're feeling all right?"

"I'm fine." *You cold-hearted bastard.* "I've been waiting for you."

Allison slid her arms around his narrow waist through his Italian silk beige suit jacket, trying not to shudder when his strong arms pulled her against his body...and his erection. The rich, exotic scent clung to his clothes, his body and made her want to gag. Did he bathe in this shit or just continue to dab it on throughout the day? Probably both, she decided. Vain bastard.

Roman's hands slid down her thin, cotton sundress. When he lifted the material, he fisted his hands around her ass and squeezed. Allison gritted her teeth and suppressed a scream at his bruising touch.

It never got any easier. Actually, that made her grateful, because the second being somebody's live-in whore became easy, Allison knew she wouldn't have any fight left.

"You know what I'm thinking?" he purred in her ear.

"I have an idea." *You're thinking you want to get in all the fucks you can before you ship me off to some other tyrant.*

Allison concentrated on the clear vase full of white orchids that decorated the antique mahogany table just over Roman's shoulder. She concentrated on the plush carpet bunched beneath her toes. She concentrated on not throwing up due to the nerves rolling in her stomach.

She concentrated on anything other than his filthy, repulsive hands roaming all over her bare flesh. When he slipped the dress over her head, Allison stood before him completely naked.

As with every time before he began his sexual pleasures with her, he would roam his eyes over her body. Inwardly she cringed at the way his eyes took on a more evil, demented look.

He shrugged out of his jacket, laying it carefully over the burgundy wingback chair beside them. His tanned fingers came up to her shoulders as he started walking her backwards.

When her bare ass came in contact with the glass French door, she wanted to die. He intended to take her here, like this, for all the groundskeepers to see. All his guards to see. All the guests in the cottages to see.

Sick pervert.

"You don't want to close the drapes?" she asked as she ran a fingertip along his smooth, square jaw line.

He undid his belt, unzipped his pants and freed his not-so-impressive erection. "I want everyone to see how wild you are, how passionate. I want them to know you're mine. I want them to want you like I do."

Like they didn't already?

Roman had muscles on top of muscles, which only added to his stamina. The rough, intense sex always lasted a long time. Then again, one minute with Roman was too long.

With little effort, his hands circled her waist as he lifted her off the ground and onto his cock. Allison locked her ankles together, pumped her hips and made all the moans and groans to make him believe he pleasured her. She even yelled his name when she faked her orgasm—just like always.

His breath came in heavy pants against the side of her neck. Humiliation enveloped her at the thought of strange men looking up and seeing her naked ass plastered against the glass door. But what did it matter? They all knew what she was anyway.

A whore. And in a few weeks, nobody would even remember her name.

ஓ

"Make sure she gets anything she wants," Roman informed his guard as he left Allison's room. "We want her to look refreshed and well cared for when she leaves here."

The young man nodded. "Yes, sir."

Roman needed to get back to his office and make some calls. This Eve Morgan was becoming more and more of a problem, hence the reason he insisted on meeting with her. Hank had been one of his henchmen for years. The man was a lazy slob, but a loyal employee. He assured Roman that Eve was eager for a meeting.

Now he had to make sure his meddling brother stayed away. If he had to, he'd kill him, but he really hated getting his hands dirty. He hadn't killed single-handedly in nearly a year.

Roman stepped into his dimly-lit office, crossed the oriental rug and took a seat in his leather chair. Eve would be a nice replacement when Allison left. Both women had bodies that would give a corpse a hard-on and Roman truly considered

Naked Vengeance

keeping Eve for himself. Nothing would torture her more than the knowledge that everyday for the rest of his life, she'd be having sex with the man who killed her father.

Ahh, yes, perhaps the lovely Miss Morgan would keep him company longer than any other woman. Then again, if her body was tainted by his brother's, well, he didn't want Nick's leftovers.

This would be a special case, one in which he'd have to play day by day.

Roman pulled his Blackberry from his middle desk drawer and put a call in to Hank. This meeting had to get underway sooner, rather than later.

Now that he knew his meddling stepbrother was hanging around, he could get his revenge on him as well. Stupid prick, Roman thought bitterly. Always wanted to save the damn world like he was fucking Superman.

Nick had always been the golden boy, the best in school, the best in Roman's mother's eyes. She chose her *step*son over her own flesh and blood. Nick had to pay.

Revenge was the best fuel to any fire and the second Nick stepped into the game, the flames instantly escalated. Some men needed an excuse to be vengeful, Roman didn't need reasons. Money, women, power, those weren't reasons or excuses, they were merely his lifestyle now.

A lifestyle he refused to give up.

ಣ

Eve pulled on a gray tank and a pair of navy-blue boxers. She wrapped her wet hair in a towel and applied the hotel's complimentary jasmine lotion over her arms and freshly shaven legs.

Ahh, the life of a dancer—she had to shave *every day. Everywhere.*

Steam billowed out of the bathroom when she opened the door and stepped out. Nick lounged on his double bed with his back against the thin, wooden headboard—the same position he'd been in when she'd gone into the shower.

After they left the club, she tried to talk to him about the upcoming meeting with this Roman character, but he hadn't said a word. Not one. She'd waited for him to scold her or to try to talk her out of going any further. But he hadn't.

He'd shut down.

Eve stared at his expression now. Brows drawn together, lips thin, jaw clenching. His intense concentration made her curious. Did he know something she didn't? Had Grady called with more information?

"Nick."

Other than the lift of his eyes, he remained motionless and tense.

"Do you want to tell me what's wrong?" Eve stood at the foot of his bed, waiting for an explanation.

"Everything," he muttered.

Eve tossed her dirty clothes she'd carried from the bathroom onto her bed. "Care to elaborate?"

"This whole mess," he exploded, coming off the bed. "You're getting in too deep and I think you should just take the name Hank gave you and give it to Grady. Let me, him and the feds handle this mess from there."

Eve wanted to tell him the truth, she really did, but she needed his help and she couldn't risk him leaving. God, she hated being caught in a position where she needed somebody, especially someone as cocky as Nick.

"I agree we should give Grady the name, but I'm not backing down."

Nick closed the gap between them. "Eve, there comes a time when you just need to back off. Now that we have the name, you can get out of this whole ordeal. Quit the club and go back to whatever it is you used to do."

"I used to tend bar at a titty club back in Virginia," she said in her most convincing voice. "That's how I know so much about stripping, and I lied and told Hank I'd done it before so he'd give me a job."

Nick lifted a dark brow. "You tended bar at a strip club?"

"Yeah. Is there a problem?"

"No, just hard to believe, that's all. You seem..."

Eve waited for him to finish his statement, but he just shrugged.

"I seem what?" she finally prompted.

"Too intelligent to waste your life behind a bar or up on stage taking your clothes off for other men."

A smile split across her face before she could help it. "You think I'm intelligent? Wow, that may be the first compliment I've ever heard come from your mouth. If you think I'm so smart, then quit trying to talk me out of backing down. Trust me enough to know I won't do anything stupid."

Nick lifted his hand toward her, but dropped it just before she could feel his touch. Damn. She wanted him to touch her. It was hell being in such close quarters with him, aching for him, but knowing a sexual relationship would screw up this whole operation. Not to mention she knew absolutely nothing about seduction—even though she played the part on stage every night.

"I trust you," he said roughly. "It's all those unknown players in this game I don't trust. I'm not all-knowing, Eve. If someone snuck into the back door of the club and grabbed you, I wouldn't know it because I'm out front."

His words sank in. Not only did he worry about her, he cared. It wasn't what he said, but the tone in which spoke, not to mention the way he looked at her. Those hard, coal-like eyes softened; his head tilted to the side.

Against the thin cotton tank, her nipples peaked. There was no hiding the natural transformation. And she saw on his face the moment he noticed how aroused she'd become. The man had the most potent effect on her.

Nick cleared his throat and stepped back. "It's late, Eve. Get some sleep and I'll call Grady in the morning and fill him in."

Even though the moment—if that's what that fleeting second could be called—had passed, Eve waited for him to say something else. Something along the lines of, "Your bed or mine?" Yeah, like that would ever happen.

"This isn't going to go away," she said, propping her hands on her hips.

"What?"

She gestured between them. "This thing."

Nick crossed his arms over his broad chest. "And what *thing* would that be?"

"You know exactly what I'm talking about, Nick." Eve took a step toward her bed, tossed her dirty clothes into the floor at her feet and pulled the tacky gold-and-green comforter back. "This sexual tension isn't going to just disappear."

She got into bed and propped herself up against her pillows. Nick still stood between the beds, looking down at her. He didn't look happy.

Eve had a feeling his grouchiness had something to do with the bulge in his pants.

"We don't even like each other," he stated.

"What does sex have to do with liking somebody? Just because we don't like each other doesn't mean we don't find each other attractive."

Clearly uncomfortable, Nick took a step to the end of his bed and sat with his elbows resting on his knees. He looked down at the floor and sank his hands into his thick black hair.

"Fine," he conceded, looking back up. "I'll admit you're attractive, but I find many women attractive. That doesn't mean I sleep with all of them."

"But you want to sleep with me," she added with a grin.

"Has your ego always been this big?"

Eve shrugged. "This has nothing to do with ego. It's the simple truth."

When Nick came back to his feet, Eve had to suppress her giggle. She'd never imagined anything would make big, bad Nick Shaffer nervous. Then again, she'd never imagined herself being this bold about sex.

"Don't worry," Eve went on to say. "I want to sleep with you also, but I'm not going to."

"Are you always this blunt?"

The strain from the past few days had caught up with her. Eve yawned, nestling further down under the thin sheet and bedspread.

"There's no need to dance around each other, ignoring the fact we find each other attractive. Now that it's out in the open, we can move on and work together to find this killer."

Eve reached up and clicked the light off. Darkness fell over the room.

"Good night, Nick."

※

The ice-cold spray from the shower head pelted Nick's back.

Damn woman. He grabbed the bar of soap, scrubbing his frustrations out on his rough skin. Did she think discussing their attractions would make life easier? It sure as hell wasn't working for him.

Now all he wanted to do was go out there, jerk her covers off and strip her naked. He wanted to run his fingers all over her firm, petite body. Then he wanted to trail his tongue along the same path until she squirmed beneath his touch.

He wanted to hear his name drift from her lips as he tasted her. He wanted to hear her scream with pleasure when she climaxed. He wanted her begging for more.

Fuck.

Nick rinsed off and stepped from the shower. Cold water didn't even squelch his desire for Eve, and he had a feeling the urge to have her would only get worse.

Night after night he would have to watch her seductive routines on stage. That right there only gave him incentive to put an end to this mission. A mission he hadn't wanted any part of to begin with.

Nick pulled on a pair of gray cotton shorts and slipped out the bathroom door, leaving the door ajar just a crack to see around the tiny hotel room. Eve lay on her side, facing him. Her breathing came slow and easy, and for a moment, Nick could only stare.

He'd never seen her look vulnerable before. With her full lips slightly open, her head pillowed in her hand, thick lashes falling against her pale cheek... Nick couldn't believe the transformation she could make from a revenge-seeking vixen to a woman who appeared to be the epitome of innocence.

Careful not to wake her, Nick pocketed a key card and his cell. Because he'd asked for a room at the end of a hallway, he stepped just out the side door of the hotel to make a call. If anything happened, he would hear her scream.

Grady wouldn't care the time of night or day. Being head of an FBI team, time didn't factor in when there were new leads on a very important case.

As Nick dialed, he scanned around the deserted parking lot. Other than his car, there were only two others. He kept his back to the hotel as he dialed Grady's home number.

"Hello," the groggy man answered

"Hey, man, sorry to wake you," Nick said, glancing around the lot again. "We've made some progress."

"Tell me." Grady's voice was full of sleep, but Nick knew he had the man's full attention.

"I would've called you earlier, but I didn't want Eve to hear and I couldn't get away until now. She's asleep inside the hotel."

"What couldn't she hear?" Grady asked. "Did you step outside?"

"I'm in the parking lot. She made some progress tonight," Nick began. "Her boss, Hank, called her into his office and told her he had a business associate who was interested in hiring her for a side job."

"Really? What kind of side job?"

"He would only say it was an escort service, but while I was at the bar before Eve's meeting, I overheard Hank and some other guy talking about her. They said they could get a good bit of money from her."

"Shit," Grady muttered.

"Exactly. Anyway, while Eve was in the office she asked who this business associate was who wanted to hire her."

"Did this Hank guy give a name?"

A knot fisted in Nick's stomach. "Roman Burke."

"Doesn't ring a bell."

"Well, this is the part I didn't want Eve to hear," Nick confessed.

"I don't like that tone in your voice, Nick," Grady warned. "What can't Eve know?"

"Roman is my stepbrother."

"*What?*"

Nick looked back inside the glass door toward the room Eve lay sleeping peacefully. "Roman Burke is a cold-hearted bastard and it doesn't surprise me a bit that he has his hands in this operation."

Grady sighed. "Why don't you want Eve to know?"

"Because I'm afraid it may have been Roman who killed Roger. Until I know more, I want to keep this between me and you. If she had any idea my stepbrother may have murdered her father, do you really think she'd let me protect her?"

"You seem to know her well already," Grady said. "But you're right. She'd freak out, but in the end, she'll be pissed. You're screwed either way."

Nick nodded, even though Grady couldn't see him. "I'd rather her be pissed than alone on the hunt for a killer."

"If that's what you think is best, but I don't know if this is the best approach. Do you need to be taken off this case? If this is going to be too uncomfortable for you, I can try to find someone else... I'd rather not, though. You're the best one to keep Eve in line."

"I don't need to be replaced," Nick assured him. "Run a background check on Roman. You won't find much in the past five years or so, but he had some shady dealings before then. He's been careful not to get his hands too dirty lately."

"Do you know where he is?" Grady asked.

"Not exactly. I haven't seen him in years, but he used to own a rather large estate in Florida and a smaller house in North Carolina somewhere along the coast."

Grady muttered under his breath the potential locations for Roman and Nick could only assume he jotted the information down. Grady would have Roman's current home addresses by mid-morning.

"Anything else?"

"Nope," Nick answered. A shadow at the other end of the parking lot caught his eye. "I'll call as soon as I know anything more."

He ended the call and slipped the cell back into his pocket as he watched the dark figure move toward his car. Nick took small steps in the same direction, cringing when a pointy pebble got stuck to his bare foot.

The figure, dressed in all black, pulled something out that caught the reflection of the dim light.

A knife.

When the stranger crouched down in front of Nick's front driver's side tire, Nick took off running. Just before he could say anything, the figure stood and turned toward Nick.

"Get the fuck away from my car."

This had to be a man, Nick figured. The tall, wide build couldn't be that of a woman. He had dark hair, but his face remained in the shadows.

With the knife blade out, the man charged Nick full force. At the last minute, Nick side-stepped and the guy missed. Nick spun around just in time to see the blade before it came in contact with his side.

Damn it!

Nick grabbed his burning side as the assailant took off. It would be ignorant for Nick to chase the guy, seeing as how Nick didn't have his gun or freakin' shoes on his feet. Not to mention the fact his side burned like hell. He'd been stabbed before, even shot once, but it always hurt like a bitch.

With Eve's safety his number-one priority, Nick raced back into the hotel. With one hand still holding his bleeding side, he used the other to unlock the door.

The bathroom door still remained cracked from when he'd showered. Light filtered into the room. He wouldn't turn on the main lamps for fear of the attacker knowing which room they were in. They needed to get out of here. Now.

"Get your stuff," he said gruffly. "We need to go."

Eve sat up on her elbow, rubbed her eyes and yawned. "Go where?"

He went into the bathroom and grabbed his damp towel he'd used minutes ago. He held it to his side, trying to clean up some of the blood.

"I don't know, but I want us gone in thirty seconds."

Eve came to the doorway of the bathroom. "Nick... Oh my God! What happened? There's blood all over your hands."

With easy movements, she pulled the towel away. She gasped as her eyes darted back up to his. "You have to go to the hospital."

"I can't risk it," he said between clenched teeth.

Eve put the towel back against the gash and held it firm. "You can't bleed to death, either."

"I won't bleed to death. Now would you please throw some shoes on and grab your bags. We need to leave."

Eve spun from the room and went to retrieve her stuff. She put her small bag down inside his and pulled it onto her shoulder, then grabbed her suitcase. Nick's car keys sat on the small table by the television. She grabbed them as well. No way would she let him drive.

By the time she got back to the bathroom, Nick's hard body leaned against the counter. His coloring didn't look so good.

His boots were by the door, so she kicked them into the bathroom. "Slip your feet in those. Then you can lean on me and I'll take you to the car."

Since he didn't argue, Eve knew the pain had to be worse than what he'd let on.

She slipped an arm around his bare waist, keeping the towel between their bodies. "Just lean on me and we'll be in the car in no time."

It was a struggle, but Eve managed to get Nick and his firm, heavy body out the door, through the parking lot and settled into the passenger seat. It wasn't until she'd thrown the bags into the trunk that she noticed her shaky hands.

Queasiness and fear were two emotions she did not have time for right now.

She glanced over to Nick after she got in and started the car. "Nick!"

Her hands rushed to his bleeding side as he sat slumped against the door.

"I'm not dead," he mumbled. "I'm just tired. Now get us the hell out of here."

Eve's heart started beating again. God, for a second there he'd looked so...lifeless.

She had no idea where to go. Another hotel? Try to find out if Nick had any family members they could stay with? They only had a half tank of gas, so Eve figured she would drive until they had to stop.

"Talk to me," Eve said, resting one hand on the gear shift.

"About what?"

"Anything. I just want to know you're not passed out and I need you to keep me awake."

The leather seat creaked as Nick shifted his body. "Eve, I can drive if you're that tired."

"I'm not that tired that I would let a stab-wound victim drive me in the middle of the night to God knows where when there's somebody who seems to want one or both of us dead."

"First of all, my wound isn't that bad. Second of all, the guy didn't try to kill me."

Tears pricked her eyes and Eve turned her head slightly to the left so he couldn't see the shimmer. "Don't give me the bullshit about your wound not being bad. I saw it."

"It's not bullshit." Nick covered Eve's hand with his. "I don't think it's that deep. It hurts like hell, but I'll live."

Eve wanted to turn her palm up and lace her fingers with his, but she resisted the urge. Her defenses against this man were weakening and it wouldn't take too much more for them to come crumbling down.

"Tell me what happened."

"After you turned off the light, I took a shower. Then I stepped just outside the hotel to call Grady."

"What did you tell him?"

Nick's hesitation made her wonder if he was going to tell her the truth, part of the truth, or a flat out lie. She found it hard to concentrate on anything right now because he was rubbing his thumb along the back of her hand. It was, no doubt, a gesture he didn't notice. But that light, friendly gesture had her aching to feel those rough fingers all over her body.

"I just wanted to let him know we had a name and you were going to be meeting with him soon."

"Go on," she prompted.

"When I hung up I saw someone creeping through the parking lot, heading toward my car. When I saw him crouch down to my tire with a knife, I took off running after the guy."

"Are you sure it was a guy?" she asked.

"Positive. The build was too big, too filled out and I heard him grunt when he charged at me."

Eve waited for him to continue, but silence filled the air. She glanced over, afraid he'd finally passed out.

"Nick?"

"It's funny how your mind works," he said.

"Why is that?"

"You automatically wanted to know if I was sure the person was a man."

Eve shrugged. "It was a logical question."

"Yes, but regular people wouldn't have thought of something like that. Most would have assumed it would be a man."

Eve eyed him for a second before looking back onto the dark road. The headlights sliced through the night, leading a path to their unknown destination. "I don't assume anything. Did you see his face?"

"There was a shadow over it."

Since they'd left the hotel nearly thirty minutes ago, there hadn't been a single soul on the highway. So far, they weren't being followed.

Eve scolded herself for letting her guard slip. She couldn't act so aware of details and her surroundings. To Nick, she was a regular civilian. Actually, in the eyes of the government, she was a regular civilian, too.

No standard-issue gun, no badge. No FBI.

She would give anything if this whole shitload of a mess was done. She wanted her life and her job back. She wanted her father's murderer brought to justice. Which, in her eyes, meant dead.

They drove in silence for a while. Occasionally Eve would glance over to make sure Nick's chest still rose and fell. His large, warm hand remained on hers; his thumb, however, had stopped stroking her.

Eve wasn't sure exactly where they were. She'd circled around quite a bit when they first left before she headed south. She hadn't seen anybody follow them. If she figured right, they should only be about an hour from the club.

As she pulled into the lot of a small hotel, she wondered if she should call Grady, then immediately dismissed the notion. That call could wait until they got settled into a room and she could clean Nick's nasty-looking wound.

He slept with his head resting against the glass, the towel still wedged perfectly between his side and the console. She slid her hand from beneath his and turned off the car.

Just as she started to open her door, he grabbed her wrist.

"Holy shit," she cried as she looked over her shoulder. "You scared me."

"Where are we?"

"About an hour away from Charleston. I'm going to get us a room. I'll be right back."

Eve popped the trunk and pulled out a T-shirt from Nick's bag. Even though it was huge on her, it was either that or go inside wearing boxers and a tank with no bra.

She pulled out a black—could there be any other color?—T-shirt and slipped it over her head. It hit her knees. Oh well, now she just looked like she had on only a shirt and tennis shoes.

The elderly woman running the desk didn't take a second glance at Eve or her attire once Eve whipped out cash. The woman pocketed the money and handed over a key.

Their room was at the end of the lot. Eve pulled in front and took all the bags in, then came back out to help Nick, but the stubborn man was trying to get in by himself.

If she weren't so worried about his injury, she would've taken more time to appreciate his male form. Well, maybe she could worry and appreciate at the same time. His bare shoulders looked broader, stronger. All that golden skin wrapped over one hundred percent muscle tone. Eve ached to run her fingers along all that bare flesh.

First things first. She had to get him inside, clean him up

and make that call to Grady.

Nick winced when he stepped his bare feet onto the gravel. When Eve came to his side, he shook his head.

"I'm fine."

Eve hovered just the same. She didn't touch him, but she stood close in case he needed her.

Once they were inside the musty room, Nick sat on the bed. That's right, the one and only bed. Just freakin' wonderful, Eve thought. It was like a scene from a bad B movie.

"I have a small first-aid kit," she said as she unzipped her bag.

Nick scooted over and lay back against the headboard and grinned at her when she came to sit by his side. "You asked for one bed, didn't you?"

Eve popped open the kit, set it on the nightstand and pulled out some alcohol pads, gauze, tape and scissors. "No, smartass, I was too worried about you to ask for anything. I just said I wanted a room. But as soon as I'm done here, I'll go see if they have another room with two beds."

When she pulled the towel away from his side, she sighed with relief. The bleeding had stopped.

"Let me get a wet cloth."

Eve went into the tiny bathroom and wet a white washcloth with cool water. When she sat next to Nick once again on the bed, she had a hard time focusing on her task.

His spicy male scent filtered through her senses. His smooth, naked flesh nearly burned her fingertips. His breath came slow and easy.

Worst of all, she could feel his heated gaze on her as she dabbed the dried blood from his side. If she kept her hands moving, perhaps he wouldn't notice how they shook.

How could cleaning a stab wound be so arousing?

Once she had the area cleaned off, she could see the actual gash. It wasn't as bad as she'd first thought, but it was still bad enough.

"Don't even think of putting that alcohol on me." His deep, soothing voice cut the silence.

"Don't be a baby. You don't want it to get infected," she

said as she looked up.

Big mistake.

Her hands stilled on his side. The way he looked at her made her wonder what he was thinking. His eyelids were heavy, his head tipped to the side and he had that damned cocky smile back.

Why did she have to find him so damn charming? Worst of all, he knew it.

"What?" she finally asked.

"You're shaking." He reached down with his large hand to cover both of hers.

"Well, if I am, it's only because I don't like blood," she retorted.

He sat up a little higher, leaned his face down within inches of hers. "That's not why you're shaking."

Eve looked down to their adjoined hands. She couldn't figure out why she let him get the upper hand. She'd never been this easy to read before, so why did she have to be with the one man she wanted more than her next breath?

"Eve."

When her eyes drifted back up, his face had taken on a serious look. He no longer wore a smile, his breathing had become heavier and his eyes were completely open and concentrated on her.

"You were right," he whispered.

Her heart thumped so hard in her chest, she was afraid he could hear it. "About what?"

"This tension between us. It won't go away."

With her hands sandwiched between his warm body and his strong hands, Eve couldn't get up and run the way she wanted to. This must have been how he'd felt back at the other hotel when she'd tried discussing this sexual awareness.

All of a sudden, she didn't feel so confident.

"I think it would be best if you let me work alone from here on out," Eve said once she found her voice. "It could be dangerous if we get preoccupied with...sexual thoughts."

Nick quirked one corner of his mouth up. "I want to have

more than thoughts. I want you, Eve."

Eve jerked her hands from beneath his and stood. "Well, it isn't going to happen. You are going to go back to...wherever it is you live, and I am going to find my father's killer. Grady will help me if I ask him."

Nick came to his feet as well, dumping all the contents from his lap into the floor. "Like hell I'll leave you alone to do this. You aren't trained to handle these people, Eve. They're not messing around. If you give them a chance, they'll kill you."

"Well, I don't want to be responsible for you," she cried back.

"Responsible?" Nick asked, taking a step toward her. "Why would you be responsible?"

Her eyes drifted to his side as she felt the burn in her eyes. Damn it, she would not let him see her upset. She turned around, wrapping her arms around her waist.

When his gentle hands settled on her shoulders, she thought it would undo her. Fortunately, he couldn't see her eyes and she had enough time to will the tears away.

"Eve, my getting stabbed is not your fault. I'm the one who went after the guy. If I had stayed in the room with you, where I should've been anyway, the guy would've only slashed my tires."

Eve swallowed and took a deep breath. "That might be, but it doesn't change the fact you're hurt because you were with me."

He turned her to face him, his hands came up to frame her face. "If I didn't want to be here, I wouldn't be."

All the willpower Eve had built up against this potent man vanished. Did she really think she could resist him for much longer?

Nick pulled her face toward his as he captured her mouth. Eve opened for him, welcoming him in. Her arms slid up his bare chest and around his neck.

She molded her body against his, needing to feel more of his strength. The kiss wasn't as hard and fast as their first one. She hadn't known Nick's lips could be tender, passionate. Whether fast or tender, the man knew how to make a woman weak in the knees.

Nick roamed one hand down her body, reaching around to grab her ass. He fisted his other hand in her hair and pulled her head back just a touch—their lips barely apart.

"I want you," he said against her mouth. "Tell me you want this."

Eve could only nod as she reached down to take off the T-shirt she'd put on over her tank and boxers. She tossed it to the side before he pulled her back into his warm embrace. Solid, safe, protective embrace.

Her nipples rubbed against the soft material of her tank and just that thin barrier proved to be too much. She wanted skin to skin. Heat to heat.

Nick's rough hands roamed up under her shirt, cupping her breasts so tenderly, Eve thought she might die from want. Shivers and nerves ran the course of her body, bumping into each other. She'd never felt such an intoxicating sensation.

She grabbed his shoulders and pulled him back down for another invigorating kiss. Her tongue swept through his mouth, tasting him. He matched her urgency with a need of his own and Eve knew this was it.

Nick would be her first lover.

The eager hands that tormented her breasts slid out from her shirt. In a second he had her enveloped into his strong arms as he slowed the kiss, taking time to nip at her full lips.

Was foreplay always this frustrating? Couldn't they just get on with it? Didn't his body ache just as much as hers?

As Nick kissed his way down her throat, Eve arched her back to allow him all the access he wanted. He dipped his tongue beneath the scoop of her tank, teasing her just enough to have her moaning...and nearly begging.

When her cell phone rang, they froze.

Nick's head snapped up, his gaze locking with hers. "You better get that. It could be important."

More important than losing your virginity in some dingy no-tell motel? More important than finally having someone give a damn about your feelings and needs? More important than realizing there is indeed a life out there for someone like her?

He loosened his grip on her and Eve felt a chill come over

her body as she dug through her bag. If it wasn't Grady saying he'd caught the killer and the slimy bastard was already on death row, she really didn't give a damn right now.

She flipped the cell open. "Hello."

"I hope your boyfriend's all right."

All the heat in her body turned to ice as Eve turned to look at Nick. "He's not my boyfriend."

"That's good to know. I don't like to share."

"What do you want?" she asked.

"You, Eve. I've wanted you for some time now. But don't worry, our time is coming sooner than you think."

Eve snapped her phone shut and slammed it down on the bed. "Fuck!"

"What did he say?" Nick asked.

"He wanted to know if you were okay. He called you my boyfriend."

Eve paced the room. Between the phone call and what could have been the best moment of her life being ruined, Eve felt like screaming. Did this ongoing nightmare have a damn ending? She'd had more than enough of playing games, she wanted justice and she wanted it now.

"He said he didn't like sharing and that our time together was coming sooner than I think."

When she spun back to face Nick, his eyes showed no sign of the passion he'd had only moments ago. "I'm calling Grady. We're going somewhere safer."

"I think we should get some sleep before we do anything," she suggested. "We're both running on adrenaline and I have to work tonight."

"Of course," Nick exploded as he threw his arms in the air. "We don't want to quit stripping. What does it matter if someone wants you dead? As long as Joe Schmo gets his thrills for the night."

"Nick." Eve kept her voice low, trying to keep this situation under control. "These calls have to be related to my father's death. They didn't start until I began snooping on my own. It may be the killer himself calling. I've come too far to quit now. If I don't find out who it is, I'll be looking over my shoulder all my life because he knows who I am. Do you think he'll stop coming after me if I quit the club?"

Nick grabbed the gauze and tape from the floor and began to bandage himself. Eve took a step forward, but stopped cold when his hard eyes came up.

"Don't," he barked. "Get all our stuff back in the car. I'll call Grady from the road."

Eve hesitated. She hadn't heard Nick that angry before. How could a man go from so loving and tender one minute to furious and hateful the next?

When she had all their bags gathered, she went out the door and slammed it behind her. Perhaps fate had jumped in at precisely the right time.

Sleeping with Nick would've been the biggest mistake of her life.

Chapter Five

Allison cried like she'd never cried before as she lay across her king-sized canopy bed. Wails of torment flooded out of her until finally her door opened a crack.

"Ms. Myers," the guard called. "You okay?"

She answered in a sob, pleased when she heard him tell the other guard he'd be right back. With a soft click, the door shut behind him and his footsteps carried him to the edge of her bed.

"Are you hurt?" he asked.

Thank God. It was the young guard—she hoped that meant the naïve guard. This could work... It had to.

Allison lifted her head as forced tears continued to pour down her face. "I'm not hurt," she sniffled.

"Do you want me to get Mr. Burke?"

"No."

"Is there anything I can do?"

The concern in his voice gave Allison hope—something she hadn't had for some time. "I just want to go home."

"I'm sorry, ma'am. I can't help you."

"I know," she sighed, lifting her head to look at the young man again. "It's just that today is my sister's birthday and I wanted to talk to her."

The fair-haired adolescent dipped his hands into the pockets of his khaki pants. "I don't think that's possible."

"No, you're right," she agreed. "I just wish I could call her and tell her happy birthday."

Junior bit on his bottom lip and Allison almost felt sorry for using him. Almost.

"Maybe if you give me her number, I could call for you," he suggested hesitantly.

Allison sprang up off the bed. A little dramatic, but this was all an act anyway. "Would you really?"

"I can't do it until my shift is over, because Mr. Burke would kill me."

She knew that wasn't just a figure of speech. Roman would kill this boy if he found out. It was a chance Allison had to take—selfish or not.

"I would be grateful if you would do that."

Allison went over to her nightstand and pulled out a piece of paper and pen. She jotted a number down and passed it to the nervous boy.

Just for extra incentive, she reached up and kissed him on the cheek. "Thanks."

A faint blush crept up his neck and covered his face. "Yes, ma'am."

He spun from the room and walked out. Allison prayed her plan would work. If Roman found out, he would not only kill Junior, he'd kill her without thinking twice.

૪૭

"Tell me how you know Grady so well," Eve said as she slipped off her shoes and pulled her feet up into the passenger seat.

They'd been driving in silence for an hour now. After Nick had called Grady and explained the stabbing and the latest phone call, Grady gave them directions to a safe house not far outside of Charleston.

Eve couldn't handle the dark, quiet car another minute. If she thought the sexual tension had been bad before, it was a hell of a lot worse now. She could still feel his hands on her aching nipples. She could taste him when she licked her lips. She could feel his body beneath her fingertips.

"We were in the Marines together," Nick told her. "We became best friends during that time. He got out before me, but we never lost contact. After he got out, he joined the FBI."

Eve turned to study his profile. It still amazed her how a hard, stone-like face could have the power to soften into something more caring, more loving. Perhaps the emotion she'd seen earlier hadn't been real on his end.

"What did you do after you left the Marines?"

His eyes never wavered. Every now and then, he would glance into the rearview mirror. Eve could've told him they weren't being followed, but then he would ask more questions that she just couldn't answer.

"I went into law enforcement. When that got too monotonous, I opened my own security company. I don't like taking orders very well."

"I never noticed."

A slight grin appeared, then vanished just as fast. "Smartass."

Eve adjusted the air vent so it blew over her shoulder. "Do you work alone now?"

"Yeah. I guess I'm what some would label a loner. If I work by myself, I don't have to worry about anybody else's screw ups."

"Do you have any family?"

Nick glanced at her, then back to the road. "Nosy this morning, aren't we? Why the sudden interest in my personal life? It's not like we're dating."

Eve shrugged, ignoring the hurt. "Just trying to pass the time. Forget it."

When he sighed, she looked out the side window at the two-lane country road they'd been on for a while now. The safe house shouldn't be too much farther. Then maybe she could put some distance between them. A nice walk by herself would do her some good, or maybe even a long, relaxing bath.

"My mom and dad live in Texas," he finally said. "I'm an only child."

"You don't have to talk to me, Nick. I can tell you'd rather not, so I'll just sit here and not ask anymore questions. When you want to kiss me again, I'll just remind you we're not dating."

"I don't always date people I kiss," he muttered. "I don't know why you have to pout."

Eve looked over, giving him a cold, dead stare. "Do I look like I'm pouting?"

"You look pissed."

Eve turned her gaze back out the window, ignoring his accuracy. A few steamy kisses and some fondling didn't give her access into his life. Unfortunately, she hadn't played a game like this. She'd never gotten that intimate with a man before. She made the mistake in assuming they could talk about something other than the case.

She didn't need a slap in the face to realize that if they had slept together, Nick wouldn't have given her another thought once they'd finished this job. She would just be another warm body in what she was sure had to be a long line of women he'd left behind. It was just as well, though. Distractions like Nick Shaffer would definitely hinder her plans.

When a man looked like him, he could have any woman he wanted—which just drove the point home that he liked being alone. Eve knew she had some naivety in the relationship department, but it still bothered her that her feelings were becoming too real and too deep for this unworthy man.

They pulled into a long, dusty lane. Large, leafy green trees canopied the road, almost forming a tunnel up to the safe house. After about a half a mile, they found the small beige cottage nestled into the woods.

An empty porch stretched across the front, only a few overgrown shrubs outlined the house and a small dormer jutted out of the second story. It looked abandoned. Perfect.

"Cozy," Eve said dryly.

Nick eyed her. "It's better than that roach-infested place you just had us at."

"I never saw a roach," Eve countered as she opened the car door. "Pop the trunk."

When the trunk lid flew up, Eve grabbed their bags as Nick went to the base of the steps to look for the key Grady assured him would be hidden.

"Maybe someone hasn't had time to bring it and hide it," Nick thought aloud.

"If Grady said it'll be here, then it's here." Eve sat the luggage on the steps and squatted beside the second shrub from the left. "He said it would be buried behind this bush."

When her fingers separated the dirt, she felt a cool metal key. She rose with it in hand and smiled. "He always comes through."

"You sound as if you know him pretty well. I take it he's come through for you in the past?"

Was that jealousy she heard in his voice? Well, that wouldn't that be fun to build upon.

"Better than most," she commented as she picked up the bags.

"I can carry my own damn bag," he grumbled.

Eve tossed his duffle onto the broken sidewalk in front of the steps. "Fine."

She unlocked the door and stepped inside to an open floorplan. Wonderful. No matter if she sat in the kitchen or the living room, she would have to look at Nick.

The small staircase to her left, she assumed, led to the bedrooms. Just as she put her foot on the bottom step, Nick stopped her.

"Where are you going?"

She looked over her shoulder. "Looks like up."

"Don't be such a smartass," he growled. "It'll be hotter than hell up there. You might as well stay down here and rest on the couch."

Eve turned and continued up the steps. "I'd rather sweat up there than sit down here with you."

Like the first floor, the second floor was wide open—with only one bedroom. Eve looked around and cringed. No bathroom. That meant if she had to pee, she had to go downstairs.

"Are you fucking kidding me?" she mumbled.

If Nick wanted to take the bed, Eve would sleep on the couch. Hell, she'd sleep in the bathtub before she got in that bed with him.

She tossed her stuff on the floor and went over to turn the window unit on the highest, coolest setting. Once she had the vents aimed straight for the bed, she pulled her T-shirt off and threw on a bra so she wasn't completely naked. Until the room got to a reasonable temperature, she would rest in her bra and her denim cut-offs.

Eve sat on the edge of the full-sized bed and toed off her tennis shoes, letting them clunk onto the hardwood floor. The thin pillow provided little comfort, but she crossed her arms behind her head, waiting for the cool air to flow over her body.

An image of Nick stretched out on the sofa downstairs filled her mind. Had he taken off his shirt, too? If she snuck down to take a peek, would she see him looking as frustrated as she was? Would the stark white bandage against his golden skin make him look more like a hero?

Stupid, she scolded herself. Nick wasn't giving her another thought—more than likely he'd already fallen asleep, with his shirt on, dreaming about voluptuous women who would obey his every sexual demand...with no questions regarding his personal life.

Just as sleep claimed her, Eve thought of the way Nick chose to stick by her side until the killer was caught. Maybe he wasn't so bad after all.

ଛଠ

Nick stood at the base of the steps for a good ten minutes, arguing with himself on whether or not to go upstairs and see what the hell had gotten Eve so worked up. He knew the conversation, or lack thereof, in the car had angered her, but he couldn't get close to someone again.

Damn it, he should have never taken their relationship to such an intense level. What had he been thinking? They didn't have a relationship. He had a hard-on that wouldn't quit and she'd had stars in her eyes when she'd looked at him back at the hotel.

But since the phone call that threw cold water on their heavy-duty make-out session and him giving her the cold shoulder, Eve had been different. How could he blame her? The

Naked Vengeance

woman wanted to find the man who had killed her father. Unfortunately, she could get herself killed in the process.

And to put the icing on this fucked-up cake, his stepbrother was more than likely the evil bastard behind this whole mess.

Nick knew he owed her an apology for being so distant, but he feared if he went upstairs, he wouldn't be able to keep his hands off her. He really tried not to let her affect him, but the woman had turned into a juxtaposition of sweet innocence and a kick-ass attitude. When she'd cleaned his knife wound, her hands weren't as steady as she probably would've liked. She'd chewed on her bottom lip as worry had drawn her brows together.

But the moment she'd looked up into his eyes, the signs were all over her face. Flushed cheeks, wide eyes, moist lips from her pink tongue. She wanted him as much as he wanted her. But something scared her.

He hadn't seen the woman back down from anything, so why should a little intimacy frighten her? Had she been in a bad relationship? Perhaps she'd never had a good bed partner. Under different circumstances he would be more than happy to show her a good time in the sack.

A momentary lapse of judgment had clouded his mind when he'd all but attacked her. This woman had been Roger's daughter. Roger, the man he hadn't protected. The man who'd trusted him. The man he'd ultimately failed.

Nick cursed himself for the lack of respect he'd showed to his old friend and his daughter. Eve might be every man's wet dream, but that's where she would have to stay. In his dreams.

Giving in to the inevitable, Nick mounted the stairs. He had to get the guilt off his chest and tell her he was sorry for being a prick, then he could come back down and get some shut-eye before they figured out what to do next.

The humming of a window unit greeted him as he mounted the stairs, so Nick assumed she planned on staying up there, since it would eventually cool off. When he turned to take the last two steps, he froze. The bed sat in his direct line of vision.

So did Eve. Stretched out, arms above her head, wearing no shirt, displaying one hell of a body.

Why was it again he wanted to keep a physical distance?

Without a sound, Nick took the last two steps and made his way over to her bedside. There was that innocent look again. Perhaps she looked so innocent because she wasn't back-talking him, he mused.

Because his hands ached to touch her, he folded his arms over his chest and caressed her body with only his eyes. From her perfectly polished red toenails, up her lean legs, to the fringe from her jean shorts laying against her tanned thighs, then onto her little bellybutton.

When he got to her breasts, he lingered. The pale yellow bra barely covered her. With the way her arms were stretched to pillow her head, her lush breasts threatened to spill out of the satiny cups.

He forced his eyes up to her flawless face and frowned when he noticed the dark circles beneath her eyes. The woman didn't take care of herself enough. Then again, neither did he. Of course, he was used to working for days without adequate rest or food. Eve didn't deserve living in fear, worrying about her father's killer running free, scared she might be next. And she sure as hell didn't deserve the lie he kept from her... No matter how he justified it to himself.

Arguing with her was a losing battle, but he wished she would let him and Grady finish this investigation. The Charleston PD hadn't closed the investigation, but since it had been a year, they had to put their manpower to more recent cases. But Nick knew if he needed more help, they would be there as well. He couldn't think of one single reason someone as delicate and loving as Eve should have to get mixed up in this lifestyle. Some may consider him sexist, but if he had his way, Eve would be far away. He didn't really give a damn what other people thought. Eve's safety was priority number one.

When she sighed and shifted, Nick refocused his attention. She looked up at him with those bright green eyes and he felt as if he'd been punched in the gut. Her mass of curls spread out like flames over the white pillowcase. She didn't try to cover herself as most women would, but then, Eve wasn't just any other woman.

Nick knew right then. He'd lost the battle with his heart. Lost in a way he hadn't before and the unknown territory scared the shit out of him.

"Why are you staring at me?" she asked in a sleepy voice.

"I came up to talk to you," he replied, trying to keep his eyes on her face. "I didn't know you'd be asleep."

Eve brought her arms down and clasped her fingers over her toned belly. "Why aren't you sleeping?"

Nick shoved his hands in the pockets of his jeans. "I wanted to apologize to you."

"Why?"

"Because I was rude in the car."

A naughty smile brightened her face. "Are you only apologizing for the car? You've been rude since I met you."

Nick shrugged. "Yeah, well, I didn't hurt your feelings all the other times."

Eve came up to her elbows and Nick couldn't help but notice her contracted abdominal muscles. Damn, that woman was built.

"What makes you think you hurt my feelings?"

He cleared his throat. "Any other time you've given shit right back, but this time you wouldn't look at me and you were quiet."

"My feelings aren't hurt," she said. "So now that you've cleared your conscience, you can get some sleep."

Nick didn't move. Did she think he was that much of an ass that he would brush her feelings aside so easily?

"Eve, I don't want you to think I didn't want to open up, it's just that... Well, I'm private. I don't open up to anybody," he explained.

"Duly noted," she said as she rolled to her side. Away from him. "If you don't want sleep, I do."

He'd been dismissed.

Damn. He didn't want to go downstairs, he wanted to crawl into that bed and curl up beside her smooth, bare skin. He wanted to draw her skimpy shorts down and see if her panties matched her bra. He wanted to taste her again. And again.

Reluctantly, Nick turned and went back downstairs.

Eve had been right. They needed to rest in order to deal

with whatever lay ahead—killers, stalkers, missing women. Romance. Nick had to be ready for it all.

⁂

"Grady called with some information on a missing girl," Nick told Eve as she followed him into the safe house.

At three in the morning, Eve's feet were practically screaming from dancing for nearly nine hours. Even though she'd changed into her tennis shoes after her shift, she'd spent way too many hours in stilettos strutting and dancing. Two other women had called off and Eve had to perform more than her usual three times.

"What did he say?" she asked, dropping her bag inside the door.

Nick moved into the kitchen and flicked the overhead light on. "We think the last woman who was taken from the club, Allison Myers, is alive and nearby."

Achy feet forgotten, Eve snapped her attention to Nick as he pulled a can of soda from the fridge. "What happened?"

Eve watched as Nick took a long, slow drink. "Somebody called Allison's sister and wished her a happy birthday. The boy said Allison asked him to call."

"Why do you think she's nearby?"

Nick came back into the living room and took a seat on the plain brown couch. "The sister said the boy sounded very young and had a strong Southern accent. He said Allison was all right. I guess the sister asked where Allison was and he told her he couldn't say exactly, but it wasn't far."

Eve crossed her arms and shifted from one sore foot to another. "Not far?"

"He hung up before she could ask anything else. The sister called the local feds and happened to speak with an agent named Max Price. His sister was the first girl taken. Carly Price."

"I assume they couldn't trace the call?"

Nick shook his head as he rested the soda can on his hard

stomach and crossed his ankles in front of him. "It came from a pay phone a couple of hours southeast of Charleston."

"Then maybe that's where she is."

"Maybe," he agreed. "Or maybe it's a deterrent to throw us off."

"I don't think so," Eve argued. "There would be no reason after two months for someone to call out of the blue. I think Allison made friends with this boy and convinced him to call her sister. She wants us to know she's alive. There were no other phone calls with any of the other girls."

"Grady's working with the local feds to search the area where the phone call came from. He's going to call me when he learns something. This Max guy is keeping him informed."

"That's it?" Eve asked in disbelief. "You don't want to go there and look for ourselves?"

Nick's eyes leveled on her. "No. We're staying put working at it from this angle. When is your meeting with this other guy who wants to hire you?"

"Friday."

"Fine. We'll be ready."

Eve waited for him to say something else, but he took another drink and looked away—as if he couldn't look at her anymore. Something had flickered in his eyes when he'd asked about the meeting. His feelings weren't a secret... He didn't want her going through with it, but backing down now wasn't an option.

Since Nick seemed to be done with chit-chat, Eve lifted her bag and went upstairs without another word. The man infuriated her. One minute he only showed concern for her feelings, the next he became angry and cold.

Nick had so many different layers to him—Eve couldn't even begin to peel away the first one to see what truly made the man.

Eve threw her duffle onto the bed and stripped down to nothing. She'd taken some of the new costumes from the club to try on in privacy. She wanted something..."wow" for Friday night. Something that would make this Roman guy take notice and want her. The thought of such a horrid man wanting her should be repulsive. Instead it just made her more eager.

She pulled out the red leather bustier and slithered into it. Once she was certain she wouldn't break a rib if she moved, she bent down to slide the matching G-string up her legs. She looked around the room, but there wasn't a mirror. The bathroom had one. The bathroom downstairs...where Nick slept.

For a second Eve contemplated not going down there, but hell, the guy had seen her strip for several nights now. It wasn't anything he hadn't seen before at the club.

Except now they were alone. No music, no lights. Just the silence of the night and some lustful feelings she couldn't shake. Eve called down the steps to him, but he didn't answer. Maybe he'd gone outside to call Grady or he'd already fallen asleep.

She tiptoed down the stairs, grateful when she didn't see him on the couch and even more grateful only a small table lamp was on, giving off a pale, glowing light.

She gathered up all her nerve and streaked across the room...just as Nick opened the bathroom door.

Wearing nothing but a towel and perfected muscle tone under bronzed skin.

For several long, tense moments, they said nothing. Eve found herself mesmerized by the iridescent drops of water clinging to his broad shoulders. Had he felt this hot when he'd seen her in only a towel after her shower? Both times?

"I thought you might be outside," Eve finally said. "I...um...needed to see a mirror and there wasn't one in my room."

The thick towel circling Nick's waist did a poor job of hiding his growing erection. "You don't need a mirror. You have to know how you look in that."

His thick voice sounded almost strained. Eve was really wishing the floor would open up and swallow her. Why had she thought she could handle the risk of running into him wearing this seductive outfit?

Because she hadn't counted on him wearing only a scrap of terrycloth.

"I'll just go back upstairs and finish trying on my costumes," she informed him, but remained rooted to the hardwood floor.

Steam from his shower filtered out around him. Black strands of wet hair fell across his forehead in disarray. His bandage had been removed, revealing a nasty cut on his perfect flesh. The fresh, clean scent from him enveloped her and the very *last* thing she wanted to do was go upstairs.

If she was honest with herself, she really wanted to pull that towel off and finish what they'd started yesterday.

"This is not good," he said, taking a step toward her.

Eve instinctively stepped back. "No, it's not. That's why I'll go back upstairs and you will stay down here. Tomorrow we can laugh about this."

Nick kept walking toward her as she retreated. "This isn't funny."

When Eve felt the side of the couch against her legs, she stopped. "Nick, we have to be adults about this. Sleeping together isn't going to accomplish anything, and we'll just be mad at each other tomorrow."

He stepped within inches of her and smiled. "Actually, I think it would accomplish a lot, and as far as tomorrow... It doesn't exist."

Eve wanted to give into her desire and his persistence, but...

"Would you back up? I can't think with you so damn close," she said, raising a hand to his chest.

Dumb, dumb move. Now instead of pushing him away, she flattened her palm against his skin—his irregular heartbeat under her fingertips. She snapped her eyes up to his. The heat shimmered in his eyes and she knew it mirrored her own. With one hand still on his chest, she brought the other one up to his freshly shaven jaw line.

"I don't want to want you," she confessed as her eyes drifted up to meet his.

Those dark, penetrating eyes roamed over her face. "I didn't want this either, but I've given in to the inevitable. Since I pulled you into that alley and caught sight of your tempting body beneath that excuse for a robe, I knew I had to have you."

Eve took a deep breath. He hadn't used the most romantic

words, but right now, she didn't care. His skin was so slick, so hard under her hands. He looked at her as if she were the most amazing woman in the world. And her panties were so damp, she just knew she would start dripping onto the floor. So she gave in.

Courage she didn't know existed built up from deep in her and took over. She slid her hands down to the towel, unhooked the knot and let it fall silently to pool around his bare feet.

"Then take me."

Chapter Six

Eve's low, throaty words registered in his head, but he couldn't believe it. He couldn't believe this would actually happen.

Nick slid his hands up her arms. She trembled beneath his touch. "If you're going to change your mind, you'd better tell me now, because in about five seconds, I won't be able to stop myself."

The wide, naughty grin she offered told him all he needed to know. This woman wanted him as much as he wanted her. Thank God.

He kicked the towel out of his way as he plunged his hands into her mass of thick, curly hair. Hauling her up against his damp, naked body, all the pent-up need he had came flooding out.

Those lush, leather-bound tits pressed against him. The tops of her smooth bare thighs rubbed against his. And when her full, pink lips parted, he took the plunge.

She answered his demanding kiss with demands all her own. As if bracing herself, she held onto his biceps, squeezing him as he swept his tongue across hers. Her warm, sweet taste filled his mouth.

Finally. He was finally going to know what Eve felt like beneath him, on him. Around him.

Nick roamed his hands down her back until he came in contact with her firm, bare ass. He filled his hands with her, lifting her up off the floor until his cock rested against the triangle of red leather covering her sweet mound.

Eve let out a short moan when he lifted his mouth from hers.

"As much as I love this outfit, it has to go," he demanded in a voice he didn't recognize as his own.

Still keeping his hands on her ass, Nick let her body slide back to the floor. He stepped back, just enough for her to undo the little hooks down the front of the bustier.

As she undid them one by one, Nick's heart thumped faster. His dick throbbed harder.

Her hands trembled as she freed her breasts. As soon as the garment peeled away from her body, she looked up, uncertainty swimming in her eyes.

"The panties, too," he croaked out.

Damn. Her high, full tits mocked him. Only inches away, her nipples peaked, begging to be sucked on. As Eve hooked her thumbs into the side strings of her panties, Nick stopped her.

"Wait. Let me."

He stepped forward, bent his head and sucked on mauve bud. He couldn't wait another second to taste her aroused flesh. He circled her nipple with his tongue, gliding his hands down her small waist. Sliding his hands through her panties, he inched them down over her slender hips until they fell freely around her ankles.

Nick moved to the other nipple as Eve stepped out of her last restraining piece of clothing. Never breaking the contact with her taut nipple, Nick wrapped his arms around her midsection and picked her up.

"Wrap your legs around my waist."

When Eve complied, Nick sat on the sofa so she could straddle him. The tip of his penis came in contact with moist, hot flesh. His hands roamed back up her body, stopping at her chest. He rubbed the moisture from his tongue into her skin. Once she glistened from his touch, he cupped her breasts—one in each hand—and thumbed her nipples.

"Nick."

"What?"

"I...I can't take it," she panted. "We need a condom."

"Shit." Nick released her long enough to reach over to the

side table where he kept his wallet. He retrieved the foil packet and had it in place in no time.

His hands came back to settle on her hips. In one forceful, determined move, he pushed her down, until her tight glove enveloped him.

Her *tight* glove.

Fuck.

Her body stilled for only a second before she rested her hands on his shoulders. She kept her eyes closed as Nick began to move.

Right now he didn't care that she hadn't told him. All he cared about was how damn good it felt to be buried so deep in her after days of fantasizing.

Using only his hands, he eased her hips back and forth until she began to set her own rhythm. Her lids remained shut as she chewed on her bottom lip and gripped his shoulders. Small, pleading moans escaped her.

Now that she had the hang of it, Nick lifted his hands to her breasts. She arched her back, tilted her head back and rode him harder. His own hips jerked in response. He didn't want to lose it, not before she received pleasure.

With her head still back, her body rocking in sync with his, Nick snaked a hand down to where they joined. He touched her, just so, until her head snapped up, her sea-green eyes flew open, and she screamed.

The hand he'd had on her breast came up to the back of her neck. He pulled her mouth against his own and swallowed her cries of pleasure.

As her inner muscles constricted around his cock, he continued to stroke her core as his tongue danced with hers. Her short nails bit into the skin of his shoulders and Nick lost it. He came hard and fast. Just the way he liked it.

Once their convulsions ceased, Eve's head fell onto his shoulder. Her warm breath tickled his skin. He let one hand rest on her inner thigh. The other still covered her breast.

Well, hell. Now what? Should he proceed with caution? Try to be sensitive? Just come out and ask her?

"Is there a reason you didn't tell me you were a fucking

virgin?"

Her lax body instantly stiffened against him. Okay, so maybe he hadn't used the best approach.

Eve jerked her head up. "It wasn't any of your business," she snapped.

"The hell it wasn't."

Nick took her slender waist in his hands and lifted her off his lap. She disentangled herself from his legs and stood, trembling before him.

Well, shit. Now he'd scared her.

"I didn't plan on sleeping with you," she said, head held high.

Nick stood himself, retrieved his towel from the floor and cleaned himself off. When he passed the towel to Eve, she jerked it from his hands.

"Like hell you didn't plan on sleeping with me," he countered. "You all but tried to yesterday in the hotel."

Eve held the grimy towel as a shield in front of her flushed body. "I was just trying to get our feelings out in the open. I wouldn't have followed through."

Nick reached into his bag by the couch and pulled out a pair of boxers. "Bullshit. All I had to do was kiss you and you would've fallen apart."

Those once passion-filled eyes turned into slits. "You aren't that impressive, Nick. I knew this was a mistake to let you help me. You probably had this agenda all along once you knew I was dancing. Did you think I'd give you a special show?"

"That would've been nice."

Eve jerked back as if he'd slapped her. Hell, he might as well have. Why did he have to be such an ass about this?

Because she'd caught him off guard. He didn't like surprises and he sure as hell didn't like that she'd given her virginity to him. She should've given it to someone who would stick around for more than a recreational screw in the midst of evading a killer.

Silence stood between them and Nick couldn't think of a single thing to say that would make up for what he'd already said. He'd damaged her enough already. The harsh words couldn't be taken back.

Carefully, Eve wrapped the towel around her body, clutched the opening together at the valley between her breasts. Without a word, she turned and all but ran upstairs.

"Damn!" Nick slammed his fist against the arm of the couch.

Okay, so he wouldn't be nominated for Romancer of the Year Award. He still should've been more patient, more considerate, more...*something*.

As time passed, an eerie stillness settled over the house. Nick stood motionless, staring at the empty wooden staircase. The emptiness mocked him, as did the scent of jasmine and sex still lingering in the dimly lit room.

He'd just had possibly the best gift given to him and he'd thrown it back in her face, which did nothing but make him feel like the jerk she'd already thought him to be. Not to mention the fact it more than likely made her feel cheap.

The damaged look he'd put into Eve's eyes had crushed something inside him. He'd never made a woman feel worthless, never made her feel vulnerable or ashamed. Somehow, he'd managed to do all that and more in the span of about twenty minutes. Nick cursed himself again, dropping his gaze from the steps to the floor.

Red leather stared up at him, mocking him. The image of her unfastening each hook-and-eye closure had him hardening again. He recalled how her hands had shook and he'd mistakenly taken it for arousal and not for what it really had been.

Nerves. The nerves of a virgin about to give herself for the first time to some asshole who had no clue how to appreciate such a delicate, special woman.

Guilt guided his hand as he bent to retrieve Eve's forgotten outfit. His heart pounded in his chest as he approached the first step.

He'd never been nervous in his life. Not when he'd joined the Marines, not when he'd joined the police force, not when he'd faced down perps in back alleys at three in the damn morning before his backup had arrived. Never.

But nerves swept through him so fast. His knees nearly

gave way as he ascended the steps. What would he say? What *could* be said? What he'd done was unforgivable.

When he reached the landing and turned to take those final three steps, he saw her. Lying across her bed, feet dangling off the edge toward him, towel still wrapped around her, stopping just under her perfect rear.

Shaking uncontrollably. Sobbing silently into the plain, white comforter.

Nick clutched her bustier and G-string. Only a low-life bastard could bring a woman such as Eve to tears. A woman who'd rather walk through broken glass with bare feet than cry. A woman who turned sadness into anger and sought revenge.

A woman who had touched a spot so deep in him he hadn't known it existed.

ଛ

How could she have been so stupid to think something about that arrogant, pompous asshole could be different than all the other arrogant, pompous assholes?

Eve had questioned herself over and over since she'd run up the stairs and fallen onto her bed. It felt like someone had taken a knife to her chest. The hurt, not to mention the humiliation, of listening to Nick's tactless, harsh comments had left an open wound she wasn't sure could ever be healed.

"You forgot something."

Eve froze at Nick's low Southern drawl. If she hadn't been so preoccupied with her own justifiable self-pity, she would have heard him come up the stairs.

There was no way she would sit up and let him see the tears on her face. She would not give him the satisfaction of seeing what his actions had done to her.

"You left your...um...leather downstairs."

God, she needed to sniff, but she refused to let him hear her. "Leave it on the floor."

His bare feet slid over the hardwood. The heavy material of the seductive lingerie thumped to the floor. Then silence.

Eve squeezed her eyes shut. She could practically feel his gaze on her back. Why wouldn't he leave? Had she not suffered enough for one evening? Could a girl not cry alone in peace?

"Eve," he said softly. "I want to apologize."

Red, swollen, tear-stained face be damned. Eve sprang off the bed. Clutched her towel against her chest.

"*Apologize*? Well, if you think your apology is going to get you another fuck, you're more of a dickhead than I thought. Get the hell out of here."

Nick took a step toward her, only to come up short when she raised her hand.

"I'm not apologizing to have another 'fuck', I'm apologizing because what I said was wrong. I didn't mean to hurt you."

A slight laugh escaped her. "You think you hurt me? You didn't hurt me, Nick. I'd have to care to be hurt."

"You're crying."

Eve swiped the back of her hand across her cheek as another tear escaped. "I'm upset because I was stupid to let myself fall into your trap. You're supposed to be helping me find out who killed my father and who's threatening me. Have you had it planned from the beginning to use this whole 'bodyguard' charade to lure me into bed?"

Nick shook his head. "I won't deny that I found you attractive the second I laid eyes on you, but I would never use my skills or profession to get a woman to sleep with me."

The tone of his soft voice made Eve want to throw up. This nice-guy persona did not belong to the same man who had berated her downstairs just a little while ago. She would not fall for his false charm again.

But, God, he'd been so easy to fall for. She'd have to be careful from here on out if he continued to "protect" her. Unfortunately, now that she'd had him, she feared resisting him would be that much harder.

Eve held onto the towel with both hands, grasping so tight she trembled. "Your apology is moot at this point. Tomorrow I'll call Grady and tell him I'm either doing this on my own or he can be the one to help me. As for you, I hope to hell I never see you again."

Nick's jaw clenched, his lips tightened. "Good night, Eve."

Bewildered, Eve watched him turn and go back downstairs. She sank back down onto the bed and sighed. His apology sounded so sincere, but she just couldn't accept it.

A fresh, hot tear trickled down her cheek—Eve didn't even bother to swipe at it. Losing your virginity only happened once. Had she known what a disaster it was going to be, she would've lost it a long time ago. She couldn't help but wonder what would've happened if she'd told him the truth in advance.

He would have gone running in the other direction.

Eve didn't even bother with pajamas. She tossed the towel onto the floor and crawled beneath the cheap, white sheets and stared at the soft glow that filtered up the steps from a lamp in the living room.

After what seemed like hours, the light went out. Darkness and silence molded into one eerie setting. Eve rolled onto her back and tried to concentrate on her mission.

She'd let Nick sidetrack her too much and it was past time she got some control back into her life. All that mattered was finding her father's killer, figuring out who the hell kept calling her, who blew up her car, and getting her suspension lifted.

Piece of fucking cake.

ଛ

The sirens blared. Lights flickered off the wet, uneven pavement. Blood pooled around the man lying in the cold alley.

Nick ran to his side, crouched down. The dying man motioned for him to lean closer. As Nick leaned in, the man whispered something in his ear.

"Rom-"

That's all he said before his eyes closed, his head rolling to the side.

Gentle fingers slid across his forehead. Nick jerked up, grabbed a hold of the hand on his face.

"It's okay, Nick," Eve said softly.

He blinked as he looked up and tried to make her out through the darkness. "Eve, what are you doing down here?"

"You were yelling. I thought something was wrong, but you must've been having a bad dream."

The dream. Oh, God. Nick's mind replayed the dream. His heart stopped.

Roman.

Roger had been trying to say Roman. Icy shivers ran all over his body.

Had Roger known Roman was Nick's stepbrother? Had he known the name of his killer beforehand? Why hadn't he been able to figure this out before now?

Nick cursed himself for not realizing this sooner, but he'd been trying for a year to put Roger's death out of his mind. He didn't want to remember anything about that night. Unfortunately, those demons from his past wouldn't let him rest. He prayed to God this dream where Nick recalled Roger's last word would be the last. He didn't want to keep reliving that night.

"Nick." Eve stood beside the couch. Her shadow loomed over him. "Are you okay?"

"Um...yeah. Sorry I scared you."

His eyes finally focused to the dark room. He looked up at Eve and...

"Holy shit!" Nick jerked into a sitting position and stared at the woman who looked like she was ready to enter his wet dream.

She was stark naked. Her pale skin nearly glowed in the darkness. His vision had focused so well now that he could see her erect nipples and the concern on her face.

"Why are you naked?" he asked, once he could speak.

"When you yelled, I just jumped out of bed and ran down here."

Nick jumped to his feet, causing Eve to take a step back. "Are you crazy?"

Her head snapped back as if he'd slapped her. "Excuse me?"

"There's a killer out there and someone who's more or less

stalking you, so when you think there's trouble, you rush down here? With no clothes? Are you completely insane?"

Eve hands came up to her hips, the angry motion made her bare breasts lift. Nick clenched his hands into fists to keep from reaching out and taking handfuls of pure sin.

He didn't know how much more he could take of seeing her naked body without having her again. Unfortunately, Eve had put a halt to that before he really even got a chance to enjoy it.

"I thought you were in trouble," she snapped. "Did you just expect me to stay upstairs and let you fight off a killer on your own?"

"Yeah," he yelled as he stepped within an inch of her, his face dangerously close to hers. "I'm experienced in handling psychopaths. What would you have done? Give him a lap dance?"

The second those hurtful words slipped out of his mouth, Nick regretted it. "Eve, I'm sorry."

She held up a hand and shook her head. "Forget it. Honestly, I don't know what I would've done, but I didn't think at all. When you yelled, I ran."

Nick smiled. "You think like a cop."

Eve's body stiffened, her eyes widened for a second...long enough for him to notice. She opened her mouth, then closed it.

"You okay?" he asked.

A fake smile spread across her face. "Of course. I feel a little silly standing here naked."

His eyes raked down to her chest, lingered on her perky buds, then drifted back up. "You don't look silly. Intriguing, beautiful, sexy as hell. Definitely not silly."

In a move he hoped wouldn't reward him with a knee to his balls, Nick lifted his hands, gently placing them on her slender shoulders. Much to his surprise, she didn't stiffen beneath his touch. Their gazes held.

"Nick, this is a mistake we already made," she whispered.

He slid his hands to the base of her neck and stroked her delicate jaw line with thumbs. "The only mistake was the way I acted afterward. I want to try again. Will you give me a second chance to make you see how good it could be?"

When her eyes closed, Nick feared she would tell him to go to hell. Every muscle in his body tensed. His cock was so hard, so ready for her, he was afraid he'd come before she answered him.

"If I give you another chance," Eve began as she opened her eyes. "Will you tell me if I'm doing something wrong? I don't want it to be bad for you because of my lack of experience."

"You did everything right last time."

"Promise me," she said again.

Nick nodded. "I promise."

"One more thing," she added.

"God, woman, I'm dying here."

Her small, soothing hands ran up his chest and stopped just above his pecs. "This is just sex. I don't want a commitment. When this is all over, we're finished. My life is too complicated for anything else."

A lump formed in Nick's throat. He'd never been on the receiving end of the "just sex" speech. For some reason, he didn't like it.

"Fine. Just sex. Really, really great sex."

Eve's smile lit up from within as her hands roamed up to his face. Before he could think, she yanked him down to her mouth and devoured him.

Her aggressiveness nearly undid him. He plunged his tongue inside her mouth as he bent down, wrapped his hands around a firm, round ass and lifted her off the floor. Her pebble-hard nipples rubbed up his chest.

Nick tore his mouth from hers. "If I'm not inside you in about one second, I'm going to explode."

With a naughty grin, Eve wrapped her legs around his waist. "We can't let that happen."

One hand remained on her bottom while the other yanked his boxers down. His erection sprang free, the tip grazed against her moist center.

He leaned down to grab his jeans from the side of the couch, fumbled with one hand through the back pocket for a condom. With one of her hands guiding his, they covered his shaft.

"I'm sorry I can't slow this down," he said against her mouth as he walked around the room with her wrapped around him.

All the restraint he'd promised her went to hell the second her back rested against the nearest wall. He plunged inside her, pausing only a moment when she cried out. But the look on her face was definitely not one of pain.

The little vixen licked her lips as she arched her back. "I can't stand it, Nick."

He began to move, slowly at first. "You feel so good, so hot and wet."

Eve's legs formed a vice-like grip...like caging in an animal. He pumped in and out of her slickness, grabbing handfuls of taut breasts.

He tore his gaze from hers only to bury his head in the valley between her breasts. While his hands continued to squeeze and rub her tits, Nick ran his tongue along the narrow patch of skin between the mounds.

"Nick...I feel...God..."

She teetered on the brink as he slid his hands back to her ass. Her own hips began to pump uncontrollably, her high, firm tits bounced, begging to be sucked.

Once again, he dipped his head. He captured a pink bud between his teeth and flicked it with his tongue before opening his mouth and taking in all he could of her softness.

Eve's hands squeezed his shoulders. Nails bit into his hot flesh. Her inner muscles clenched around his cock as she screamed. Nick forced himself to move from her breast—he captured her mouth with his and swallowed her cries of satisfaction.

Even when her convulsions stopped, her hips kept a fast, hard rhythm. She ground against him, keeping him right where he wanted to be—in her tight pussy. It wasn't going to take too much more for him to blow.

She matched him thrust for thrust, stroke for stroke. When she broke off the kiss, she looked into his eyes. That simple, innocent look drove him over the edge.

With one last thrust, he clenched her ass in his palms and erupted. She rode him until the last spasm faded, then framed his face with her hands and placed a simple kiss on his cheek.

Chest heaving, Nick smiled at her. "What was that for?"

"You promised great sex. You provided."

"I also promised I'd go slow," he countered.

Eve ran her lips along his neck and murmured, "Then take me upstairs and we'll try it until we get it right."

Nick jerked his head back and drew his brows together. "You don't act like a virgin."

With a slight tilt of her hips, she grinned. "I'm not anymore."

He hardened again inside her. "You'll be sore."

"I think it's worth it, don't you?"

"We've still not slept very well," he argued.

Eve unwrapped her ankles and pushed against his chest until he stepped back. She disengaged their bodies.

"Well, then, I'll let you get back to sleep."

The cool tone of her voice had Nick cursing and reaching for her before she reached the first step. "I'm fine, but I don't want to wear you out."

"No problem," she said as looked up. "You're right. I am sleepy. I'll see you in the morning."

He let her get to the first landing before he went after her. By the time he got to her room, she was adjusting the covers that she'd obviously left in disarray to come to his aid.

When he yelled out from the horrid dream where his friend was trying to reveal the killer.

He stomped down the thought and found himself distracted by the sight of Eve's perfect ass as she reached to fluff her pillow.

Nick took two steps, grabbed her by the arms and spun her around. "I'm not done with you yet. I told you when I met you I never go back on a promise. You've got slow sex coming. And I'm going to deliver it right now."

℘

His dark eyes held both fury and passion. Eve cursed herself for liking the way his strong hands wrapped around her biceps, but she really hated the way she had to look up to see his face.

"Now kiss me and we'll begin your lesson on how to make great sex even better." Even though the words were a demand, he said them with gentleness.

Before she had time to react, he hauled her against his bare, sweaty body. One of his hands came up and gripped her hair and pulled. For one intense moment before he kissed her, he simply raked his hard gaze over her face.

A shot of pure lust ran through her, straight to her heat—making her wetter.

He ran his tongue along her lips in a slow, agonizing manner. When she sighed, he nipped at her bottom lip and sucked. Heat filled her, consumed her until she couldn't take it anymore.

"I don't like going slow," she complained. "I want it fast and hard. Like before."

Nick dropped his hands. A chill crept over where his warm fingers had just gripped. When he stepped back, Eve's shaky knees gave out and she sank down onto the edge of the bed.

He dropped to his knees in front of her. "I have something better in mind."

Before she could reply, his hands came up to her knees. He spread her legs wide. Clever fingers trailed a path up to her moist heat and Eve had to clutch the comforter to keep from begging. Again.

"Slide forward," he murmured as his lips followed his hands. "I've been dying to taste you."

Too anxious and aroused to be nervous, Eve did as he asked. He flung her legs over his shoulders as she rested back on her elbows. He positioned his hands on her inner thighs. Using the pads of his thumbs, he eased her folds open and massaged.

Eve kept her eyes locked onto his. A sinful grin split across his devilish face as he slipped one long, lean finger inside her.

"Damn. You're so tight and hot."

Her hips bucked beneath his touch as she let out a low moan.

"How do you feel, Eve?"

Did he expect her to make a sentence? She barely had a coherent thought, especially when a second finger snaked its way inside her.

"Do you like this?"

She nodded as she watched his dark hand work magic against her pale center.

"Keep watching me," he told her as he dipped his head down. His dark hair fell against her cream-colored legs.

The second his tongue ran between her folds, Eve cried out. His hands continued to rub against her inner thighs. His thumbs worked with his tongue to create a sensation she'd never felt before.

Eve pulled her knees up to rest her feet against his shoulders. She rocked against his mouth as his hand slid around to grip her ass. He took one long, slow swipe of his tongue all the way up between her lips, then blew.

Shivers crept through her body, over her body. Hell, her damn hair even shivered. She couldn't take it, but God she wanted this newfound pleasure to last.

As his mouth moved faster and harder, her hips pumped out of control. The orgasm slammed into her, making her scream his name, grab the comforter on either side of her and push against his shoulders. The explosion ran the course of her body as Nick continued to taste her until she relaxed.

Eve's lifeless feet slid from his shoulders. She didn't even have the energy to open her eyes. Her whole body quivered as he removed his mouth from her tingling heat and slid his hands out from her behind.

For a second, Eve wondered where he went, but then the mattress dipped beside her. Nick's hard, taut body molded against hers, his impressive erection nudging her hip.

Could she keep going? She had to in order to pleasure him. Pleasuring Nick would definitely not be a hardship, though. The sight of that male form all aroused made her want to attack him...no matter how fatigued her body seemed.

"Did you like that?" he breathed into her ear.

She couldn't respond. For now she only wanted to bask in the glory of his touch. His fingertips ran up and down her abdomen, taking a side trip to circle each of her breasts.

When Eve arched her back, Nick's thick laugh filled the room. "You come alive, Eve. I'm glad I'm the one to see it. I can't imagine all the pent-up passion you have within you, just waiting to burst out. We haven't even begun to explore."

Eve wasn't sure if that was a threat or a promise. Hell, she didn't care. After three Nick-gasms in one night, she trusted him to bring her more and more toe-curling pleasure.

"I didn't know," she sighed.

"What's that?"

"How fun and intense sex could be. It's incredible." Eve opened her eyes and rolled to her side, causing Nick's hand to rest on the blanket between them. "I'm sure it's just another roll in the sack for you, but for me—"

He silenced her with a finger to her lips. "You're not just another lay. And yes, even though this is just sex for us, you are opening my eyes to a new experience. I've never been anybody's first time before, and it's making me take a little more time to appreciate each step of this process."

Eve looked down, unable to look into his eyes. "I'm sorry for not having any experience, but I already know what I like, and I hope you'll tell me what you like, too, so I can make you feel good."

His warm breath washed over her naked body. Her nipples peaked, almost touching his chest. "I feel more than good, Eve. Having you come against my mouth was incredible. I can't wait to show you more. Teach you more. You're already such a fast learner."

She needed to know. She didn't want to ask, it would sound clichéd, but she just had to find out. Maybe she really sucked in this department. Nick would be honest with her...but could she handle the mortification that came along with asking this asinine question?

"So, the...um...sex we had downstairs. Did I do okay? I have nothing to compare it to, and I know you'll be honest with me."

Nick propped his head up on his hand and studied her face. "Do you really think I could compare you to other women?"

Eve's eyes remained on his chest as she shrugged. She couldn't look him in the eye if he told her she had been inadequate.

"Well, I can tell you this. No other woman has ever worn red leather for me."

When her eyes lifted to his, he smiled. Ever so slightly, he moved in, touched his lips to her soft skin at the edge of her mouth and eased back.

"I'm going to show you what a desirable woman you are," he said, running a hand along her side. "You can't possibly believe you aren't perfect in every way. In bed and out."

Mesmerized by his velvety touch, Eve rolled onto her back. Nick's hand moved from her side to her abdomen, caressing his way up until he outlined each breast.

"I want to be the one to touch and taste you everywhere. I want to discover where you are most sensitive, most vulnerable. I want you to remember your first lover for the rest of your life."

As if she would have ever forgotten him? Even if they *hadn't* had sex, she would've remembered Nick Shaffer up until she took her last breath.

"Are you ready?" he crooned.

The exhilaration from deep inside her sated body bubbled out into a smile. "Don't leave anything out."

Nick's low, throaty laugh vibrated against her. "Do you really think I would skip anything when I have every man's walking wet dream right here?"

Eve ignored the flutter in her chest. "Nick, I've already agreed to a sexual fling, there's no need for flattery."

A somber look stole all the pleasant features on his face. "It's not flattery, Eve, if it's the truth. Don't ever doubt for a second the power you have over a man. And, lesson number one, don't ever settle for anything less than the best."

This had to be a dream. Had someone written him a script? Did men really say things like that and mean it?

No, no and obviously so. So why had she agreed to sex

only?

"I'm dying to touch you," Eve whispered as Nick's magical fingers made her skin heat and tingle with each stroke.

Nick leaned down, kissed the tip of her nose and grinned. "I'm dying for you to touch me, too."

Eve stared up at his amazing smile. She reached for his face. Coarse stubble tickled her palm. He placed light, hypnotizing kisses against her lips as she slid her hand down the side of his neck, past his chest.

When her hand stilled on his lower abdomen, he lifted his head. He kept his eyes on her as he guided her hand to his shaft.

"Will you tell me if you don't like something?" she asked.

Nick looked down at her pale hand against his skin and smiled. "I wouldn't like it if you stopped."

Eve stroked him, slowly. It pleased her when his eyelids flittered shut, his jaw muscle clenched. She placed a hand on his chest and pushed until he lay on his back.

She came up to her knees, taking in the sight of this golden, muscular god. Even in the dark of night, Nick's perfection shone through.

Like any hero, he had scars. One through his right brow, a nasty round one by his shoulder—a gunshot, she knew—and now he would have a new one, thanks to the psychopath in the hotel parking lot. The scars on Nick's perfect body only added to his sex appeal.

Guided only by her hormones, Eve leaned down and licked his nipple. Then the other. Her mouth danced kisses all over his shoulders and chest before she slowed her lips down and took her time working across his rippled abs.

Nick sucked in a breath and fisted a hand in her hair. As her mouth moved lower, Eve brought a hand up to cup his balls. She smiled when he groaned, jerking his hips.

Finally, she made her way to his cock. She hesitated only a moment before running her tongue along the length of him, licking off the moisture that had accumulated at the head.

Eve's body responded the second she took him into her mouth. Her nipples tightened; the ache between her legs intensified. His hand on the back of her head squeezed when she lowered her mouth all the way to the base of his shaft.

When his hips started pumping, Eve found herself mimicking him. She swirled her tongue all over him as she worked her way up and down, trying to taste and savor him.

"Stop," Nick said, breathless.

Eve lifted her head. "Am I doing something wrong?"

"God, no," he panted. "I think you've definitely got the hang of that."

The hand on his sac came up to wrap around him, stroking the moisture from top to bottom. "Then what's the problem?"

He brought a hand down to stop her. "I want to show you more."

"Oh." Eve shuddered at his seductive tone.

Nick sat up and Eve sank back onto her heels. If his heavy breathing was any indication, she figured he had been close to an orgasm.

Tremors crept through her when his eyes drifted down her body. She didn't mind being dissected, she knew her body was in great shape—it had to be if she was ever going back into the field. But when he'd called her beautiful, she knew that had to be the hormones talking.

She had long, naturally curly red hair that had a mind of its own and never looked fixed. How could that be attractive?

"Come back up on your knees," he said. "Now spread your legs just a little."

Eve scooted her knees wider apart, the thrill of the unknown made her quiver with anticipation. Nick placed a hand out to his side to support his impressive body. The other arm rested on his drawn-up knee.

"Let me see what you do to yourself when you're alone."

"Nick!"

"Surely you have nights when you're lying in your bed, dreaming of someone touching you, caressing you, making love to you."

As his voice washed over her, Eve closed her eyes. Yes, those nights were lonely and sometimes frustrating. But she truly hadn't known what she'd been missing.

"Do you squirm beneath your sheets?" he went on. "Do you get hot and wet?"

Eve nodded.

Nick took her hand, lifted it to his mouth and sucked her fingers. "There. Now show me where you start. How do you pleasure yourself, Eve?"

The moment enveloped her as she brought a hand to her breasts and rubbed. The familiar touch made her moan.

"What about the other hand? What does it do?"

As she fondled her breast, her other hand, moist from his mouth, slid across her stomach. Her freshly shaven pubic area heated beneath her touch as her index finger slid into the slick crevice.

"Do you scream when you're alone, Eve? Do you make noises of ecstasy when you make yourself come? Come for me. I know you want to, just let go."

Eve sank back onto her heels, unable to hold herself up any longer, forcing her finger to slide up.

"It's not enough," she cried, rocking back and forth against her own hand. The other still held onto a breast. "I need more."

"You're all alone, Eve," Nick's voice said. "What would you do?"

Eve shoved a second finger deep inside. Her knees squirmed against the sheet. She rose up, then plundered back down. Her cries filled the room as her convulsions racked her body.

The hand from her breast caught her as she fell forward onto his hard body. The climax ran through her body, then again and again as she gripped onto Nick's chest.

She couldn't catch her breath. What had she just done?

Chapter Seven

Nick nearly came himself watching that erotic show. Eve's body still convulsed, her eyes were still closed and he knew this would be the point where she realized what just happened and got embarrassed. Or worse...mad.

"Eve," he whispered. "Open your eyes."

Hesitantly, her lids lifted. Her breasts rose and fell. Sheen covered her body, glistening in the moonlit room.

"I don't blame you for not taking a lover before," Nick stated. "You know your body so well, you came in seconds."

"I can't believe I did that," she murmured.

He placed his hands on her shoulders, urging her to lie back against the pillows. He followed her down and rested his elbows on either side of her head.

"You have so much passion in you. Did you know there was this sex goddess inside?"

Eve finally opened her eyes and shook her head. "I've never wanted anybody to touch me like that."

An alarm went off in Nick's head, but now was not the time to question her statement. Not when his body had become so primed and ready to take her again.

He'd never been like this with any other woman. The realization both excited and scared him, knowing he could lose control so easily with Eve. But right now, he didn't care. He wanted her again and again, until she told him to stop.

"Do you like when I touch you?"

A lazy smile spread across her face. "I love it."

"Good, because I'm not done with you."

Nick settled in between her legs, tormenting them both when his shaft rubbed against her wetness. Eve lifted her knees, opening for him.

"You learn quick."

"I need you in me," she moaned.

Ignoring her plea, Nick dipped his head and ravished her sweet breasts. Eve arched her back, offering more. His lips roamed up her chest and throat until he captured her mouth.

"I have a condom in my bag," she said against his lips.

Nick raised a brow. "Were you expecting this?"

"No, I carry them as part of the whole stripper act. Do you really want to discuss this now?"

Without wasting another second, Nick retrieved it and sheathed himself before joining her on the bed again.

When he allowed his weight to press into her body more, he jolted at the fit they made. They molded together as if they had done this a thousand times before. Her legs came around his waist, her heels fell against his back.

When his tongue slipped into her mouth, Nick slid himself ever so slowly into her heat. Hips remained still, hands caressed, mouths lingered.

A niggling voice in Nick's head told him he was getting too intense, too fast. He pushed the annoying bastard out of his head and began to move with Eve, as if they'd choreographed the dance.

Now would not be a good time to try and dissect his feelings. Not when he had a hot, willing woman underneath him.

And not just any woman. Eve.

The sweat between their bodies formed a suction—binding them even closer. Nick let his lips hover just over Eve's. Breathing, moans and sighs merged together. They were one.

Climax slammed into climax. Eve clenched around him— Nick poured into her. The eerie silence that followed scared the shit out of him. When he started to roll over, her knees pressed tighter against his waist.

"I don't want to crush you," he murmured into her hair.

Eve unwrapped herself and Nick not only rolled off her, he

stood, slid the condom off and threw it into the small trash basket by the bed, then pulled on his boxers.

He made a big mistake by looking back down at the flush, sated woman he'd just slept with. Her breasts glistened from sweat and wet kisses. Her lips were swollen from his mouth. Her exotic hair fanned out around her face.

"I think we'll take a break and get that sleep now," he suggested.

This intensity of their bedroom romp had gotten out of control. As much as he hated to, he had to put a stop to this. Every ounce of willpower he had drove him away from her bed, toward the steps.

"Are you sure you don't want to share the bed?" Eve's fingers trailed over the sheet. Promises filled her eyes.

"If I stay, neither one of us will get sleep," he assured her. "And it's almost morning now. If you insist on going back to the club tonight, we need to let our bodies settle down and recoup."

For more than a second, he contemplated throwing his good intentions and manners out the window. Why should he deny his body this insatiable woman? Why should he deny her? They were both adults. They both wanted the same thing, so why did he have to act so stupid?

Because his latest nightmare confirmed his all his fears—his brother had killed Eve's dad. Now Nick had a new sense of dread. He'd been in this business long enough to know coincidences didn't exist.

Roman, or one of his cronies, had been calling Eve. Had left her death threats. Had blown up her car.

Nick had to keep his lustful emotions a distant second to Eve's safety. He wouldn't so much as let her get a hangnail on his watch.

"See you in the morning," he whispered to her in the dark.

Before she could persuade him to stay—which wouldn't have taken much—Nick headed back down to his lumpy, small, lonely couch. Sleep wasn't an option for him. He had to figure out a way to cancel this meeting or find a way to go along with her without his brother knowing.

Shit. After this assignment, if he didn't die protecting Eve, he'd retire.

A glimmer of hope flickered. Allison hadn't died, and neither had Junior, which meant Roman didn't know about the phone call. Two days had passed and the young guard had visited her during his shifts. The visits were brief and when they both knew Roman was busy with something else.

Allison sat on the edge of her bed, brushing her hair. As always, there wasn't a tangle to be found, but nerves kept the brush sliding through her long, silky strands.

Just because she hadn't been found out, didn't mean she wouldn't be. Roman had an eerie way of knowing everything that took place on the estate.

When the locks on the door clicked, Allison glanced to the nightstand—sure enough, the clock showed the time for another sex session with Roman. Disgust and humiliation filled her.

Roman came through the door, unsmiling. Without a word, he closed the door behind him and pocketed his keys into his designer black dress pants as he made his way toward her...and the bed.

The deranged look in his eye crushed any hope she'd had only seconds ago. Did he know? Would he kill her now, or make her suffer more?

"You look lovely this morning," he said as he extended his hand for her to take.

Allison dropped her brush onto the comforter, came to her feet and steadied her own hand before she slid it into his. "Thank you."

Her white form-fitted tank ended just below her breasts, leaving her whole midsection exposed. The long, yellow sarong skirt sat low on her hips.

The outfit left absolutely nothing to the imagination, especially considering there wasn't one piece of underwear in her room.

"I've been given some disturbing news," he offered as he undid the tie at her waist. The skirt fell instantly to the floor.

Oh, God. She never should've pulled that young boy into this. Was he already dead?

"What's that?" she asked.

Roman's hands slid up and down her slender hips. "It seems the new girl I want to bring here to join our party isn't at all what she seems."

Their party? Did that mean he wasn't going to sell her soon?

"I've known for a little while now," he went on as his hands moved around to grab her ass. "It seems she isn't really a dancer at all. She only wants to find me."

"What are you going to do?" Allison couldn't help but ask.

Roman's exotic blue eyes turned to ice as a grin split across his face. "Oh, I'll still bring her here. I think she'll be a nice addition to our fun. I can't wait to watch the two of you. Together."

Allison couldn't believe what she was hearing. First of all, she couldn't believe he wasn't going to sell her or kill her. Yet. Second of all, she couldn't believe he hadn't killed this other woman already.

Why did this woman want to find Roman? Who would purposely seek out this monster?

Questions whirled around Allison's mind as Roman freed himself. He pushed her back onto the bed and forced his way into her.

No foreplay, no moisture to ease the pain. Allison bit her lip to keep from crying out. The grunts in her ear grew faster and louder as his hips pumped.

Allison knew it was selfish, but she couldn't wait for another woman to come along. Maybe they could work together to escape. Or better yet...to kill their captor.

ഗ

The first floor didn't seem so dull and gloomy with the sunlight pouring through the windows, casting a variety of shapes onto the glossy, oak floor. Eve glanced around the spacious room only to find it empty. The bathroom door stood wide open.

No sign of Nick.

Eve padded into the kitchen in the hopes she would find a coffee pot. Granted it was nearly two in the afternoon, but it was morning to her and she needed a jump start...especially after last night.

Within minutes the strong scent of fresh-brewed coffee filled the house. Eve leaned back against the cracked Formica countertop, waiting for the slow drips to make two cups.

Across the room, Eve spotted Nick out on the front porch. For a moment, she allowed herself the luxury of staring, considering he'd done his fair share of staring last night.

He'd thrown on a pair of jeans, no shirt and no shoes. Even from this distance, she could see the tight muscles in his back. He leaned one hand against the wood railing, rubbing the back of his neck with the other.

What had him so tense? Surely the sex didn't have him worried.

Had something new happened with the case? Did they have more information on Roman?

Eve rummaged through the cabinets until she found two mugs. She assumed he took his coffee black, so she didn't add anything to it.

Carrying two full mugs and a mountain of nerves, she pushed her butt against the screen door. Nick didn't even glance up as the door creaked open then slammed shut.

"I thought you might want some coffee," she said.

Still leaning on his hands, Nick eyed her over his shoulder. "Thanks."

Eve moved in beside him, setting his mug on the railing. The first sip burned her tongue, but the pain dulled in comparison to her jitters. She nearly laughed aloud at herself. If Grady could see the way her hands shook, he'd never let her live it down. She'd been known as the agent of steel. Nothing ever penetrated her emotionless mask.

"Heard from Grady?" Eve asked as she looked out onto the small yard surrounded by hundreds of trees.

Nick's fingers tightened around the handle of the mug he'd yet to lift to his lips. "I talked to him about an hour ago."

Short and to the point. Eve waited for him to elaborate or at least look in her direction. But then it hit her.

He regretted sleeping with her.

Shame covered every part of his face. The dead stare, thin lips, clenched jaw. Fine, she was a big girl. She didn't need to be coddled or fawned over. It would be better all around if they devoted all their energy to finding this madman who killed her father.

What a shame. She had really enjoyed herself last night. How would she do that with anybody else? She couldn't imagine being that comfortable with another man.

"I have a question," Nick murmured, breaking into her thoughts.

"What's that?"

Finally, he looked over. "Why hadn't you slept with anybody before last night?"

Now Eve took her turn and looked away. That was one question she thought she'd covered the night before—and the one question she didn't want to answer truthfully.

Eve shrugged and took another scalding sip. "I never wanted to."

Picking up his mug, Nick turned and leaned against the railing. His eyes, however, remained on her face.

"There had to have been someone," he pushed. "You're how old? Twenty-eight?"

"Yeah."

"All those adult, not to mention teenage years, and nobody sparked anything in you?"

"So?" Eve hated the defensive tone in her voice. "Just because I didn't hop into bed with the first guy that I found attractive, that makes me odd?"

Nick crossed his arms over his bare chest, still holding the steamy mug with one hand. "That's not what I'm trying to say."

She slammed her mug down onto the wooden rail. Coffee sloshed out onto her hand. She must have winced enough from the hot liquid, because Nick cursed, set his own cup down and grabbed her hand.

"Now, you see what happens when you get all riled up for no reason?"

She jerked her hand back, rubbing it against the side of her gray boxers. "I'm fine."

With a disbelieving look, Nick snatched her hand back and examined the red skin. "You've got a burn. Let me go get some ice."

"It's fine," she insisted again. "Leave it alone."

She so wished he would let go of her hand. It was impossible to touch him like this and not want him all over again. But once he knew the truth, all of it, would he still want her?

Nick sandwiched her hand between his and stepped closer. "You said something last night and I want to know what you meant."

"I said a lot of things last night." She smiled.

The serious look he gave her faded her smile and filled her with dread. What had she said that made him look at her with both worry and pity? The only thing she remembered was great sex and more great sex. Conversations weren't really in the forefront of her mind right now.

"You said something about not wanting a man to touch you before." Nick's thumb slid gently over the back of her hand, soothing her burn. "Is there something more to that statement?"

A confession was on the tip of her tongue. Eve bit it to keep her secret from slipping out. Now that he mentioned it, she vaguely recalled saying something like that. At the time, she'd thought the statement had only been in her mind.

"Eve?"

She pasted her grin back on and pulled her hand away, crossing her arms over her chest. "Don't read into that too much, Nick. I guess I was just trying to explain why I was still a virgin. Nothing more."

He shrugged. "I don't believe you, but if you don't want to talk about it, that's up to you. I just want you to know I'd listen."

With a tilt of her chin, she forced herself to keep her eyes locked onto his. If they wavered even the slightest bit, he'd know.

"There's nothing to tell," she said.

Nick looked away first...thank God. He stepped back, rested his thumbs through his belt loops and looked out onto the yard. A shiver of relief rippled through her.

"When did it happen?" he asked softly.

Every muscle tensed, every nerve went on alert. "What?"

"You heard me."

Yeah, she had, she just didn't have an answer. "I don't want to have this discussion, Nick. Just let it go."

"You haven't talked about it ever, have you?" he pushed.

"Dammit, Nick!" Eve forced her way past him and went back into the house, allowing the screen door to shut with a bang behind her.

She really had no idea what to do now that she'd made such a dramatic exit, especially since Nick followed right on her heels, so she opted to go into the kitchen to clean the coffee pot.

Seeing as how she lived her daily life as a slob, Nick probably figured her actions were guided by nerves. She didn't care what he thought right now.

While she waited for the water to heat, she dumped the remaining coffee down the sink. Even though Nick said nothing, his looming presence irritated her more than words.

He just had to keep pushing. Maybe if she told him what he so desperately wanted to hear, he'd finally shut up.

"I didn't want to make you mad, Eve."

She turned off the water. The warm coffee pot sizzled as she dunked it and when her new burn came in contact with the warm water, she nearly yelped.

Doing her best to ignore Nick, she searched through drawers looking for a dishrag. The jerk simply stood, leaning against the small counter that separated the kitchen from the living room.

"I just think you'd feel better if you talked about it," he said.

"I'd feel better if you'd shut the hell up and quit asking me questions about my past that have nothing to do with you."

Not a word came out of his mouth while she washed and rinsed the pot, dried it, and put it back in the cabinet. Unfortunately, she didn't figure he was finished with this particular topic.

"I'm going to call Grady," she told him as she left the room and headed for the steps.

"Why?"

"Because I want to," she yelled without looking back.

It took all her effort not to stomp up the steps, and Nick more than surprised her when he didn't follow.

At the top of the stairs, Eve froze. Memories of the night before came flooding back the second her eyes landed on the red leather on the floor. She could never wear that on stage, especially not while Nick loomed in the back of the club. Even though the outfit was trashy, in her opinion, the scraps of leather held more sentimental value than she cared to admit.

Ignoring the mixture of hurt and regret, Eve grabbed her bag off the floor and dug out her cell phone. The ID screen on the front showed she had one new message.

She wasn't foolish enough to wonder who would be on the other end when she answered. She already knew.

After listening to the ten-second message, not only did she worry about her own safety, she worried for Nick's. It would probably not be a bad idea to come clean to him about her true identity.

If he knew she worked for Grady—okay, maybe not right now—they could come up with a plan to catch this bastard. She hated acting like she needed protection. Even more so, she hated that she actually did need Nick—in more ways than one.

Eve punched Grady's number and waited for him to pick up. She paced the small room, making a U-shape with her path from one side of bed to the other.

"Yeah," he answered.

"It's me."

"Something happen? I just talked to Nick a while ago."

"I think maybe I should tell him," Eve blurted out.

"Tell him that you're a fed? Probably not a bad idea," Grady said. "But are you sure?"

"No," she admitted, stepping over a pair of tennis shoes. "I'm not. But I think if he knew the truth, we could work together and come up with some sort of plan. As it is, he's exerting the majority of his energy into my safety."

Grady's silence always made her grin. She could easily picture him leaning forward in his chair, resting his elbows on his desk calendar while rubbing his forehead. Stress seemed to be Grady's best friend.

"Do what you think is right, but keep me informed. I don't like being the last to know things."

"I'll tell him today," she promised. "I should probably let you know I just received a voice mail on my cell from the psycho."

"And?"

Eve sank onto the edge of her bed and examined her feet. Wouldn't hurt to throw a coat of polish on them before her shift tonight; unfortunately, she hadn't packed any.

Oh well, it wasn't as if the men would be looking at her toes. Her greatest asset was a little more to the north.

"Just another threat," she said.

"Eve," Grady warned. "I know from that tone there's more to it. I've known you since well before you went to Quantico, so don't try to hide anything from me."

She sighed as she fell back onto the mattress. "He threatened Nick, too."

"What did he say? Exactly."

Eve closed her eyes, recalling the chilling words. "He said, 'You can't hide for too long, Eve. I'll find you and when I do, the end will come for both of you.'"

"You didn't delete it, did you?"

"No, sir."

"Good. So far we haven't been able to trace where these calls are coming from, but we're going to keep trying. I think it would be best if I came down there."

Eve shot up. "Sir, I don't really think that's necessary."

"Why not?"

"We've got it under control for now and I've never known you to take any time off."

Grady laughed. "Well, Eve, when one of my own is in trouble—not to mention, Nick is one of my best friends—I think I can make an exception."

Even though he'd suspended her, he still referred to her as one of his own. The decision to give her a leave of absence hadn't been an easy one for him, she knew.

"You really think this is going to get worse, don't you?" Eve whispered.

Just as the question came out of her mouth, Nick came up the steps. He leaned against the wall and stared at her. Instead of concentrating on his still-bare chest—which was what she really wanted to do—she tuned back in to what Grady said.

"I don't want to take any chances with you or Nick. When all this is over, I want you back in the field immediately."

Hearing Grady say he wanted her back made her smile widen. "I can't wait."

Nick's eye's narrowed for only a second, enough for Eve to wonder what had brought on his sudden bad mood.

"I'll try to wrap things up here in the next day or two," Grady went on to say. "I'll be in touch, but if anything else happens, you call me."

"Will do. Bye, Grady."

Eve snapped her phone shut, tossed it on the bed beside her and leaned back on her hands. "Is there something you needed?"

In an instant, Nick's face went from suspicious to cocky. He quirked a brow and grinned at her. "I always need something. But first I want to know what you and Grady talked about."

"Nothing much. I just wanted to check in."

"I already told you I did that this morning."

Eve sat back up and came to her feet. She felt an argument on the rise. "So you said earlier, but I wanted to talk with him myself."

"It's kind of tacky to mess around with a married man," Nick accused.

"Yes, it is," Eve agreed as she rested her hands on her hips. "If you're trying to insinuate I have a thing for Grady, you couldn't be further from the truth."

"Really." Nick shoved off the wall and took two steps to close the space between them. "You always talk to him in private, and your face lit up a second ago, right before you said you couldn't wait. Do you think now that you've got some fucks under your belt, you can move on to someone else? I suppose married men would be more of a challenge."

Her fist connected with his jaw before she even realized it. Her whole body shook with anger as Nick looked back at her, and she didn't feel the slightest bit sorry for hitting him.

"Cocky, arrogant bastard."

"That's the second time you've done that," he stated.

Yeah, not to mention the second time she'd felt like her fingers broke the instant they came in contact with his hard jaw. She wiggled them at her side to make sure they still worked.

"Consider yourself lucky," she told him. "You've deserved a lot more than two. Now, if you're done condemning me for things you have no idea about, you can get your ass back downstairs. I don't want to see you again until we leave for the club."

"I won't apologize for my comment," he told her. "Especially since you didn't bother denying it."

Eve lifted her heavy hair off her neck and held it up with one hand. "Grady will be coming down here in a couple of days. When he gets here, you can go."

It pleased her immensely when Nick's face hardened. Without a word, he turned and went back downstairs.

Even with the air conditioner on high, heat filled the room. Eve dropped her hair back down and stripped off her tank and boxers. She flopped onto the bed, belly down, and let the cool air calm her.

Fighting must arouse her, because if he hadn't turned and left, she would've taken him again. His words had only hurt for a moment before she realized he'd said them out of jealousy.

Eve turned her face into the rumpled comforter and laughed. Nick Shaffer had a jealous streak. Could it get any sweeter? She doubted Nick had ever had to worry about his status with a woman before.

More than likely all he'd ever had to do was throw his signature smile their way and rip off his shirt to reveal an impressive set of pecs.

Eve hated the fact that she'd fallen into the category of easy women. True she'd waited twenty-eight years to give into desire, but when it came to Nick, she'd definitely been easy.

Easy or not, she'd managed to make Nick jealous.

Maybe she would just bask in this feeling a little longer before she told him she really worked for Grady. She couldn't wait to see the look on his face when he realized what a jerk he'd been.

On the downside, he'd be really pissed. She knew Nick well enough now to know he didn't like being left in the shadows.

Oh well, if he got mad and left, she would survive. She wouldn't like it, she admitted only to herself, but she would survive. Keeping Nick happy was not her top priority... Actually, it wasn't a priority at all.

First, she had to find a killer.

Chapter Eight

Roman couldn't wait for his meeting with the beautiful, sexy Eve Morgan. He hated being played for a fool. But he found himself admiring her for seeking revenge; after all, she'd focused the past year of her life on hunting him down. The obsession flattered him.

It would be so sweet to finally have her in his home where she could dance for him. Privately. He hated going into the club when he wanted someone new. The stale cigarette smoke, the pathetic—usually married—men that sat around waving dollars at the women. Not that he cared about their marital status. So long as they brought in the bills, he was thrilled.

Yes, men who had to pay to see a woman naked weren't a pretty sight, but he would make sacrifices in his life for what he wanted.

And he wanted Eve Morgan.

Despite the fact she was a fed and he'd killed her father, Roman just had to have her. He would make her his in every sense of the word before he decided what to do with her.

Selling, of course, was an option, but he almost hated to share such a work of human art. The money he could get from her would be tremendous, but he had time to decide.

Someone had tried to kill her... Someone Roman still hadn't found.

Roman leaned back in his leather office chair and looked out onto the grounds through the small, round window. He couldn't wait to see Nick. When they came face to face at the meeting, Nick would know for sure who had been behind this whole operation.

Even as young children, Roman hadn't been known for his bright mind, Nick had. Nobody had thought Roman would amount to anything in his life—well he'd certainly showed them. He had his own employees who would kill at his command if necessary, he had women at his beck and call, and more money than Bill Gates and Oprah combined.

But there was one thing his life lacked. Well, maybe not lacked, but something that needed to be seen to as soon as possible for Roman to be able to get on with his life without having to look over his shoulder.

Roman had to kill his brother. No henchmen would be given the order. This was personal, and Roman intended to handle the situation personally.

Meddling little prick always had girlfriends in high school, always the jock, always so fucking perfect. Well, now they were adults and Roman wasn't the geeky stepbrother anymore.

Nick had always been a smart man, Roman would fess up to that, so Nick should have figured out by now who killed Eve's father and who had been calling her.

Such fun, such an enjoyment. Roman hated to see this game come to an end. He truly delighted in the fact he'd tormented his brother and his girlfriend.

Over the years, Roman had kept tabs on his younger stepbrother. He'd known when Nick had enlisted in the Marines, known when he joined the police force and dropped out, and even known when the bastard had a woman in his life. Actually, he had women. Seems Roman and Nick did have one thing in common—it took more than one woman at a time to keep them satisfied.

Roman smiled. He couldn't wait to see Nick at the meeting. There wasn't a shred of doubt that Nick wouldn't allow Eve to attend all alone.

Tomorrow. He would finally see his beloved big brother after all these years.

And kill him.

Nick glanced at his watch one more time. They were going to be late.

"Eve!"

He rested a booted foot on the bottom step and draped an arm over the rail. What could the woman be doing? She never ran late. How hard could it be to get ready for work at a strip club? The men didn't care what her hair or make-up looked like.

She had tits and legs. What more did she need?

"Eve," he yelled again.

After another minute, she appeared at the landing. "What?"

"Are you coming or not?"

"I called off tonight," she said.

Nick took in the sight of her blue boxers and skin-hugging gray tank. Did the woman only lounge in men's underwear? And why the hell did he find this cotton ensemble more erotic than the red leather?

The little patch of skin just above her waistband gave him a jolt for a second. Damn. He really wished this woman didn't have such power over him. A power he seriously doubted she knew about.

"You could've told me earlier," he snapped.

Eve shrugged. "Well, I'm telling you now."

"Whatever," he said. "Why aren't you going in? Aren't you the one who was so adamant about not missing any work in case something happened at the club?"

She started down the steps. Fingers trailed lightly over the wooden banister. Her slow descent appeared graceful. The picture she made reminded him of old movies where the beautiful young woman made her entrance onto the first floor, wearing a sweeping skirt with a tight, fitted bodice.

Eve looked every bit as delicate and lovely, even in her state of dress with her hair piled haphazardly atop her head.

Nick nearly laughed at himself. First of all, what the hell had come over him that he'd thought about Eve in such a poetic way? Second of all, since their first few meetings, he had come to think of her as delicate...even vulnerable.

She'd kick his ass if she knew where his thoughts had

wandered.

"If you must know," she said as she stopped on the step with his foot. "I'm nervous."

That was a word he'd never expected to come from her mouth. "You're nervous? About tomorrow?"

She nodded and crossed her arms just under her breasts, causing them to lift above the scoop neck. His eyes had a mind of their own and he couldn't help that they wanted to stare at the soft swell of skin that threatened to spill out of the tank.

"You have a problem with those wandering eyes," she said.

"It's not a problem for me," he threw back. "I kind of like it."

Eve cocked her head and sighed. That deep breath only did more marvelous things to her tits.

"Well," she said in a low, seductive voice. "I'm off all night and since you're staring, you might as well take what you want."

Nick's hand tightened on the rail. "What makes you think I want you?"

A sinful grin spread across her face. Her eyes glistened. "You're a man, aren't you? Don't you all want the same thing?"

"No," he answered. From the look on her face, he'd not surprised only himself with the reply. "I mean, yes, we do love sex, but that's not all we think about."

She sank down onto the step and hugged her knees. Her pale green eyes looked up at him in question. Not only did they hold questions, they held answers as well.

Answers Nick wasn't sure his heart or his mind were ready to hear.

"Eve." He took a seat himself on the bottom step. "I know you won't talk about what happened, but I want you to know there are guys out there who truly care about women's feelings. Not all guys are assholes."

"Are you saying you're one of the good guys?"

Nick couldn't help the laugh that escaped him. "No, I'm not saying that, but I am saying I don't use women for sex."

She raised a brow. "You're saying you've never had sex with a woman just for the sake of having sex?"

"I have had meaningless sex, but the lack of feelings was mutual."

The question still remained in her eyes... It didn't have to be said aloud.

"What we've done," he began, choosing his words carefully. "I wouldn't consider it meaningless—"

"It's okay." Eve's hand came up and she shook her head. "I don't need to be babied about this, Nick. I'm a grown woman. You don't have to explain what's going on here and you don't have to worry. I haven't picked out our monogrammed towels."

The playful tone she used, along with her dimpled smile, put him at ease. Not that he wouldn't mind getting to know Eve better—in bed and out—but right now that was just not a luxury they had.

"So, about that proposition you were offering," he said as he trailed his fingers up her smooth shin.

She reached for him at the same time a thunderous jolt shook the house and blew out the living room window.

"Get down!" he yelled, shoving her down the last few steps and onto the floor. "Crawl on your stomach away from the door. Get on the other side of this staircase."

He assumed she followed his orders. He didn't have time to look as he crouched low himself and made his way to his black bag. Shards of glass were everywhere—on the couch, the coffee table, the floor, on top of his bag. He lifted one end of the duffle, sending the broken pieces clattering to the floor.

Once he dug out his gun, he crouched back to the airy hole where the window had been only seconds before. A strong scent of smoke filtered into the house. Nick kept his back against the outside wall, eyes on Eve. She lay on her stomach, safely tucked on the other side of the staircase. Her hard eyes were locked onto his.

The soft sound of crackling and popping filled Nick's stomach with dread. He peered through the opening, only to see his car on fire.

"Damn it!"

"What is it?" Eve asked as she came up to her elbows.

"My fucking car exploded," he fumed. "Stay in here. I'll be

right back."

"Don't go out there," she cried. "If someone is there, that's what they want you to do."

Nick jerked back to look at her again. "You're right, but I still need to see what's going on."

"Well, I'm going with you."

Eve came to her feet, but still remained somewhat crouched. As she started for the steps, he stopped her.

"Like hell. You're going to keep your little ass inside and I'll go see what the hell is going on."

Like lightning, she ran up the steps, emerging seconds later with a gun in her hand. The same one she'd pulled on him in her apartment. God, that seemed like a lifetime ago.

"Put that down before you accidentally shoot me," he scolded her. "If there is someone out there, do you think I'm going to let you have a face off with them?"

"Fine," she conceded. "Go on out there and be Mr. Big-Bad-Bodyguard. If someone out there doesn't shoot you, I will when you get back in, for acting like I'm incapable of taking care of myself."

Nick shook his head and scowled. "I don't have time for this."

"You know I'll just follow you out, so you might as well go on and quit wasting time."

After giving her one last what he hoped was an intimidating look, he eased the front door open and aimed his gun outside.

No sign of anything, except the burning car and blackened grass surrounding it.

"Stay here," Nick said to Eve as she stepped behind him. "I'm going to take a quick look around the house. If you hear or see anything, get your ass back inside and don't try to be a hero."

She held her gun in one hand and gave him a mock salute with the other. "Yes, sir."

Worry and fear had his emotions too tied up at the moment for there to be any room for anger. The fact that someone had blown up his car, and could very likely be waiting for an ambush, kept his mind off Eve and on their safety.

Each corner of the house he came to, Nick feared he'd see his brother on the other side. Fortunately, nobody waited.

When he finished his search, Eve stood on the porch, her back against the doorframe. "See anything?" she asked.

Nick shook his head. "No. I'm going to go back around and look closer. I want to see if there are any footprints in the dirt or flattened grass outside any of the windows. I can't imagine somebody planted a bomb and didn't look inside."

Eve's eyes widened. He could only imagine her thoughts. Whoever had been here had more than likely seen them. Together.

"Don't think about that now," he ordered.

He didn't stand around to discuss the possibility further. It was a dreaded thought he wanted to forget himself.

Had someone seen the way he'd taken her like an animal that first time? Had they seen how damn sexy Eve had looked in the red leather? Had they watched her come from the shower wrapped only in a short, thin white towel?

Sick prick.

Now that he'd set his blood pressure soaring, Nick looked over every speck of dirt, every blade of grass that surrounded the house. For a mission he'd hoped would be quick and easy, he couldn't have taken a more frustrating, fucked-up job if he'd written the damn script.

॰॰॰

Another hotel room, another day, same old scenario.

Eve dumped her bag on the bed closest to the air conditioner. After some local feds had come out to the not-so-safe house, they'd poked around a bit, taken some pictures, hauled off Nick's car for inspection and given them a ride to a hotel about twenty minutes outside Charleston.

When the lock to the hotel room door clicked into place, Eve spun around. Nick dropped his bag in the entryway, went into the bathroom and slammed the door.

Well, she thought, at least he'd showed some emotion. He

hadn't said a word to her since she'd been standing on the porch trying to digest the fact someone had probably watched them.

He hadn't told her if he'd seen anything when he'd taken his walk around the house, hadn't asked her opinion on what they should do next, hadn't even gotten near her until they were in the car with a local agent, and even then he'd sat in the front seat.

Because he'd been such a jerk since his precious car blew up, Eve had taken it upon herself to call Grady, who'd informed her he'd be there by morning.

Then, while Nick had been talking with some local Feds, she'd taken her own walk around the house. To anybody watching her, she'd just looked like a woman trying to clear her head after a near-death explosion. In actuality, Eve had been looking for clues herself.

Eerily enough, there had been areas around the back of the house where the grass lay flat. Other than that, she didn't see any signs of an unwanted visitor. Could have been a deer or a dog, but she highly doubted any animal would leave sneaker-sized imprints.

Then again, Eve had never been an optimist.

Weary and frustrated, Eve shoved her bag to the foot of her bed and fell face down in the middle of it, her feet dangling over the edge toward Nick's own bed. When she heard the bathroom door open, she didn't move. If he wanted to pout and be left alone, fine. The last thing she needed was to console a man over the loss of a piece of tin.

"You hungry?" he asked gruffly.

"No."

"What have you eaten today?"

His denim-clad leg brushed against hers. She didn't have to feel him to know he stood at the edge of her bed peering down.

"Coffee."

"That's why you're too skinny," he snapped. "I'm going to get us something."

Eve rolled onto her side. Rested her head in her hand. "I said I wasn't hungry. If you want to go out and get something, then go. I'm sick of seeing you sulk anyway."

Nick's brows drew in. "Sulk? Why the hell do you think I'm sulking?"

"You tell me," she said as she came to her feet, causing him to back up. "You haven't said a damn word to me in hours, you hardly looked in my direction, and now you look like you want to throttle me. I suppose it is my fault your car blew up, seeing as how this sick bastard is after me, but that gives you no right to be a rude ass about it. It was you who insisted on protecting me in the first place."

"Are you finished now?"

Eve merely crossed her arms—it was either that or deck him to wipe that smirk off his face.

"First of all," he began. "I don't give a fuck about that car. Okay, well, maybe I do, but it's not important now. I can buy another one whenever I want. If you really think I'm sulking, it's because of you."

"Me?" she exclaimed. "You're blaming your bad mood on me?"

Nick grabbed her by the arms and shook her. "You're damn right I am. Don't you get it? That explosion was too close. What if we'd been on the couch or in front of the window, or God forbid, sitting in the car? That bomb went off under the passenger seat, just like in your car. You could be dead!"

Even though his fingers dug into her arm, Eve knew his actions were out of sheer terror. The look in his eyes she'd mistaken for pouting had in fact been fear.

For her.

Her body relaxed under his touch. The slightest touch of a smile formed on her lips.

"You're scared," she said.

"Damn right I am. How would that look on a resume if I lost a client?"

Eve shook her head. "You can make jokes all you want, but you're scared because you care about me more than you want to."

Nick's eyes held hers for a time, then looked off to the side. He released her and stepped back. "Maybe. Maybe I'm just concerned where I'll find another car like the one I had. It was a babe magnet."

The urge to reach out to him came on so strong, Eve couldn't stop herself. Just a few fingertips against his bare arm had him looking back at her.

"Babe magnet, huh?"

He shrugged. "Got you, didn't I?"

Eve couldn't help the flutter in her chest. "Do you have me?"

The uncertainty on Nick's face made her smile. "I don't want anything to happen to you. I can't explain what I feel when it comes to your safety, but I know I can't let anything happen to you. Guess that makes me pussy-whipped."

"Caring for me is nothing to be embarrassed about," she told him. "I wouldn't want anything to happen to you, either."

"I'm not embarrassed," he snapped. "Don't put words in my mouth."

Trying to keep the situation as calm as possible, Eve dropped her hand from his arm and laced her fingers together. "Fine. Tell me the words you want me to hear then."

Nick ran a hand through his hair, let out a frustrated sigh. "I just got freaked out a little when the what-ifs started going through my head. Even though the threats keep coming and the level of danger increases each minute, I still thought we'd be safe where we were."

"But..." she prompted when he stopped and simply stared.

"I can't figure out how this bastard knows everywhere we've been," Nick said. "It's like he's got a tracking device planted on me. Or you."

Eve's blood ran cold at the realization. "You think somebody is tracking us?"

He shook his head. "I don't know how. All we have are these two bags, you have another bag you use for a purse and God knows what else. I don't have the car anymore, so I wouldn't think the device would've been on that, or he wouldn't have blown it up. Other than our cell phones, we don't have anything else."

"Maybe we should look through our stuff just to make sure

Naked Vengeance

it hasn't been tampered with," she suggested.

Nick stepped out of her way when she reached around him to grab her duffle. She dumped all her belongings onto the bed.

It looked like a Frederick's of Hollywood catalog had thrown up its latest fall fashions. Some denim shorts, cotton tanks, silky thongs and boxers tumbled out as well. Nick got a hard-on just looking at her skimpy wardrobe.

"I don't know where anything would be hidden in these," Nick said, picking up a white sheer bra with nipple slits. "Let me look through my bag."

After he retrieved his bag by the door, he too, dumped his belongings onto her bed. Black T-shirts, jeans, whitey tighties, another gun and some ammo.

He searched through the box of bullets, finding nothing. They each turned their bags inside out, examining each tooth of the zippers, each stitched seam, but in the end nothing looked suspicious.

Nick stood back with his hands on his hips. "Let me see your cell phone."

Eve pulled it from the pocket of her jean shorts, watched as he popped the back off. A determined look came over his face as he examined the insides of the phone.

"Son of a bitch," he mumbled. "I thought for sure there would be a tracking device. How the hell do they keep finding us?"

"I understand all the other places, but the safe house? I don't get it."

Nick ran a hand through his hair. The sinking feeling in his gut told him he and Eve were in deeper than either of them had anticipated.

"What do you want to do?"

Nick took a minute, trying to determine the best course of action. "We're getting the hell out of here. Now. Can you fit through that window?"

Eve glanced over. "Probably. You think someone will have followed us here?"

Nick nodded.

"You want them to think we're still here?" she asked.

"You sure you're not a cop?"

The questions struck her guilt chord even though his tone was playful. "Not a cop," she assured him...*just an FBI agent who's currently on suspension for not following orders and by putting herself in danger by trying to track down a killer.*

"We should call Grady and let him know we're on the move," Nick said. "I won't risk discussing our whereabouts over the phone, though."

Eve went into the bathroom, messed up some towels, pulled the shower curtain back halfway and moved the coffee pot out into the bedroom area. When Nick gave her a skeptical look, she merely shrugged.

"Do you want this to look real or not?" she asked.

"Let's go. It's fine."

"Where do you suggest we go?"

Nick dialed Grady's number and held the cell to his ear. "Well, right now we need to go find a bus or a cab or something."

Eve barely listened to Nick's short, vague conversation with Grady. Their next step plagued her mind now. Tomorrow was her meeting with this Roman guy and she had a hunch he'd been the master manipulator behind it all. The murder of her father, the missing women from the club, the exploding cars, the phone calls, the letters, and the possibility of being stalked by more than one psychopath. Roman obviously had a lot of men working in his sick and twisted operation.

Nick snapped his cell shut as she eased out the window. After Nick's long, broad frame squeezed through the slot, he joined her in the back alley. Thankfully they were alone.

Muggy, sticky air enveloped her. She needed a good, long shower. Maybe even a shower with Nick. Just to get her mind off things for a while.

A long while, she amended. Nick's amazing body and talented hands could do things to her mind that made her forget her own name. That's what she needed right now. A distraction.

"So where to now?" Eve looked up and down the street.

"We're going to go to the hotel a few blocks down," he told

her as he turned to head in that direction. "I figure when they realize we're not in the room they think we're in, they'll probably look elsewhere. That's why I think we should stay around here. I didn't tell Grady, but it's best if we don't stay in one place too long."

The plan made perfect sense and if Eve hadn't been too busy thinking about water sluicing off Nick's perfect pecs, she would have thought of it as well. Good thing Nick had his priorities in order.

"Besides," he went on to say, "I don't want to run the risk of getting on a bus or in a cab. We need to stay low until tomorrow morning for your meeting."

The meeting. Each passing second brought them closer to the inevitable.

"I'm going to need some things," Eve told him as he held the door open to yet another hotel.

"Like what?"

"A razor, some deodorant, make-up, an outfit." She counted the items off on her hand. "Since all my stuff is in the safe house, and I can't very well go wearing what I've got on."

Nick nodded. "Fine, I'll get us a room, get you settled, and go back out to get your stuff."

They paid for the room in cash—dwindling her stock pile down to near nothing.

"Do you have any cash?" she asked as they entered their room.

Not as bad as the others, still just as small. Two full-sized beds, a TV, a small desk with phone.

"Some. Why?"

Eve sank down onto the farthest bed. "Because I'm about out and you're going to have to buy my stuff, unless you want to risk using a credit card. I won't make anymore cash until tonight."

Nick sighed, still standing near the doorway. "Fine. Write down *exactly* what you need. Sizes, colors. As for the make-up, be specific as possible. I don't know shit about that stuff."

Eve leaned onto her side and opened the drawer of the small table beside her bed. A complimentary pad and pen were tucked inside. She tried to be specific enough, but in reality, she didn't care. What she really wanted wasn't at all possible at the moment.

Her job back, her father's death avenged. And Nick.

The first two wishes went hand in hand. Once she accomplished one, the other would fall into place.

As for wanting Nick, that seemed to pretty much be a twenty-four/seven want.

No, make that a need. Needing Nick fell into the same category as air, food, water, sleep. Of course, she would forego any of the last three for passion-filled sex.

"You're not writing," he scolded.

She jerked her gaze back up to find that he'd moved closer to the bed. So close, in fact, his denim-covered legs were within an inch of her bare ones. She really wished she weren't so turned on by the fact this potent man would be picking out her underwear. It would be interesting to see what he came up with.

"Is something wrong?" he asked as he leaned down and braced a hand beside her on the bed.

She tore off the top sheet of paper and jotted down her sizes. "Here," she passed the page to him. "I don't care about colors and all that, just so it fits."

"What the hell do I know about your taste in clothing?" he demanded.

God, why couldn't he just take the damn list and get out? She needed some space. No, she amended, she needed him, but since that would be a bad idea right now, she opted for privacy.

Until she could tell him about her FBI status, she didn't feel right about having sex with him. True, they didn't have a "relationship", but sex was still new to her and still something she valued.

"You're a guy," she replied as she flipped her corkscrew curls over her shoulder. "You know what you like to see women wearing. Pick out something you think I'd look good in."

Mysterious eyes roamed over her heated body. "Well, if that's the case, then I don't need to get anything... That's how I think you look the best."

Naked Vengeance

Eve rolled her eyes, trying to keep her emotions somewhat in control. "Please, don't try flattery to get me on my back again. If you want sex, just say so. There's no need for bullshit."

Nick's face hardened. "I don't have to flatter you, Eve. All I have to do is touch you."

One hand remained beside her on the bed, the other came up to her knee. The soft, feather touch of his fingertips trailed up her thigh to the frayed edges of her shorts.

"I bet if I dipped my finger under your shorts, I'd find your panties damp," he whispered. "You're ready, aren't you?"

Eve tilted her chin, trying her damnedest not to squirm under his touch. "What if I am wet? That doesn't mean I have to do anything about it. I've been horny plenty over the years. I don't need you to satisfy me."

Nick took hold of her shoulders, pushed her back on the bed and came up onto the bed to straddle her. He stayed up on his knees, but his strong legs kept hers locked in place.

"Maybe you don't need me to satisfy you." His Southern accent washed over her. "I don't need you to satisfy me, either, but I'm sure as hell not going to let you self-entertain when I'm rock hard and ready. Don't put up such a badass front when you want this just as much as I do."

"Fine," she conceded. "I do want it. I want it so bad I can't think straight right now. I hate that you make me feel so reckless and out of control of my own body. Does that make you happy?"

His mouth twitched. "Actually, I love the fact that I've been the only man to make you feel that way."

"I didn't say you were the only man," she countered.

Nick leaned down within a breath of her face, placing a hand on either side of her head. "But I'm the only man you've let yourself go with. If you were so reckless before me, I wouldn't have been your first."

Even if a reply had been on the tip of her tongue, she didn't have a chance to argue with him. His lips connected with hers. The gentle, light touch of his warm mouth made her squirm beneath him. She wanted more.

The need to feel his skin against hers was so great, Eve bunched the bottom of his T-shirt in her hands and pulled up.

He broke the kiss only for a split second as he grabbed the shirt himself and flung it to the floor.

Finally. Eve ran her hands up his muscular torso, taking her time when she reached his nipples. He groaned into her mouth, but still didn't increase the speed or intensity.

Eve gave him a slight shove. Perplexed, Nick sat up and stared down.

"What's wrong?" he asked in a husky voice.

"Everything," she cried. "You're going too slow, and we've still got too many clothes on."

"Oh, well, if that's all," he replied with a cocky grin.

He brought his feet to the floor and stood up, taking her hands and pulling her with him. As he unbuttoned his jeans and jerked them off, along with his tight, white briefs, Eve went to work on her clothing.

"Better?" he asked once they were naked.

"I don't want you to be gentle," she whispered as she stepped closer to him. "It's been a really bad day and I want to forget, even if it's only for a little while."

When his strong arms encircled her waist, she fell against his chest. "That I can do."

The kiss he gave her now demanded everything she had in her and even more. He gripped one hand on her bare ass; the other snaked up her spine to fist in her hair. His thick erection on her belly made her that much more excited. The size of him still amazed her. The fact that he wanted her that much astonished her.

"I want you to watch what I can do to you," he murmured against her lips. "I want you to see how passionate you are."

She heard what he said, but the words didn't quite register. Still holding onto her, Nick began to move toward the end of the bed—he took her with him, for she had no control over her legs right now.

Nick pulled back from her, settling his hands on the dip in her waist. "Sit on the bed."

The second she sank onto the bed, he fell to his knees. Her image filled the large mirror over the chest of drawers. She'd never thought of herself as a wanton woman before, but the image she made proved otherwise.

Perky nipples, flushed skin, recently ravished lips, heavy eyelids. Her eyes drifted down to the top of Nick's head as he positioned himself between her legs. His hands slid up her inner thigh as he blew his hot breath onto her moist center.

"Spread for me," he said. "And keep your eyes in the mirror. It's the most erotic picture I've ever seen. Watch yourself come, Eve."

Eve leaned back on her hands, opened wide for easy access and drew her eyes back up to focus on herself. When his finger slid up to separate her slick folds, her eyes drifted shut, but only for a second. Now she watched herself as the pleasure grew.

She bit her lip as her hips started to pump. Nick slid his tongue up the length of her while his thumbs peeled her lips back.

"Nick," she pleaded, eyes still locked onto the mirror. "Faster. I need more."

The next thing she knew, his finger slid into her, his mouth covered her clit and he sucked gently. Now the wild woman in the mirror who convulsed and moaned didn't resemble anybody she knew. Her full tits bounced with each jerk. The spasms took over her body as Nick shoved a second finger inside, prolonging the climax.

Tremors faded to euphoria. Still, her eyes remained in the mirror. Her chest rose and fell rapidly, her skin not only flushed, but also glossy from the sheen.

Nick continued to savor her, taking his time with his tongue and fingers. The tingling sensation only added to the enjoyment of his soft touch.

"Wait," she said on a breath.

Nick looked up at her, she down to him. Their eyes held for a second, but it was long enough for Eve to feel it.

No. No. No. She would not let him get to her like this. The sneaky bastard had somehow gotten to her, making her fall in love with him. She was a grown woman, she had control over her emotions and she would not allow this. The only relationship she wanted or needed involved strictly physical activity.

"Is something wrong?" he asked.

With her heart pounding out of control—thanks to the amazing orgasm and the smack in the face from the damn love fairy—Eve shook her head. "No, but I want to do something for you."

The smile she used to despise, but now adored, spread wide. "Like what?"

Eve shrugged. "What do you feel like? I want to make you feel as good as I do."

Nick continued to stroke her as his eyes roamed over her chest then back up to her face. The wicked gleam in his eye frightened her...a little.

"Let me sit there," he said as he came to his feet. He offered her a hand and she stood on her jelly-like legs.

The roles were reversed now. Eve looked down to Nick's bare body, aching for more of his touch... A touch she would have to get used to living without once all this business was said and done.

"What's the gloomy face for?" he asked, trailing a fingertip up her leg, stopping at her hip. "Doesn't this feel good?"

Eve focused on the here and now. She would enjoy each second she spent with him and the memories she made would have to last her a lifetime.

"It feels wonderful. I'm just wondering what put that naughty look in your eye," she replied with her hands on her hips.

Nick's hands came up to her wrists and held on. "I want you to dance for me."

Her once-rapid heartbeat came to a halt. Nothing he could've suggested would've shocked her more. "D-dance?"

He nodded. "Please? I've fantasized about you since the first time I saw you dance. Even once I started protecting you, I pretended you were dancing for me. In private."

Eve stepped back. She needed space and she needed to process this. She couldn't think with his hands on her.

"Nick," she began in a shaky voice. "I don't know, I mean I do that only to find information on my father's killer. I don't really enjoy it. I feel..."

"What?" he urged.

"Dirty," she whispered.

"Do you feel dirty with me, Eve?"

She shook her head.

"This is just between us," he told her softly. "If you really don't feel comfortable, then I won't force you, but it would mean a lot to me."

"I've thought about this," she told him honestly. "At first when I started working at the club, I would block out all the shouts and the strange hands reaching for me. Now when I go on the stage, I focus on you. On us. In my head, it's just us in that room."

Nick reached for her again and took her by the hand. "It's just us now."

"But it's not really the same when I'm not taking anything off," she said, glancing down at her naked body.

"I want you to dance like you're lover is about to take you for the first time. I want you to express your feelings through your body. Tell me what you want me to do, how we can pleasure each other."

Once again, Eve stepped back, offered him a genuine smile and said, "I hope you can handle it."

Chapter Nine

So did he. He'd seen the look of pure panic come across her face when he'd asked her to dance, but like the strong, fearless woman he'd come to know and care for, she gave in to his desire.

Her eyes closed. Her hips started to sway to an imaginary beat. Her hands slid up over her naked, flushed body until she came to her fiery curls. She lifted them off her neck and began to dance in a circle, guided by her gyrating hips.

She looked like an erotic gypsy.

Her ass danced before his face, mocking him, making his hands itch to get ahold of it. His cock twitched in anticipation.

It took all Nick's willpower—including some left in reserve—to keep from jumping off the bed and saying to hell with it. He wanted her. Now.

As she circled back around, she let her hair fall around her shoulders, framing her petite face. Innocence and desire made a fascinating combination. Only Eve could do both at once.

Nick gripped the thin comforter as Eve's hands trailed back down to the slope of her rounded breasts. She lifted them higher, rubbed them beneath her palms, all the while keeping the same slow pumping rhythm of her hips.

Eve closed her eyes, tilted her head back and moaned.

"Enough," Nick growled. "Let me."

Frozen in place, Eve simply stared at him as he stood and covered her hands with his own. Together they massaged her full chest. Their eyes remained locked, their breathing in sync—heavy and fast.

He guided their hands on down her body—one to her soft, smooth mound, the other to his pulsing shaft. Nick inserted one finger from each of their hands inside her moist heat while he urged her to stroke him.

"This feels good," she whispered. "I like feeling us inside me."

"I can tell. You're so wet, so ready to come."

"Are you?"

Nick gritted his teeth as her soft hand slid up and down. He tightened his hand around hers and quickened the pace.

"I can't take it," she moaned.

"Yes, you can."

Nick leaned forward to rest his forehead against hers. Together they looked down between them, watching the friction and the intensity build with each thrust of their hips.

When her inner muscles clenched around their fingers, Nick let go. Warm, sticky liquid spilt into their hands.

Minutes ticked by as only the sound of their labored breathing filled the room. Nick pulled his hands away from hers and went into the bathroom to retrieve a towel. After they were both clean, he led her to his bed.

Together they slid beneath the cool sheets. Eve settled beside him in the crook of his arm with one delicate hand resting on his chest. Over his heart. A heart he'd come to believe wasn't his own anymore.

"Let's get some sleep," he told her as he adjusted the covers.

"I need to tell you something," she whispered.

Nick waited. He had no idea what she wanted to tell him, but the way her body tensed sure wasn't a good sign. Her body heaved with a deep breath, relaxed as she exhaled.

"You were right."

Nick stroked her arm with his thumb. "About what?"

"There was an incident when I was little," she began. "One of my mother's boyfriends."

Shit. Nick closed his eyes and tried to force the image from his head of a childlike Eve and a bastard who had a sickness for little children.

"It's not as bad as you think," she assured him.

"If anybody touched you inappropriately, it's bad, Eve. Tell me what happened."

In a lazy pattern, she trailed her fingertip around his nipple as she spoke. "My mother worked the evening shift at the hospital. She was an E.R. nurse. Phil, that was her boyfriend, would watch me while she worked. He basically lived with us, but he'd always been so nice."

"Don't defend him," he growled.

"I'm not," she said. "I guess I'm defending my mom. She never would've put me in a position like that if she'd known what he was really like. Anyway, one night I was getting ready for bed. I'd just put on my nightgown and I went out to tell him goodnight."

Eve's warm breath washed over his chest. He didn't want to hear this, but he was glad she trusted him enough to tell him. Nick cuddled her closer, as if trying to protect her from past demons.

"He'd been drinking," Eve continued. "He asked me to sit on his lap for a goodnight kiss. He'd never asked that before, so I went over to him and he lifted me up on his lap. I could feel his...um..."

"Erection," Nick finished.

"Yeah. The whiskey on his breath stunk so bad and for the first time I was truly afraid of him. He smiled at me and said my mother said it was okay if he kissed me like adults do."

Nick closed his eyes. "Eve, I don't think I want to hear anymore."

As if he hadn't spoken, as if she were in a trance, she went on. "When his tongue slid in my mouth, I couldn't believe it. It was so gross and disgusting. I scrambled off his lap and ran to my room. I locked the door, then hid in my closet."

"Please, Eve," Nick begged. "Stop."

When she turned to look at him, unshed tears shimmered in her eyes. "Sorry, I didn't mean to upset you, too."

That's when Nick realized he had tears in his own eyes. "Tell me your mom kicked that lowlife bastard out."

"She found me in the closet when she got home. I guess Phil had lost his job that day and he had a gambling problem my mom didn't know about, so he decided to get drunk to forget his troubles. When she demanded to know why I was in the closet, I told her and he didn't deny it. She called the cops and they took him."

"This story would only get better if you told me his bookie found him and severed his dick," he said.

Eve smiled, causing a tear to escape down her pale cheek. "No, but he did die years later in a car accident."

"Good. That'll save me the trouble of looking him up and killing him."

She drew back. "You're serious, aren't you?"

"Hell yes, I am. There's no need for scum like that to be in society. How old were you?"

"Seven."

Nick gathered her close again and kissed the top of her head. "I'm glad you told me. I hate knowing it, I hate thinking it, but I'm glad you opened up to me."

"Me, too," she told him. "It doesn't make you think weird things about me, does it?"

He squeezed her tight. "No. It makes me want to punch something, but it doesn't make me feel any different toward you."

But how did he feel about her? The unspoken question filled the darkened room. All he could admit, even to himself, was that he'd never felt this way for any other woman.

That was it. That was all he could feel. If there was more to his emotions than that, he didn't want to know. Eve needed promises and happily ever afters...something he sure as hell couldn't offer.

"I hate admitting this." Eve's soft voice broke the silence. "But I'm nervous about tomorrow."

That made two of them. There was no way around it. He'd have to have to face his brother tomorrow with Eve in the same room.

All he could do was pray, because if he told her now, she would run. At least this way, he could protect her for a little while longer.

He hoped.

"You'll do fine," he assured her. "Just remember he already likes you, he's seen you dance."

Eve's body trembled against his. "I know."

"Don't jump into anything major," he told her. "Don't mention the missing girls, don't act like you're scared. You should be interested in the job because it would bring in extra income, but that's all."

"I know, I know," she said, patting his chest. "I'll act interested, but not nosey. We've been through this, Grady and I have been through it, and I've been through it with myself over and over in my head. I can't think of it anymore."

"Then let's get some sleep."

Eve started to sit up. "I don't know how much sleep I'll get, but I'll try."

"Whoa." Nick kept his arm around her, blocking her quick retreat. "Where are you going?"

"Um...to my bed?"

"Stay here," he whispered.

"I thought you didn't like to sleep with women," she replied.

He urged her back into the crook of his arm. "Normally, no, but I want to sleep with you. I want to feel your body against mine all night. That way, if I want you again, I won't have to go far."

He'd added that last bit to keep the moment light, to keep her from thinking this was too serious. To keep himself from coming to the realization it was getting too serious.

"Are you sure?" she asked.

"Positive." He placed his hand over hers on his chest, guiding it down to his erection. "See, it's a good thing you didn't leave yet. I already need you again."

Eve laughed as she came up to her knees and straddled him. "That's convenient, since I need you, too."

His schedule had changed.

Junior came into Allison's room early Friday morning to inform her Roman would be gone most of the day and he sends his regrets. That had been the good news. The bad news...he had a surprise for her when he returned.

Did he intend on getting the new girl now? Was this going to be a hands-on abduction?

She couldn't believe Roman would risk getting caught with his hands in any dirty dealings. The prominent "business" man must really have a personal interest in this transaction.

Allison dreaded what would happen when the new girl arrived. Did that mean they would share a room? Would Allison be shipped off to God knows where?

She hadn't perfected her plan of escape. Junior would have to help. Maybe she could persuade him to come with her—that way she could save him as well.

The breakfast Junior left for her didn't look appealing at all. Even the fresh pineapple and toasted blueberry bagel—her favorite—made her stomach turn by just looking at it. If she wanted to get out, she would have to work fast.

Without wasting another second worrying about what would happen if Roman caught her, Allison went to her attached bathroom and prepared to make a quick escape.

She fingered her hair up into a ponytail and pulled on a pair of khaki shorts and a simple red tank top. She slid her feet into a pair of white sneakers—better to run in than the heels Roman preferred her to wear around the house.

When she felt like she was ready, she went to the locked bedroom door and tapped on it.

"Excuse me," she called.

When the keys jingled in the door, she stepped back. Junior stepped in, shutting the door behind him.

"Yes, ma'am?"

"I was wondering if I could take a walk down by the pool today," she asked in her sweetest, most innocent voice.

Junior rubbed the back of his neck and sighed. "I'm sorry, ma'am, I can't let you out of this room. We have strict orders."

Allison let her fake smile falter. "Of course, I understand. Could you perhaps make another phone call for me at the end of your shift?"

He bit on his bottom lip and held out his hands. "I don't know. It was pretty risky the first time. We're lucky the boss didn't find out."

"Does Roman know everything you do with your personal time?"

The young guard shook his head. "No, but if he thinks anything, we're both dead. Besides, if I let you out, the new guard might say something. He's down by the main gate and he's already the boss's favorite."

Allison put her hands on her hips, knowing the simple gesture pulled her already tight tank even tighter across her chest. Anything to make him feel something for her.

"I really need to see my sister," she insisted. "Surely you have family. A brother? Wouldn't you hate it if you didn't see him for months?"

She prayed the guilt card would work. When he'd nodded at having a brother, she nearly jumped with relief.

"Maybe I could have your sister brought to you," he suggested.

"No!"

"I don't know what else I can do," he told her. "I just don't think this is a good idea."

He spun on his heel and Allison grabbed his arm. "Wait, please, I just want to go home."

Junior glanced over his shoulder, sympathy in his eyes. "This is your home."

ಐ

Nick had gotten up at the crack of dawn to hunt Eve some clothes and toiletries at a Wal-Mart down the street. Now as she stood in the small bathroom of their hotel room, she wasn't so sure this was a great idea. Nick shouldn't accompany her.

This part of the op should be done alone so she could fully

concentrate.

Eve pulled the black tube top over her full breasts, trying to adjust it so it covered the top and bottom of her tits. Figures, he'd pick something this tight and tiny.

Then again, she had told him to get something he liked to see a woman in. Obviously this was something like his other women had worn.

Bimbos.

She sighed and gave up on stretching it any more. Oh well, she would just have to hang out of it.

She pulled a black thong out of the bag and tore off the tags. Eve laughed when she pulled them on and glanced into the mirror. "Bite Me" covered the front of her panties, written in silver glitter. Classy.

Who knew what other tricks awaited her in the bag. Fortunately, she found a little pair of red shorts that fit her perfectly. She was surprised he hadn't bought a spandex black skirt to match the top.

At the bottom of the bag was a pair of black wedge sandals. A half-size too small. The band across the top of her foot dug in, but maybe they would loosen up as she moved around in them.

Or, better yet, maybe the pain would keep her mind off the fact she could very well be sitting across from the man who'd murdered her father.

After applying a liberal amount of make-up, she finger-combed her curly hair and left it down. Nick wanted it wild and loose—as if she had a choice in the matter.

One last look in the mirror and Eve decided she wouldn't be any more ready to go. She stepped out the bathroom door and found Nick leaning against the wall across from her.

His eyes widened as he raked his gaze over her. Twice.

"Damn, that stuff didn't look that hot on the hangers," he finally said.

"That's because my big tits and ass weren't poured into them," she scoffed as she went to her bed to grab her bag.

"Your tits and ass make that outfit, honey," he assured her.

When she turned back around, he had an eerie smile on his face and as he made his way toward her.

"Oh, no," she said with her hands up. "No touching. I will not be late and I will not have all this make-up smeared."

"I really wish you'd reconsider," he told her, all joking aside. "Couldn't you just call and talk to this guy on the phone?"

"No. I need to see him. I want to see the bastard who's responsible for innocent women disappearing and possibly for my father's death. In fact, I'd like it if you let me go alone."

"Like hell," he exploded. "I'm going, just like we discussed. I am your very jealous boyfriend and I want to know what this new job is. Just like we practiced, remember?"

"What if they don't hire me because you *are* my jealous boyfriend?" she asked. "Won't that make them reconsider if some hulky guy is giving them the evil eye?"

Nick's mouth twitched, only for a second. "It's that or you don't go at all. I wouldn't mind if they didn't want you for the job. Then we could think of another way to get this guy without using you as bait."

Eve took a step forward and placed a hand on his freshly shaven face. "Thanks for worrying, but I'll be fine."

His jaw clenched beneath her touch. "Stick close to me. No matter what happens, I want you to remember I will always protect you."

"What does that mean?" she asked.

"Just promise me you'll let me help you," he persisted as he brought his hand up to cover hers.

"Okay, I promise."

He opened his mouth as if he wanted to say something else, but shut it just as quickly. There was something new in his eyes she hadn't seen before.

Hurt? Maybe. Fear? Definitely.

"Let's go," he said, still holding on to her hand, now down at their sides. "And don't leave my sight. No matter what."

Just what the hell did he think was going to happen? If she'd had more time she would've called him on it, because if her instincts were right—and they usually were—he knew something she didn't.

Nick drove slower than normal in an attempt to put off the inevitable.

There would be a meeting. Eve would meet his brother. She would hate him. End of the fucking story.

He gripped the steering wheel until his hands cramped. All he could do now was pray Roman wouldn't show up, Roman wouldn't recognize him or Eve wouldn't go ballistic when she found out the truth.

The chances of that were about as good as an Eskimo laying out in a bikini for a nice golden suntan. Nick just knew all the prayers in the world wouldn't change the inevitable.

"You okay?" she asked from the passenger seat of the rental car Grady had had sent over to them under aliases.

"Yeah," he mumbled. "Just going over some stuff in my head."

Like how you are going to shoot me dead when you find out I've lied to you. No, that would be too quick. Someone like Eve would want to drag out the torture and make her victim suffer.

She reached across the console and rested her hand on his thigh. "It'll be fine. We're together and I think we've made a hell of a team so far."

That was a major understatement. Too bad he'd gone and betrayed his partner.

They remained silent for the rest of the drive. When Nick pulled into the club lot, Eve pulled her hand away and grabbed her black bag off the floor of the car.

"You ready?" she asked when he parked.

"If it's my only choice."

"Do you have to wear that?" Eve asked pointing to his shoulder holster and gun.

He nodded. "Yeah. Problem?"

"You look like more than a jealous boyfriend," she said as she closed the car door. "You look like a cop."

Nick shrugged. "Fine. Put my gun in your bag."

"I've already got one in here," she replied, coming around to stand beside him.

"Your father's Glock?"

Eve nodded.

"That's good enough, but I get to hold the bag." Nick shrugged out of his shoulder holster and put it into the trunk. "Happy?"

Eve smiled and handed over her bag. "Not really. Let's just get this over with."

They held hands as they approached the main entrance. Nick tried to keep his mind off the fact half of Eve's body was hanging out and his slimy brother would be staring at her like a prime piece of meat.

It was just something he had to prepare himself for. Eve couldn't help the fact her body looked like a walking wet dream, nor could she help the fact her father had gotten killed and she felt it her responsibility to find his killer.

Eve opened the door and walked back toward Hank's office. Even though the place sat deserted, the stale cigarette smell filtered through the dark room. Scuffed up tables were empty, save for the ashtrays. Various bottles of liquor behind the bar were lined up perfectly.

A slant of light coming from Hank's office spilt onto the cement floor. Men's voices rose high enough so that Nick knew they were discussing Eve's new position.

"You're hurting my hand," she whispered.

Nick didn't realize he'd squeezed her so hard, but he let up. He had to control himself if he intended to keep her safe. To keep her, period.

When Eve knocked on the door, Hank's voice boomed, "Come in, come in."

She pushed the door open with her free hand. Nick stepped in with her and came face to face with Roman for the first time in years.

Nick cursed himself when the look on Roman's face was anything but surprise. The little prick had known Eve would bring him along. It was all a trap, and Nick couldn't believe the rookie mistake he'd made by sinking into it.

His brother had always hated him, always wanted to see

him destroyed. Roman had been jealous from day one when his mother welcomed Nick with open arms. Nick hadn't thought Roman's evil streak would run this deep, for this long.

Roman probably had his sights on Eve from minute one, knowing she was Roger's daughter. He'd played with her mind and her emotions. Ironic, considering Nick had done the very same thing.

And now here he and Eve were in the lion's den.

"Eve, thanks for coming," Hank said, keeping a watchful eye over her shoulder. "I assumed you'd be alone."

She smiled at her boss. "Oh, you know boyfriends. He doesn't hardly let me out of his sight."

Nick and Roman continued to size each other up. How long would it take Roman to drop the bomb? Would he even do that here or make Nick sweat a little longer?

He really needed to get Eve out of here.

If Roman knew Nick had been protecting Eve, then Roman knew Eve wasn't really a stripper. Fuck.

"Are you Roman?" Eve asked as she turned to the madman in the expensive suit.

"Yes." Roman extended his hand, smiling when Nick cringed as Eve shook it. "It's a pleasure to finally meet you, Eve."

Roman's thick, deep voice dominated the tension-filled room. It was nothing but a game to him. A game, Nick knew, Roman intended to win.

That would only happen if Nick were dead.

"I'm a little curious as to what kind of job you want me to do," Eve told the devil in disguise.

Nick leaned down to her ear. "Honey, could you step outside for just a minute?"

Eve looked at him as if he'd just grown another head. "What on earth for?"

"Man talk," he replied with a shrug.

"Darling," she crooned, patting his face. "Don't be rude."

Roman stepped forward and guided Eve to the seat across from the desk. "Why don't we all get comfortable?"

Nick wanted to tell his stepbrother to keep his fucking hands off her, but he kept his mouth shut. For now.

Eve sat in a squatty orange arm chair across from Hank's desk. Nick stood behind her, one possessive hand rested on her shoulder.

He tried to tell himself he remained so close out of support for her, but in all reality the possibility of what his brother could do scared him shitless. What if Roman did something to Eve right in front of his eyes?

Nick's free hand tightened on the strap of the bag. The bag with the fully loaded Glock.

"What I'd like from you, Eve," Roman began as he came to stand behind Hank's desk, "is a few evenings a week. Maybe two, just for starters. What you'd be doing is more private, but along the same lines as what you do here."

"A hooker?" she gasped.

Roman's lips thinned. "You'd be keeping the company of some very wealthy clients of mine who want professional women who aren't looking for anything more than a little extra money. The clientele here is nice, but some men prefer their privacy."

Eve tensed beneath Nick's touch.

"She will not be whored out," Nick said. "She's my fiancée and I won't have her sleeping with other men, no matter how good the money is."

Nick thanked God Eve didn't contradict his impending marriage statement. She didn't even flinch. The cool composure came as a surprise, although he didn't know why. Life had dealt this woman a shitty hand, but she always managed to maintain her self-control.

At least in public.

"I think what Nick is trying to say," Eve cut in, "is that we love each other very much. I wouldn't mind doing some bachelor parties or even private parties, but I'm not comfortable with the whole escort thing. Being one on one with a strange man outside the club sounds kind of dangerous."

Nick wasn't sure how he felt at the big L-word coming out of Eve's lips. It sounded too...perfect.

"Perhaps you could take some time to think about it," a

nervous Hank suggested. "Take another week and let us know. The money is good, Eve."

Yeah, people die for it, Nick thought.

"I can take a few days and discuss it with Nick," Eve agreed. "I hope you won't give this position away until I give you my final answer."

Roman smiled, turning Nick's insides to ice in the process. "Of course not. You're our first pick. But I do have one condition, though, if you agree to the job."

Nick knew. He just knew what would happen. This world he'd come to live in with Eve, the main focal point, would come to a crashing halt in about one second.

Nights filled with passion and shared secrets. A partnership unlike any other he'd ever known. A relationship on the brink of something he couldn't even fathom.

It all ceased the second Roman spoke.

"You'll have to stay away from my brother."

Those damning words stopped time. The air in the room practically stilled and even though he felt Eve beneath his touch, he knew she'd just put walls between them.

"Your...brother?" Eve asked with a shaky voice.

Roman nodded. "Nick, or should I say your fiancé, is my long-lost stepbrother."

She whirled around in her chair. The look in her eyes confirmed Nick's worst fear.

He'd lost her.

Chapter Ten

Eve's lungs felt as if they were filled with mud. The one man she'd chosen to trust had betrayed her in the worst way possible.

She had to get out of here, but she didn't want to give Nick the advantage of knowing how bad he'd hurt her.

Hurt her? More like destroyed her.

Once she felt like she could form a complete sentence, she looked back to Roman and Hank as she came to her feet. She extended her hand across the desk and smiled.

"Thank you for meeting with me, but like I said, I'll need to think about this. And if I decide to do it, I will definitely keep Nick out of the picture."

She wasn't so dazed that she missed the gleam in Roman's eye. Damn the man, he knew how his words had affected her. Had Nick been in on the scheme, too?

Oh God…had Grady?

Without another word, or even a glance in Nick's direction, Eve willed her shaky legs to carry her from the room. From the club. From the whole fucking town.

Once she stepped outside, she tried to inhale the fresh air. Instead, she dropped her hands to her knees and concentrated on not passing out. Just when she thought she wouldn't be dealt any more damning blows, here came a sucker punch from out of nowhere.

Footsteps crunched in the gravel behind her. Eve closed her eyes and begged to God she would die. If there had ever been a time when she wanted to give it up, now would be that time.

She'd failed. Her father's murder would go without justice served, she would never get her job back, but worst of all, she would never be able to piece back together her shattered heart.

Damn her for allowing vulnerability to sneak into her life.

When the footsteps stopped beside her, she opened her eyes to a pair of worn black boots and her large black bag. Eve gritted her teeth, letting the rage override any hurt she felt.

"If you're smart, you'll get the hell out of my sight," she growled as she snatched her bag.

"Eve," Nick began. "I know what this looks like."

She pushed off her knees and stood straight up. A wave of nausea rolled through her and she had to close her eyes for another second until it passed.

All her strength came rushing back when Nick's hand grabbed her elbow to steady her.

"Keep your damn hands off me," she snarled, jerking her arm away.

"I want to explain. Let me take you somewhere so we can talk."

Eve dug into her black bag and pulled out her Glock. She glanced around, making sure no one could overhear. The parking lot was deserted. "Give me your cell phone."

Nick's hands went up. "Eve, what are you doing? Put that away."

"Give. Me. The. Fucking. Phone."

He pulled the phone from his pocket with one hand, keeping the other in defensive mode. She jerked it from his hand, kept her eyes and gun on him, and dialed.

"Prescott."

"Grady, it's me."

"Eve, where the hell are you?" Grady asked. "I'm at the safe house and it would be a little helpful if I could talk to you guys about what happened. Since I'm the outsider here, I'm not getting too much information from the locals."

Nick kept his hands up as Eve talked. This could not be the

same man who had saved her time and again. This could not be the same man who loved her so passionately with soft, loving words. This could not be the same man she'd chosen to give her virginity to.

"We have a more important matter to address," she explained.

"What is it?"

"Nick is working for the enemy," she told him.

"What the hell are you talking about?"

Eve sighed. "His brother, Roman, is the man I had to meet with at the club. He's the man who I believe has taken all the women, threatened me and killed my father."

Silence answered her on the other end of the line. Eve waited for Grady to explode with a fury that matched her own.

"Is Nick with you?" he asked instead.

"Yes."

"Let him explain," Grady told her. "He's not working with them, Eve."

The gun nearly fell from her hand. "You *knew*?"

"Yes," he said. "I knew. But neither Nick nor I knew before about a week ago."

Eve stepped backward, keeping the gun on Nick, until she felt the bumper of the car. She leaned against it, fearful she'd fall if she didn't. "And between the two of you there was no time to tell me in these past seven days?"

"It wasn't that easy," Grady persisted.

"The hell it wasn't!" Eve dropped the gun to her side, her eyes to her black sandals. "I can't believe this."

"Just let Nick explain. Better yet, let him bring you here and we can all sit down and talk this out."

Eve glanced back up to Nick. He'd dropped his hands to his sides, but still remained rooted in place. Hurt swam in his eyes...Eve steeled her heart. She didn't care if got down on his knees and professed his undying love to her.

She never made the same mistake twice.

"Sure," Eve conceded. "Why not? It's not like my life could get any shittier at this point. But just because I agreed to meet you and listen, don't get your hopes up that I'll ever forgive you for betraying me."

She eyed Nick. "Both of you."

Eve snapped the cell shut and got into the car without a word to Nick. She scooted over against the door, as far away from him as possible in such a confining space.

When he got in and started the car, he paused to look over at her. "Eve..."

"Just drive, Nick. I'm not in the mood to be lied to anymore."

In actuality, even though she was so angry, she felt her eyes burning. No way in hell would she ever let him see her cry over him. Not again. He'd caught her once, she wouldn't be vulnerable again.

"I'm not going to lie to you again," he told her softy. "I wanted to let you know when I found out—"

"But you didn't." She turned in her seat to face him. "You chose not to, you chose to keep the most important piece of information from me. And I am the only one to blame for letting it happen. I let myself trust you when I knew I shouldn't. I let you cloud my judgment and I let myself start to feel something for you."

Eve's head fell back against the seat as she closed her eyes. "Damn it."

"What did you feel?"

"It doesn't matter," she said. "Just...drive."

Nick stared at her another second before looking ahead and starting the car. "It matters more than you think," he muttered as he pulled out of the lot.

In a pissed-off-induced state of numbness, Eve kept her attention on the guardrail alongside the road, on the small fields, farm houses, other cars they passed.

Basically, anything to keep her from reaching over and strangling the life out of him.

Anger had become her closest ally. If she didn't focus on the fury, she'd do something really stupid.

Cry.

Nick had already seen her shed tears over him—she

wouldn't allow him the satisfaction of seeing it again.

When they pulled onto the long gravel drive to the "safe house", Eve nearly laughed. Safe. Nothing had ever been safe for her. She hadn't even found safety in the comfort of the man who'd taken her virginity...the man who still held onto her heart.

Eve hardened when her eyes locked onto the only other man she'd ever trusted with her life. Grady. He stood on the porch, examining the gaping hole where the window had once been.

Wide, broad shoulders filled out his white dress shirt. His sleeves were rolled halfway up his forearms, his hands on his hips. When Eve slammed her car door, he turned and glanced over his shoulder.

The grim look on his face did nothing to ease her state of mind. When she'd first met Grady, he'd not been an easy man to read. Thankfully, she knew him well enough now to know exactly what he felt.

Worry and anger, but most of all concern. For her.

Damn. She did not want to feel guilty. She would not let Grady or Nick make her feel like any of this was her fault. If they were truly concerned for her safety, they would have been upfront from the beginning.

The gravel crunched under Eve's black wedge sandals as she made her way to the porch. Grady moved toward her as well, saying nothing.

"Let's go inside," she said, leaving the men no option but to follow.

Once inside, which didn't provide too much privacy considering the wall to the living room was pretty much gone, Eve forced herself to remain strong, no matter how angry and hurt she was. At least the other feds snooping around outside for clues wouldn't see her rage... They would only hear it.

"First of all," Eve started as soon as Grady and Nick took a seat on the sofa. "Let me just say that if it weren't for me pursuing this matter, neither one of you would be involved."

Nick squirmed in his seat, casting a suspicious look in Grady's direction. Eve stood on the other side of the coffee table, hands on her hips.

The glass had been cleaned off the floor and furniture since yesterday. Too bad it wasn't that easy to wipe her mind clean.

And her heart.

"Have something to say, Nick?"

Without looking directly at her, he shook his head. "No."

"Fine, then." Eve raked a hand through her curly hair, a frustrating gesture caught short by a damn tangle. "I want to know why the two of you think it was best to keep something like this from me. Once you answer that, you can tell me what else you're hiding."

"Eve," Grady said in his boss voice. "Sit down, and let's talk about this like the adults we are. I know you're angry—"

"Angry?" Eve repeated. "I'm furious, working my way toward a nice stage of seriously pissed off."

Her boss held his hands out. "Okay, you're entitled to be pissed, but you may understand if you hear why Nick kept Roman's identity from you."

"Don't be mad at Grady," Nick chimed in. "I asked him to keep quiet."

Eve snickered. "That's no excuse. If he wanted to tell me, he would've."

And that is what hurt the most. The fact that Grady sided with Nick over her. Grady knew the death of her father took precedence over anything else in her life...including her career. So what could be the reason for keeping this secret?

"You're right," Grady agreed. "But for the time being, I thought Nick's reasons were valid and I still do."

Eve locked her eyes onto Nick's as she brought her hands back on her hips. "I'm just dying to hear this," she said dryly.

Nick sighed. "I was afraid you'd run."

"Run? Where would I run to?"

He came to his feet, but remained between the sofa and the coffee table. "I was afraid if you knew Roman was my stepbrother, you'd run. I didn't want you to look at me like you're looking at me now, thinking I had something to do with all this. I haven't spoken to Roman in years."

"But you knew I'd be meeting him?"

Eve's heart sank even lower when Nick shook his head. "I knew the day you set up the meeting with Hank. I was standing outside the office."

If he would just punch her in the face, it wouldn't hurt as bad as hearing this. She now truly understood the meaning of heartache.

"Is that why you tried to talk me out of going to the meeting?" she asked, point blank.

"Yeah."

Grady came to his feet and cleared his throat.

Eve held out a hand to stop him from leaving. "I never would've taken you for a coward, Grady."

Yes, this man was her boss. Yes, this man held her career in his hands. And yes, that said career had probably just disappeared.

Eve didn't care right now. She had nothing left to fight for other than justice for her father. Everything else be damned. Including her career, Grady and most of all, Nick.

"I know you don't mean what you're saying right now," Grady said.

"I know exactly what I'm saying," she countered with a bit of bite to her voice. "I can't believe of all the people in my life, you lied to me. You know what all I've gone through, what all I've given up to be here."

Grady smiled. "That's precisely why you shouldn't be so angry, Eve. Think about what you're doing. Nick isn't the only one with secrets."

Eve felt Nick's glare, but refused to turn to meet it.

"We aren't talking about me," Eve insisted. "From here on out, I'm doing this my way. I don't want or need either of you deciding what's best for me."

"Why don't you let me handle things from here?" Grady suggested.

"Do what you want. I'm outta here."

Without waiting for another word to be said, Eve spun on her high heel and marched out of the house. Angry tears filled her eyes, but she wouldn't let them fall now. Maybe when she finally got some alone time she could enjoy a good pity party.

Until then, she would be strong.

She didn't need Grady or Nick. She didn't need them controlling her life. She didn't need their help in finishing this case.

So why did she feel so deserted?

༄

Hopeless. Utterly hopeless.

Allison knew her days were numbered. She would never see her family again. Not that her parents cared about her, but her sister actually did.

What would her sister think had happened? Would she give up on searching after a certain amount of time had passed? Would she assume Allison had gone off on her own?

She had to get out of here, but something or someone had scared Junior and he hadn't been back in to see her for a couple of days. Maybe that new guard had warned him to keep his distance from the prisoner.

There had been more commotion lately. She'd overheard the guards talking outside her room about how the new guard Max was an ass-kisser to Roman and he would get special treatment with "the new girl". It seems they'd heard how beautiful Allison's replacement was, how she might stick around longer than any other because the boss had special interest in her.

So where did that leave Allison?

More than likely dead, if she didn't get her ass in gear. There would be no way she would be sold. Somehow in the exchange, she would try to escape.

It sounded like a good plan, but her inner devil's advocate told her if it were that easy, all the other missing women would have escaped.

Maybe she could talk Roman into letting her stick around for a while. Maybe if he thought she was into more than one bed partner, he would find it tempting. Wasn't that the secret wish of all men?

Without Junior, Allison knew she'd be on her own. No biggie—hadn't she been that way her whole life? This predicament happened to be a little more challenging and a hell of a lot more dangerous.

Allison crept closer to her locked bedroom door. The guards on duty now were speaking quietly, but she laid her ear against the solid oak door and listened.

"She'll be here tomorrow," one of them said with excitement.

"I can't wait," said the other. "The boss is really excited about this one. I can't imagine another woman being better stacked than the one in there."

Allison looked down to her "stacked" chest. Size-D breasts had always been a curse, from the time she'd had to start wearing a bra in the third grade until now.

"The boss says the girl's name is Eve."

"Does that mean one of us gets to play Adam?"

The guards made sick jokes and laughed at themselves. All the while Allison felt her stomach churning, threatening to toss up the fresh pineapple she'd had for breakfast.

She could only pray that whoever this poor, unknowing girl was, that they would be put in the same room. Even if only for a day, they could work out a plan of escape.

Allison wasn't naïve enough to think she could do this on her own... She needed an ally. Now she'd wait. Wait for Roman's next victim.

෨

Eve put on the finishing touches of her make-up at her vanity table. The crowd at the club tonight seemed to be larger than usual, but that had nothing to do with the nerves in her stomach.

Hank had told her Roman would be here to watch her dance again and he intended to speak with her after the club closed. Would Roman insist she work for him?

Eve stood in front of her lighted mirror and smoothed her

hands down the front of her policeman's jacket. The same jacket she'd had on the night Nick dragged her from the club.

In two days, he hadn't called her or tried to talk to her. Oh no, talking wouldn't be nearly as bad. The sneaky bastard slept in a rental car outside her hotel room.

Every morning and night he would simply look at her as she came and went to work. He even followed her to her apartment that first night. After she'd gathered some necessities, she found him still waiting outside her building.

Not only did it infuriate her, Nick's controlling actions made her feel vulnerable. Did he really believe she couldn't take care of herself? She'd been trained as an FBI agent, for crying out loud. But then, he didn't know that. And as far as she was concerned, he never needed to know it.

If and when the time came for her to leave this town and go back to Virginia, she would never see Nick Shaffer again.

The whistles and shouts grew louder over the blaring blues music as Eve made her way to the stage. A large portion of this mission might have gone to hell, but Eve still had a job to do, an image to portray.

She knew Roman wanted her to be the next girl; she all but had this gig in the bag. Eve stepped onto the stage when the lights dimmed. The music began for her routine. Now she only had to dance to seal the deal.

☙

Nick nursed his second shot of whiskey while he waited for Eve to perform. He'd watched her every damn night, then waited in his car with the most uncomfortable boner while she changed her clothes at the end of her shift.

She knew he followed her. He didn't miss the glares she cast in his direction when she got into her own rental car in the hotel parking lot each day.

It might be his imagination, but it seemed she dressed more provocatively since they'd parted ways only two days ago. Her shirts were either halter tops or strapless and they were always paired with a short denim skirt that barely covered her sweet ass.

Did she want to kill him? Had it been her intention to make him suffer? More than likely, yes. He deserved the torture, after all.

The music started and only the red lights glowed onto the stage. A long, toned leg slid through the curtain.

Nick would know that leg anywhere. He'd touched it, tasted it, dreamt of it.

Times had surely changed. Now instead of the good ol' days when Eve would taunt him by looking his way, licking her lips, she purposely avoided him. An easy feat, considering he stood at the same end of the bar each night.

More than anything he wanted to rush the stage, wrap a long coat around her and haul her out of here like some barbarian. Now that he'd had that body, he didn't want other men ogling it.

As long as Eve still held his heart, her body belonged to him.

Nick's zipper threatened to pop the second she ripped off the dark blue jacket and tossed it aside. Tonight she wore red sheer underneath—leaving nothing to the imagination.

Images of Eve wearing the red leather bustier filled his mind. The way it had molded to her body just before he took her out of it. Eve lying back on the bed as he pleasured her in the most intimate way.

Nick tipped back the rest of the amber liquid, welcoming the burn. Maybe that would knock some damn sense into him. She'd made it clear she didn't want him around anymore.

Unfortunately for both of them, he wasn't going anywhere until his brother was behind bars or dead. Preferably the latter.

When Eve sank to her knees at the edge of the stage for the eager men to stuff bills into her G-string, it was all Nick could do to remain still.

How could she let other men touch her after what all they'd shared?

Because they'd really only shared sex. They hadn't shared too much about their pasts—at least he hadn't. Eve, on the other hand, had confessed her fear of why she hadn't let men touch her before him.

So how could she do this now?

Because she'd loved her father that much and still wanted his approval, even in death.

Nick still didn't know the reason Eve's father and mother split, nor did he know the reason Eve sought acceptance from a dead man.

Once Eve sauntered offstage, Nick breathed a sigh of relief. He'd made it through another routine without killing some perverted bastard for whistling or yelling at her to take it all off.

He didn't know how much more of this...heartache he could take. Heartache? God, yes. It was heartache he felt.

There had been an empty place inside him since Roger's death, then Eve had come along. She'd fit into the gap perfectly. Now, the ache forced its way back into his life and he knew it would never be filled again.

He'd fucked up and had no one to blame but himself.

When Eve came into his sight again, Nick shook off his pitying thoughts. She moved along the outside wall, wearing jean shorts and one of those damn halter tops. This one in white.

Like the pathetic guy he'd become, Nick kept his eyes on her until she disappeared into the back office.

Déjà vu.

He moved over so he could hear the conversation.

"I've considered your offer, Mr. Burke." Eve's voice filtered through the door. "I think it would be a good career move for me. It would be silly of me to turn down such a generous amount of money."

"I'm glad to hear it," Roman said. "I'd like you to start at the end of the week."

"This week?"

Dread and apprehension filled Nick as he continued to listen. The end of the week would come all too soon.

"Is there a problem?"

"No," Eve replied. "Not at all. I just didn't expect it to be this week."

"I have another girl who I'm sure will show you the ropes, and she'll be leaving soon."

There was still another girl alive and unsold? Nick's worry for Eve shifted to the back of his mind, only for a second. If the other girl was still around, maybe Eve could get her out.

With his help, of course.

Now he only had to convince Eve she needed him...as much as he needed her.

Chapter Eleven

Nick's car sat empty in the parking lot of The Excalibur. Eve didn't wonder where he had gone to. Really, she didn't.

Okay, maybe a little part of her wondered.

She used the keyless remote to unlock her rented beige Ford Taurus. Bor-ing.

Thankful another night of letting well-manicured hands rub her thighs had ended, Eve slid behind the wheel. Soon it would all be over and hopefully it would all be worth the humiliation and misery she'd suffered.

And once all was said and done and she was back in the field, she'd request never to see another gentlemen's club again.

"Miss me?"

Eve screamed and spun in her seat. She didn't have to wonder about Nick any longer. Not only did his overwhelming presence fill the car, his fresh, masculine scent did as well.

"What the hell are you doing hiding in my car?"

"I want to talk to you and I knew you wouldn't invite me into your room if I followed you back. This way I'll talk while you drive, sleep in your car and you can bring me back here tomorrow to get my car back."

Eve started her car, willing her heart to beat at a normal pace again. "You have ten minutes."

Nick sat up in the back seat. "It takes twenty to get to the hotel."

"I feel like driving faster tonight. Call me crazy." She pulled out of the lot and sighed. "Do you have to sit in the middle? All I see is your damn head."

He shifted...somewhat.

"Please reconsider working for Roman," he pleaded in the dark.

She couldn't let that sweet, Southern accent affect her hormones. "No."

"Do you have any idea what he's capable of?"

"Gee, no, why don't you tell me."

"Don't be a smartass."

"Let me run down the list," Eve said. "Kidnapping, selling women as sex slaves, illegal prostitution, stalking, attempted murder, possible murder... Should I go on?"

"Only if that impressive list hasn't changed your mind."

"Nothing will change my mind."

The streetlights lit up Nick's ominous face every so often. Eve tried not to look in the mirror at him—she didn't like the look she received in return.

God, she'd give anything if he would just go away. She'd give anything if she didn't have to look at him again. She'd give anything if she could get over him, mend her heart and get her old life back—the life she'd had before her father had died.

Unfortunately, she couldn't turn back time. If she could, she would have never trusted her heart to such a dangerous man.

When she pulled into the hotel parking lot—exactly nine minutes after leaving the club—Nick spoke up again.

"Let me come in."

"No."

"We still need to talk," he insisted. "If you're so adamant about this, I want to help. Don't be stupid and think you don't need me."

Eve met his eyes in the rearview mirror. The streetlight behind the car illuminated his head. His face still remained shadowed.

"I know I'll need some help, but it won't come from you."

"Who, then?"

"Much as I hate to say this, Grady will be helping me."

Nick nodded. "At least you're not still angry with him."

"Oh, I'm angry, but I know without his help, I could end up in a world of trouble. I've become enlightened lately as to what exactly I've gotten myself into."

"God, Eve, you can't know how sorry I am."

Eve looked out the driver's side window. "I think the only thing you're sorry for is the fact you got caught."

"I won't deny that's true, but I'm more sorry that you got hurt. That was the absolute last thing I wanted to do. You mean something to me."

Eve's eyes snapped back to the mirror. "Don't throw my words back at me like they should mean something now. You're too late if you ever thought I would be anything more than a great fuck."

"It was more than that and you know it."

That was the bitch of it. Their time together *had* meant something, but she couldn't dwell on that now. If she did, she would break.

Eve shut off the car and got out, not at all surprised when he followed her to her hotel door.

"You're not coming in."

She made the mistake of turning to him and laying a hand on his chest to stop him from moving farther. For just a second, she allowed her hand to linger on his signature black tee. She breathed in his fresh scent, pretending they were in a different time and place.

The hard pecs under the soft material molded into her palm. His heartbeat quickened beneath her touch.

When he brought his own hand up to cover hers, she had to lock her knees in order to stay upright.

"Eve, please."

"No."

"Just let me in for ten minutes," he pleaded.

Her gaze traveled from their joined hands up to his handsome face. The features she'd once thought of as hard were now softened.

Something inside her shifted. "Five minutes."

His chest fell as he let out a pent-up breath. She slid her

hand out and turned to unlock the door. She wasn't foolish enough to believe he'd actually leave after the allotted five minutes.

Eve flipped on the light switch, causing the lamp by the bed to come on. She tossed her keys and her bag on the sturdy desk in the corner, breathed in a good dose of strength, then spun back around to face Nick.

For the first time since she'd met him, he looked nervous, out of place.

Good.

"You'd better start talking."

She wanted to be as firm as her voice sounded, but she really feared if he crossed to her just now, she'd go into his arms, then tumble with him onto the bed. Her body ached for his touch. Now that she'd had it, she didn't know how to do without.

"I know you hate me," he began.

She remained silent, allowing him to draw his own conclusion.

"If I didn't care for you, I wouldn't have hung around this long. I would have told you the truth the second I found out and let you go off on your own to bring Roman down. But I didn't tell you and if I could go back and let you in from the beginning, I would."

As he spoke, he inched closer. Once his face made it into the light, she could see the bloodshot eyes, dark circles and just plain fatigue. He still made her heart skip beats.

"You're tired," she said before she thought better of it.

He shrugged. "I'm not asking you to forgive me, I know you won't, but I'm at least asking you to let me help on this. Roman will kill you without a second thought if you're not properly prepared. No one knows this bastard like I do. Even though I haven't seen my brother for years, a man like that doesn't change his ways. I can't sit back and wonder if you're okay. I need to be near you, to know you're safe."

Eve listened to his defense and she had to admit, he did have every reason to be involved. Roman Burke had more than likely anticipated this blow-up between her and Nick, so Roman wouldn't be expecting Nick to still be around.

"Okay."

Nick's brows shot up. "Okay? You don't care if I work with you again?"

"It would be stupid of me to put my pride before bringing down the guy who killed my father."

"I promise I'll do everything I can to keep you safe."

"I believe you will."

He took a step closer, his eyes roamed over her body. With that one look, her nipples responded, pressing against the thin cotton of her halter.

Why did her body always have to betray her?

"I think your five minutes are up," she said.

"You don't want me to go."

"You have to."

"You want me," he said.

"So what if I do? You hurt me. You destroyed a part of me. Wanting you doesn't change that."

"No, it doesn't. I can't undo past mistakes, Eve, but I can make you feel better."

She stepped back as he advanced on her. "Stop, Nick."

"Tell me you want me to leave this room without making love to you. Without making you come at least three different ways."

His voice had dropped to a near whisper as he continued to stare at her with compassion and heat. She truly believed he was sorry, but he'd still made a mistake that could have cost her everything.

"I can't," she whispered.

Close enough to touch now, Nick trailed his rough hands up her bare arms. "Let me show you how much I still care for you."

"This isn't right," she insisted.

"You can't stay mad forever, Eve. Just let go for a while."

Eve's hands came up to toy with the hem of his shirt. "I can't resist you. I want to, I know I should, but I can't. Make me forget everything that's happening now. Make me forget about what might happen tomorrow."

"With pleasure."

His mouth came down on hers, hard. Not an ounce of gentleness came through in his touch anymore. She all but tasted the sexual frustration in his kiss, felt it radiate from his hard body.

He untied the bow at the base of her neck, allowing the straps to fall. Their tongues intertwined, their hands impatient.

Nick freed her breasts as walked her backward. When she came in contact with the wall, she arched her back, needing to feel more.

The bruising way he squeezed her tits made her so hot, so moist, she thought she'd come without him. She unbuttoned his jeans, pulled down the zipper and reached inside his briefs to free his erection.

She swallowed his low moan, all the while stroking him. Up, down.

His frantic hands moved from her breasts to her shorts. In no time he had them undone and shoved down her legs, along with her string panties. She kicked out of them and jumped up to wrap her legs around his waist.

"Now, Nick."

He slammed into her so hard, so fast, she cried out and convulsed around him. Her climax hit not a second too early.

Nick's mouth feasted on her taut nipples as he drove her over the edge two more times. Her quivering body clung to his.

"Fuck," he muttered as he tried to pull out.

"No, Nick. Don't."

"I need a condom," he told her.

"Where is it?"

"My back pocket."

Eve reached around with one hand, keeping her other arm wrapped around his shoulder. She dug into his pocket, thankful when she felt the foil square.

She pulled it out, ripped it open with her teeth and handed it to him.

"Here."

"Put it on me," he growled.

He pulled out just enough for her to roll the condom on. The second she let go of him, he drove into her again.

Eve let go of his shoulders, her arms hanging to the side as she used the wall and her back to create the leverage she needed.

Nick's creative hands fondled her. One on her breast, one on her clit. The fourth orgasm came out of nowhere just as he reached his own release.

Their hips pumped in synch, their breathing heavy.

He leaned against her body for support once their spasms subsided.

"In about two minutes, when I catch my breath, I'm going to take off the rest of our clothes and do this all over again," he promised her.

Eve barely noticed her top bunched around her waist and she really didn't care that Nick was still fully dressed.

"Don't go to all that trouble on my account," she said into his ear.

"It's no trouble. I want to feel your skin against mine, in that bed, for the rest of the night. I want to inhale your sweet scent, I want to watch you fall asleep after hours of pleasure."

A new set of shivers raced down her body.

He lifted his head to look her in the eyes. "Does this mean you forgive me?"

"No, but I'm shameless, and I'll let you screw me as long as you want until we're finished with this case."

Something shifted in his eyes, his lips thinned. "Fine. In that case, I don't want to waste anymore time talking about it inside this room."

The matter-of-fact tone made her cringe. Had she sounded so cold as well?

All thoughts vanished when he literally tore the rest of her top away from her body, leaving her in only her high-heeled sandals.

She unwrapped her legs from his waist and slid them to the floor. The determined look in his eyes should have frightened her. Instead it heated her up all over again.

He jerked his own shirt over his head while he toed off his

shoes. With quick movements, he shucked his jeans and briefs, kicking free of them. He yanked off his socks, then with more gentleness, he discarded the used condom into the trash beside the desk.

"Get on the bed," he told her.

Eve kicked off her own shoes, did as he asked and propped herself against a pile of pillows against the headboard. She allowed her legs to fall open, inviting him.

"On your stomach."

Eve drew her brows together, then without a word, she scooted down and rolled over. Nick came up beside the bed and grabbed a pillow.

"Lift your ass in the air."

Again, she did as he asked. He shoved the pillow under her hips and she knew he wanted her from behind.

Could he not bear to look at her face?

Eve cursed herself for being such a wimp. This had been her idea, hadn't it? She didn't want anything more from him other than his body and obviously he only wanted her body in return.

This arrangement would work out just fine.

Maybe.

With no kind words, no gentle caresses or kisses, Nick got on his knees behind her and entered her with a groan. All anger melted away at the new sensations streaming through her.

Eve grasped onto the pillow in front of her. Nick's hands dug into her waist as he held on and pumped in and out. With each thrust, he hit her so deep she didn't know how much longer she would last.

Finally, he entered her, stilled and rocked his hips. That's all it took to send her sailing over the brink once again.

His fingers tightened around her, his body shook against hers—that's when she felt the warm, sticky liquid.

"Nick!"

He pulled out...too late.

"Oh, God. Eve, I'm sorry."

"Sorry? You think that'll fix it?"

Naked Vengeance

She scrambled out from under him and ran into the bathroom. Nick's pleas for her to stop followed.

Eve grabbed a white hand towel from the edge of the marble sink to wipe herself off—as if that would undo the damage. Her heart beat so hard, so fast, Eve feared she'd throw up. This couldn't be happening. Not now, after all she'd been through.

In the back of her mind, she did some quick math to know if she'd wanted to get pregnant...she would've had sex tonight.

Dammit.

Most women would cry right about now, but what would that accomplish? If they'd made a baby—and God help the poor child if they had—she would have to just face the consequences.

Alone.

"Eve." Nick tapped on the bathroom door. "Open up."

She tossed the towel back onto the counter and unlocked the door. When she turned the knob and peered out, Nick leaned against the doorframe—still gloriously naked.

"What can I do?" he offered.

"Nothing can be done now."

"Where are you at in your cycle?"

Eve laughed. "Don't worry. I wouldn't tie you down to anything."

Nick reached in and grabbed her by the bare arms. "That's not what I asked. I want to know if this was a bad time."

Dammit, why did the tears pick now to show up?

"The worst," she confirmed.

Nick swallowed and nodded. "Then we'll deal with this together."

"No, we won't. I mean it, Nick. Once this case is closed and over, I'm going back to Virginia. I want my job back. Hell, I want my life back."

He drew back. "You are in a hurry to get back to tending bar at a titty club? What kind of life is that?"

Guilt flooded through her. Of course that was how he'd see it... She'd told him no different. That only made her a hypocritical bitch for the way she'd acted when he'd lied.

"I just want to be done with all this so I can go home," she insisted.

Nick pulled her against his sweaty, hard body. "I'm sorry. It will be over soon. One way or another."

Yeah, that was what scared her the most.

Chapter Twelve

Allison forced herself to relax when Roman came into her room with a new guard—or at least one she hadn't seen before. If she showed any sign of fear toward the new man, Roman would punish her later.

The slinky white dress Allison had been ordered to wear slithered over her naked body as she moved toward the two men.

The new guard caught her breath when he came into the room, but she had to remind herself, Roman's looks had been striking at first as well, until she got to know him. If this guard and Roman were friends, or even acquaintances, the new guy couldn't be much better than her captor.

This must be the "ass kisser" she'd overheard the other guards talking about.

"Allison," Roman said. "This is Max. You will be entertaining him this evening while I go out. I trust you will take good care of him."

Like the dutiful whore, Allison smiled. "Of course, Roman."

Allison kept her smile locked into place as Roman leaned forward, planting a kiss on her cheek. Without another word, he turned in his Italian leather shoes and left the room.

"You're so beautiful," Max whispered the second they were alone.

Allison jerked her gaze away from the newly locked door to the new stranger. "Excuse me?"

As if to clear his thoughts, Max shook his head. "I'm sorry. I didn't expect someone like you."

"Like me?"

"When Roman said he had someone for me to meet, I had no idea it would be someone as purely innocent-looking as you."

Allison couldn't help it. She laughed. "Pure and innocent are not words to describe me. You do know why Roman brought you here, don't you?"

Max nodded, but unlike most men, his eyes never wavered from her face. Not once had she caught him looking at her breasts.

The man had to be gay.

Great, Roman had brought her his newly employed gay friend to try to convert over to the straight side. Not that she had a problem with gay men, but obviously that was not where her expertise lay.

"If it's all right with you," Max said. "I wouldn't mind just talking to you during our time together."

Allison froze. "Why?"

It had to be a trick. Some sort of setup by Roman to test her abilities to get this gay man into bed.

He shrugged and moved toward the sitting area. "I don't know you and Roman didn't supply very much information. Is there a problem?"

Allison continued to eye him as he took a seat in one of the matching burgundy wingback chairs. This guy couldn't be for real. No sex, just talking? Unheard of.

It always seemed like such a shame when a man this hot turned out to be gay. Allison sighed and made her way over to the other chair beside Max.

The man did dress nice, she mused. Black slacks covered his long legs, a baby-blue button-up shirt looked as if it had been made for those broad shoulders, not to mention the fact the material matched his eyes perfectly.

He'd removed his jacket that all guards were required to wear and laid it over the arm of his chair. It made him seem a little more human when he rolled his sleeves up his forearms.

Nice, golden-tan forearms. Strong forearms.

"Allison."

Her name slid from his lips like he'd said it a thousand times before. She couldn't explain it, this instant attraction to someone so unobtainable. He'd been brought here for one reason and one reason only.

To get laid by a high-class whore.

"I'm sorry," she said, shaking off her unwanted thoughts.

"It's okay." He grinned, flashing a slight dimple to the right of his mouth. "You were staring like we knew each other."

"Do you know me?" she wondered aloud.

He shook his head. "Should I?"

Allison's hope faded. "No. I just didn't know if you'd ever seen me before now, maybe at The Excalibur."

Again, Max shook his head. "I've never been in there. Do you work there?"

"I used to."

Who knew she would wish her life back into that hellhole? Who knew she'd give anything to be back dancing on a pole?

"What do you do now?" he asked.

"This is it." Allison spread her arms, glancing around the room. "I sit within these four walls all day. I do what Roman asks me to and I entertain his friends and some employees."

"This is my first week as a guard."

"Down by the front gate?"

"Yeah," Max replied. "Roman told me when he hired me that he had a bonus for employees he deemed worthy."

Allison smiled. "I guess you did something right, but won't your partner be upset with this setup?"

Max's blond brows drew together. "My partner?"

"You're gay, aren't you?"

For a second, Allison didn't know if he'd heard the question, but when Max nearly rolled out of his seat with laughter, she knew he had. And now she knew the answer.

"You're not?"

"Oh...God..." His warm, rich chuckle filled the cold, somber room. "No, I'm not gay."

"Oh, well, I assumed when you said you only wanted to

talk," Allison defended herself.

Max leaned over, placed a hand on her bare knee that peeked through the slit in her dress. She couldn't suppress the shiver that erupted under his warm palm, nor could she ignore the way he looked her right in the eye.

Like she was a real person.

"I said I wanted to talk, because I do."

Still confused, and a little nervous, Allison leaned forward in her chair. "But, why?"

"Why don't I want to jump right into that bed?"

She nodded.

"Because when I take a woman to bed, I take her to *my* bed. I don't share and I prefer to know her first. Women should be treated with respect."

Oh man, did men like this really exist? This had to be a setup, a trap. Roman sent this man in as a test to see what she would do.

"So, what do you want to talk about?"

Max kept his hand on her knee. "I want to discuss the fact that you have nothing to worry about."

"Excuse me?"

"I'm going to get you out," he said in a low whisper.

The room closed in around her until complete and utter darkness consumed her.

ଛଠ

Max knew he shouldn't have just blurted the truth out like that. Now because of his poor timing, Allison sat slumped against the side of the chair.

Dammit.

"Come on, Allison," he said as he patted her soft, pale cheek. "Wake up."

She stirred under his touch. Like Sleeping Beauty, only he didn't get to kiss her. He never would've dreamed the last missing girl from the club was still being kept captive. Yet here she sat.

Not only did she have the body of a pinup, Allison Myers had the face of the girl next door. Her tall, willowy curves begged a man to glide his hands over them. And her little excuse of a dress left absolutely nothing to the imagination.

He knew Allison had been ordered what to wear, say and do to all the men who came through this room. Roman had no problem whoring her out like a piece of trash.

Sick fuck.

Max brushed Allison's blond hair off her creamy shoulder. It didn't need to be done, but he couldn't sit here another second without touching those silky strands.

The instant he'd come through the door of her room, Max had nearly swallowed his tongue. If a more intriguing, beautiful woman existed, Max didn't know where. Allison couldn't have been more perfect if he'd conjured her up himself.

Slowly, her lids fluttered open, exposing gorgeous blue eyes. She blinked several times, as if trying to focus in on his face.

"Allison?"

"What happened?" she asked.

"You passed out," he said without moving back to give her the air she probably needed.

She smelled so damn good, he couldn't stand up now if he wanted to. Between her exotic scent, the feel of her skin, her hair, and that damned dress, he now had one hell of a hard-on. The last thing he wanted to do was scare her.

But at least she would see he wasn't gay.

Allison jerked upright. "You said something about getting me out."

"Yes, but we have to stay quiet."

Hope glistened in the moisture that gathered in Allison's almond-shaped eyes. He would get her out of here, find the other women and bring this perverted bastard down.

"Wh-who are you?" Allison's voice shook, more than likely from anxiety.

"I've been trying to work for Roman for a while now. My name really is Max and I'm one of the good guys, but that's all you need to know. The less you know the better."

Allison nodded.

"We'll have to convince Roman we're lovers, though," he told her. "He can't think anything's up, or he'll fire me. I'm working as a gate guard to gain information on him."

"Are you a cop?"

He smiled. "Just concentrate on keeping Roman happy."

"How long?"

He hated the fact he'd have to leave her here to "entertain" Roman and his friends, but he didn't have a choice. Max certainly didn't want to think about what all she may have to endure until he could get her out. Or what the other women had gone through—like his sister.

"Hang in there a few more days."

Cynicism still swam in her eyes. He didn't blame her for not trusting him, not after all she'd been through. He still wanted to gain her trust. He wanted her to know he wouldn't let her down.

"Why can't we just leave now? Roman's gone."

"We need to gather more evidence and find out what happened to the other women. I promise we'll get you out."

Allison looked him straight in the eye. "I want *you* to get me out."

Max swallowed the lump in his throat. "Fine. I'll get you out."

She released a breath and Max forced himself to back away. The woman was supposed to be beautiful, tempting, alluring... It was her job. Damn, she was good.

But why the hell—no, *how* the hell had someone as pure-looking as Allison gotten mixed up in such a screwed-up world?

"I want you to know you can trust me," he said once he came to his feet. "I will be working the front gate every morning, and I'll make sure I see you after each shift. Okay?"

Allison looked up with her big, sparkling eyes and nodded. "Will you do something for me?"

Between her whisper-like voice and her pouty pink lips, Max would damn well do anything she asked right now.

"Will you call my sister and tell her I'm okay?"

Anything except that. "I can't. I'm sorry."

Her hopeful gaze dropped to her lap. "Oh, it's okay."

"If I called, that might compromise the investigation, and I want this man put away for a long time."

He waited a beat for her to respond, but when her head came back up, her eyes had turned to steel. Anger didn't even diminish her beauty.

"I want him to rot in hell for what he's put the other girls through."

Max tilted his head. "What about what he's put you through?"

Allison looked away. "At least I'm still close to home," she whispered. "Who knows where the other two girls are."

That's what worried Max the most. His sister had been sold—she had to be out there somewhere.

Max forced himself to sit back in his vacated chair now that her color had come back. Only now he feared he would have tears to deal with.

"Did you know the other two girls?"

With her head tilted to the side, her long, blond hair shielded her face. "Yeah. Carly disappeared about a week after I started, so I didn't get to know her really well. Ashley and I hung out a couple of times, though."

Max fisted his hands on the arms of the chair. He hated the way her voice had hitched, hated the hell she would have to endure for a few more days. He wanted her out of here now. He wanted to pick her up, carry her out and say to hell with the investigation.

But Carly needed him. As usual.

"Weren't you scared to keep working there after two women disappeared?"

She turned her face back to him. Her red-rimmed eyes were dry. "I couldn't afford to be. With it being a gentlemen's club, I knew I'd bring in a good bit of money. I needed that job so bad, I just took extra precautions."

"Like what?" he asked.

"I bought pepper spray. When I'd pull into work, I'd always wait and walk in with another girl, then walk out with other girls after work. I always parked near a light."

Max hated this part of his job. He hated making victims remember the initial attack. Unfortunately, it had to be done in order to catch the psychopaths that littered society.

He tried to put the image out of his mind of his sister and Allison being treated as whores. They were people. He didn't know Allison's story, but he knew Carly's.

The poor girl never seemed to keep her mind in the right place. And always seemed to fall for some poor schmuck with a sad story.

"How did Roman get you?" Max asked, getting back to the present.

Allison took a deep breath in. Her chest rose, then fell slowly. "I was taken to Hank's office. He's the manager of The Excalibur. He told me an associate had a job offer for me and I could still work at the club, this would just be extra income. I couldn't turn it down, so I agreed.

"My first night on the job I was given this address, and Hank assured me the client would meet me here and it was completely safe."

Lying bastard. Max vowed to bring Hank down right along with Roman.

"Roman met me at the door," Allison said with a shudder. "He was everything a dancer like me wants in a client."

"What's that?"

"Rich."

"You want some man to come whisk you away from your daily life?"

"No." A sad smile spread across her angelic face. "We aren't naïve enough to think a white knight is going to come in and take us to a castle to live happily ever after. Basically, we are just looking for a good customer who thinks our dances are worth a lot of money."

Max hated thinking of her on a dimly lit stage with strange, probably married, men leering at her, flapping dollar bills her way.

Like waving kibble at a puppy.

"Are you okay?" she asked.

Max offered a smile. "Yeah, just thinking."

Allison kept her questioning eyes on him. For the life of him, he couldn't make himself look anywhere else.

Maybe she would see something in his own eyes, something that would make her trust him, believe in him. He didn't want to leave without her having some reassurance that it would be okay. Maybe not today or even tomorrow, but it would get better from here.

Because he couldn't stand sitting here a second longer without reiterating the truth to her, Max leaned forward and patted her arm. "It'll be okay. This will all be over and by this time next week, you'll be back home where you belong."

Allison closed her eyes and leaned her head against the side of the chair. "I pray you're right."

"I wouldn't have told you if I thought there was the slightest chance we couldn't get you out. I'll personally get you away from this bastard."

Truer words had never left Max's lips. He would get Allison home where she belonged. And he'd to do the same for his lost sister.

☙

Could her life get any more humiliating?

Not only did Nick have to stand in the back of the club, now Grady hovered near the bar. The men were at least smart enough to keep their distance from each other.

Grady all but screamed FBI with his dark suit and crisp white shirt, especially the way he kept his glaring eyes roaming over the room. She doubted anybody else noticed, but the way he stood, his gun pushed the side of his jacket out.

Eve had already done one set. One set with her boss and her...what should she call Nick? Her temporary lover?

They'd both kept their eyes focused in her direction, Nick more than Grady. Her body burned every time she looked back and saw Nick, his face unreadable.

But Eve knew he hated this. He might act tough and

strong, but deep down Nick hated watching her strip for other men. But he couldn't hate it nearly as much as she did.

Eve touched up her make-up and piled her hair loosely on top of her head with only one large gold clip. She stood to examine her navy, gold and white "sailor" outfit.

The white skirt hugged her hips, the navy and white vest barely buttoned over her chest and the gold stilettos were taller than her usual four-inch shoes.

She prayed she didn't teeter off the stage into some man's willing lap.

Eve bent over toward the mirror and reached inside her vest to pull her breasts together. The more cleavage, the better.

One more set and she'd be done for the night. Except she wasn't really looking forward to going back to the hotel with Nick, who had been insistent on discussing the fact she could be pregnant.

Eve placed a hand across her flat stomach and prayed. Surely life wouldn't be that cruel to place a baby in the hands of a woman who couldn't even take care of herself, much less an innocent child.

Dirty diapers and three a.m. feedings would definitely put a damper on her field career.

When Eve's music began, she pushed the unpleasant thoughts aside and concentrated on not throwing up at the fact she had to go out on the stage and strip with her boss watching.

The second she stepped onto the stage, Eve looked to the bar, where four familiar eyes would be watching her. But something didn't look right.

Where had Nick disappeared to? Grady stood in the same spot as before, but Nick was nowhere in sight.

The two-minute dance seemed to take two hours. Eve had to get off that stage and find Nick. Something really important had to have come up or he would be there.

Surely he wasn't in any danger or Grady would have come to the dressing area and gotten her out as well. And if Nick had needed back-up, Grady would've gone with him.

So where the hell had he gone?

Naked Vengeance

Once Eve finished, she didn't even take time to change into her own bra and panties. She left on the sheer gold lingerie and pulled her jean shorts and white tank over them. She slipped into her own white sandals and headed to the front of the club.

When Grady caught sight of her, he straightened from the bar.

"Where's Nick?"

"He's taking care of something," Grady replied.

"Did he leave?"

Grady shook his head. "No. He's right behind you."

"Are you done?"

Eve turned at the sound of Nick's angry voice. "Yeah, where were you?"

Nick took her by the arm. "Let's go."

Shocked and a little more than irritated, Eve waited until she and Nick were outside and in his rental car before she said anything.

"What the hell was that for?" she asked as he started the engine.

"I just wanted you out of there," he said.

Eve kept her eyes on the side of his face. "Why all of a sudden?"

"We'll discuss it when we get back to the room."

Anger boiled through her. Eve crossed her arms and jerked around to sit against the seat. "Fine, but I don't know what I did to put you in this pissy mood all of a sudden."

"It's not all of a sudden," he replied.

She threw her hands up. "What the hell is your problem? You were fine on the way to the club. Did something happen I need to know about?"

He flashed a quick glance her way. "I said we'll talk in the room."

"Fine," Eve conceded. "But don't blame all your bad moods on me."

Nick smacked the steering wheel as he pulled into a parking spot at her hotel. "My bad moods *are* because of you."

He threw the car into park and got out, slamming the door

behind him.

Eve could only stare for a second as he stalked toward the side entrance. Her body's actions finally caught up to her mind. She got out of the car and ran after him.

He used the keycard for the side entrance, then marched four doors down to their room. Without a word, he unlocked the door and stepped inside.

The second Eve stepped in behind him, she slammed the door.

"Now tell me—"

Nick turned and crushed his mouth down onto hers, pushing her back against the door. His hard body always felt so perfect up against hers. It amazed her how one person could be made to fit with another's body so well.

Eve relaxed, letting his forceful kiss carry her to a better state of mind. Her body had already become moist for him.

"When we're in here, it's about sex," he said against her lips. "Remember?"

She put a hand on his chest and pushed him back. "No. Tell me what has you so upset."

"I'd rather not talk right now."

Eve held up her other hand to his chest when he moved in again. "I'm not having sex with you until you tell me why the hell you pulled me from the club and where you were while I was doing my last set."

Nick held his hands out to the side. "Fine. You want to know what I was doing? I was in Hank's office informing him this would be your last night of employment."

"*What?*"

"I also told him to tell Roman you wouldn't be taking that job, either."

Rage flooded through her body as she charged at Nick. Before she knew it, her fists were flying. Unfortunately she only made contact once before he caught both her wrists. She struggled to free herself, but he had a good hundred pounds on her.

So she brought her knee up.

"Fuck!" Nick dropped her hands and fell to the floor.

"How dare you do this to me," Eve shouted down to him. "After all that talk about trust and working together as a team. Why the hell did you do that? Do you know what you've done? We may never get another chance to find the three missing girls."

Beads of sweat glistened across Nick's forehead. After a minute, he got to his knees, then to his feet. Still bent at the waist, Nick panted and held himself.

"When we talked about working together, circumstances were different," he groaned out.

"What circumstances?"

He tilted his head up. "You weren't pregnant then."

Chapter Thirteen

Nick watched a play of emotions come over Eve's face. Anger, confusion, disbelief. His balls ached like a bitch, but he had to explain his feelings.

"Look," he said as he attempted to come to his full height. "It's not that I don't trust you or think you aren't capable of taking care of yourself, but if there's the slightest possibility you could be carrying my child, I don't want to take the chance."

"Our child," she said.

"What?"

"You said your child, but the baby would be ours."

"Sorry."

Eve moved toward him. His dick twitched with fear. "Whether I'm pregnant or not, we have to help these girls, Nick. I may be their only way out. I have to take the chance. Yes, there's a great possibility I'm pregnant, but there's an even greater possibility these girls will never be heard from again if we don't do something."

Exasperated, he ran a hand through his hair. "Would you listen to yourself? Even you admit the fact there could be a baby. Don't you care you could be putting him or her in danger?"

"How dare you say that to me? Do you think I haven't thought of this poor child? Do you think I haven't thought of the fact if I am pregnant I have absolutely nothing to offer a baby? I don't even have a real job anymore and, thanks to you, I don't even have the fake job."

Nick held his ground. "I won't apologize for what I did."

"You might not apologize to me, but you will go back to the club tomorrow and apologize to Hank and tell him you were drunk, high or just plain stupid. I don't care. I will finish what I started. I've come too far, Nick. I've sacrificed too much to give up now."

Nick grabbed her by the arms. "Don't you think your father would want you to back off if there's a chance you're carrying a child?"

"How would you know what my father wanted?" she retorted.

The lie came too easily to Nick. "I wouldn't, but I can't imagine any parent wanting their child in danger if they can help it."

Tears formed in her eyes. "I'm doing this for my father. Don't you get it? Yes, I care about those girls, but all this started because he knew something illegal was going on. Nobody had gone missing when he was on the case, but he knew someone was running an illegal prostitution ring out of that club.

"The stakes are just higher now that women are missing. There's more to fight for."

"Then let me and Grady and the FBI handle it," Nick begged. "That Max guy I told you about has somehow gained entrance to Roman's estate. That access alone could blow this case wide open."

Eve swatted at a tear as it trickled down her pale cheek. "Fine. I can finish this on my own, I started that way."

Guilt lay heavy on Nick's heart. He wanted to tell her about the night her father died. He wanted her to know he was supposed to help, but he'd been sidetracked by one of "Roman's girls". Of course, at the time, he didn't know Roman was in charge.

"If you want to help Grady, there's the door." Eve thumbed behind her.

He glanced at the door, then back at Eve, who didn't bother to wipe away the steady stream of tears.

She'd finally done it. She'd finally broken down and he had no one to blame but himself. He'd officially shattered her.

"I don't want you hurt anymore," he whispered. "Don't you

get it?"

"Don't you see that it would be worth it to me to get hurt, even die, if I knew my father's murderer got what was coming to him?"

Nick exploded. "Why do you have such devotion to him? He hadn't seen you in five years and all of a sudden you want to die for this man."

She cocked her head to the side. "How did you know I hadn't seen him in five years?"

Shit. "You told me."

"I don't remember telling you."

"Then Grady did," he said quickly. "I don't know where I heard it, the point is I don't want you involved here anymore."

Eve crossed her arms over her chest. "It's too bad you don't have say-so over my life. I will do this, with or without you. I think you know me well enough by now to know I won't back down."

That was the bitch of it. She would not stop until the end. Hadn't Grady told him that in the beginning? At the time Nick hadn't cared...now he cared too much.

"So, what will it be?" she asked. "Are you in it with me or are you going to work with Grady on your own?"

"What if I tell Grady you could be pregnant?"

Eve threw her arms in the air and crossed to the door, yanking it open. "Get out. Just get out and don't come back. If you can't have an adult conversation without acting like a tattling toddler, then just get the hell away from me."

Tear tracks stained her cheeks; her eyes, however, were dry and full of anger.

Slowly, Nick moved toward her. He took Eve's hand from the knob and shut the door, securing it with the chain. With his hands on her shoulders, he eased her back against the door.

"Look at me," he whispered, inches from her face. "Look me in the eye and tell me what you see."

Her damp eyes came up to his and softened. She immediately looked down to his chest.

"You saw it, didn't you?" he asked.

"I don't know what you're talking about."

Nick cupped her chin and tilted her face up. "Yes, you do. You're not a coward, Eve. Tell me what you saw."

"No."

"I see it in your eyes, too." He moved his hand along her cheek, rubbing her smooth skin with his thumb. "When you don't think I'm paying attention, I've seen it. I know you don't want to admit it, maybe you haven't even admitted it to yourself, but I know the feelings are there."

"Don't tell me what I feel," she pleaded.

Nick trailed his fingers along her slender neck, along the curve of her tank. "Fine, I'll tell you what I feel. I care about you more than any other woman I've ever known. I've never felt this need to protect someone and strangle someone all at the same time. If that's love, then I guess I'm in love with you."

Tears welled in her eyes, spilling over. The warm wetness tickled his hand.

"Don't tell me that just because you think I'm pregnant," she cried. "I don't want pity love."

Nick seized her trembling lips with his. The familiar mouth opened to him with a warm welcome touch, only now it was different. This woman actually held the purpose of his life, baby or no baby.

When her body relaxed into his, Nick wrapped his arms around her and moved away from the door. He walked backwards, never breaking contact with her.

The back of his knees hit the edge of the bed and he pulled back slightly.

"Let me make love to you, Eve."

"Yes," she moaned, her eyes still closed.

"Tell me first."

Her lids fluttered open. "Tell you what?"

"How you feel."

An easy smile formed on her swollen, pink lips. "I love you, Nick."

Nothing had ever made him feel more like a man than those sweet words from Eve's lips.

He reclaimed her mouth as he sat down on the bed. Her legs came around to straddle his thighs, her arms encircled his neck. At this moment, Nick couldn't think of anything better than being enveloped by Eve's tempting body, knowing in a matter of minutes he would feel her skin against his.

Eve moaned as she wiggled against him. Her rounded breasts raked against his chest, causing his cock to twitch with anticipation.

She broke from the kiss long enough to pull her tank over her head. When she came back to his lips, Nick took it upon himself to unhook her bra and free the mounds his hands ached to touch.

Another groan escaped her lips as Nick rubbed her pebbled nipples. One second he had his hands where he wanted them, the next second they were empty.

Eve jumped off his lap and made quick work of the snap and zipper on her jean shorts. Not one to waste a prime opportunity, Nick stood before her and did the same.

Within moments they were both naked, panting and falling back onto the bed, laughing. Hands roamed, mouths savaged.

Nick took his time with her, wanting this moment to last. Wanting their first time "making love" to be more than just sex.

Eve followed Nick's lead. With the lights still on, he could savor each part of her perfect body. The curve of her hip, the swell of her breast, smooth legs that led to dainty feet.

Each part of Eve deserved to be treasured. Nick did just that all through the night. In return, she showed him her feelings, using no words at all.

The look in her eyes, the touch of her hand across his heated skin; it all came together in such a way, Nick knew this woman would be in his life for a long time to come.

Funny how that realization didn't scare him anymore.

ಬ

Allison whirled around when the bedroom door opened. She'd been daydreaming as she looked out the French doors, wondering if she would truly experience fresh air again or feel a soft breeze across her face.

Now her heartbeat quickened when Max stepped through the doorway. Once inside, he smiled at her as he clicked the lock into place.

"How are you?" he asked.

Allison still couldn't believe this guy actually existed. He was simply beautiful, not to mention a true gentleman. He'd made good on his promise and visited. With today being the second day, she hoped it would be her last in this hellhole.

"I'm fine," she replied.

Max took cautious steps toward her, never taking his eyes off her face. "You look tired. Is everything okay? Other than the obvious."

Allison nodded. "I just want all this to be over."

"Me, too."

When he came to stand within inches of her, Allison had to look up to see his handsome face. A woman could get lost in those innocent baby blues. If that didn't get her, his soft, good ol' boy smile would.

"I feel like this is a dream," she murmured.

"Why is that?"

She studied his face. He seemed so interested in her. Not her boobs or the rest of her curvy body, but *her*. The sincerity in his voice almost brought her to tears.

Could this guy really care what happened to her?

"I'm afraid I'll wake up and you'll be gone," she replied. "I'm scared I'll be stuck here forever...or worse. I'll be sold and no one will find me."

"You will get out of here, Allison. It won't be long now."

She offered him a warm smile, knowing he wouldn't lie to her. For some reason, she trusted him. Trust had never come easy to her, but this guy had hers one hundred percent.

She trusted the look in his eyes. She trusted the warmth of his smile. Most of all, she trusted each word that slid from his mouth.

She jumped when Max's fingers trailed up her arm.

"What's this?" he asked, bending down to look closer.

Allison closed her eyes for a second, humiliated. "Bruises."

Those soft eyes turned hard as ice as they lifted back to her face. "From what?"

She shrugged. "It's no big deal. They're just small bruises."

"They look like fingerprints," he said between gritted teeth.

Allison turned back around to look out the French doors again. Why did this nice man have to witness the most shameful part of her life?

"Did Roman do this?"

Without turning around, she nodded. "Sometimes he gets a little rough."

"This has happened before?"

"Yeah," Allison whispered, on the verge of tears.

The sexual torture and disgrace she'd been put through was not a topic of conversation she wanted to discuss. She wanted to forget it had happened. All of it.

She wanted her life back. No matter how bad she'd thought her life was before, she'd take it back in a heartbeat in exchange for this living nightmare.

"Has he done more than bruise you?"

Allison turned back to him as she willed her tears away. "Max, don't."

Concern etched each and every feature of his face. His brows drew together, his lips thinned, jaw clenched.

"Don't pity me," she demanded. "I couldn't stand it. Just help me get out."

Max nodded, swallowed. "I'll do more than that. I'll kill him if he puts his fucking hands on you again."

Allison's heart swelled at his declaration. The tone of his voice held truth and promises. She had no doubt he would follow through on the threat.

In an answer to her earlier question... Yes, he did care about what happened to her.

Why?

Nick sat at the foot of the bed; across from him, Grady leaned against the wall. With Eve in the shower, and out of earshot, Nick had to talk quick.

"I don't think she should be doing this anymore," Nick stressed for the umpteenth time.

Grady shook his head. "Look, I can see your personal feelings are getting in the way, but I can assure you, she can handle herself."

"What makes you so sure?"

"Trust me."

Nick sighed. "If anything happens to her, you're responsible."

"Nothing will happen to her," Grady said.

"Can you tell me what happened to her parents? Did she ever tell you why they split?"

Grady shrugged. "Did she say anything?"

"No, I haven't asked. I'm just trying to figure out why she feels the need to please her father when he's dead. She talks about always wanting him to be proud of her."

Grady nodded as if he understood. "That's true. I knew Eve when her father was still alive. She...made some choices he wasn't happy with when she became an independent adult. Certain dreams of hers were not the same ones Roger had for his only little girl."

Nick rested his palms on his knees. "Like what?"

"She can tell you that. All I know is Roger and his ex split up when Eve was little. Eve's mom had a problem with alcohol and a string of boyfriends. For some unknown reason, the judge in the custody case gave the mom full rights and Roger had very few.

"The fact he was a cop didn't carry much weight. To my understanding, Roger left Virginia and moved down here. He joined the force and tried to start a new life. He tried on several occasions to gain custody of Eve."

Nick couldn't imagine an innocent Eve being tossed about between feuding parents and court dates.

"When Eve turned eighteen," Grady continued, "she came

Sophia Rae

to visit her father. She told him what she intended to do with her life. He wasn't happy, they argued quite a bit. Eve always wanted to be with her father, but her mother wouldn't bring her down here. The way I was told, Eve asked to live with him, but it never happened."

"What on earth did Eve want to do that was so upsetting to Roger?"

Grady hesitated. "It's not my place to say."

"I only worked with him a couple of months," Nick said. "He mentioned he had a daughter, but that was it. He said they hadn't spoken in a long time, but that he wanted to make up with her."

Grady shoved his hands in his black trousers. "He would've, too. Roger was a good guy."

Nick nodded. He'd gotten that impression in the short time he and Roger had worked together. The man had been a tough cop, a perfectionist when it came to the job. He went above and beyond his duties. In the end, it had cost him his life.

"You're going to have to tell her sometime," Grady said.

"I know."

"Soon."

Nick sighed, dropping his head between his hunched shoulders. "How do I tell her? How can I tell the woman I've fallen in love with that it was my fault her father died?"

"What?"

Nick's head jerked back up at Eve's soft, shocked voice. She stood just outside the bathroom, wearing a pair of gray cotton shorts and a white tank. Her damp hair clung to her porcelain skin. It reminded him of the time he'd broken into her apartment.

"Eve," Nick said coming to his feet.

She held up a hand. "Did you say it was your fault my father died?"

Grady pushed off the wall. "I'm going to go make a call."

Neither Nick nor Eve noticed their friend slip out the door.

"Nick?"

"Sit down, Eve."

He motioned to the bed, but she didn't budge. God, he'd put that look in her eyes again. Mistrust, anger, fear, resentment. Loneliness.

Dammit, why did he continue to hurt the woman he claimed to love so much?

"I knew your father," Nick began.

Eve leaned against the wall, he assumed for support. Her face held questions only he could answer, but he feared the truth would drive her out of his arms for good.

"Grady and I were in the Marines together. He was just leaving as I was coming in, but we bonded quickly. When he left, he joined the FBI. After I served a few years, I became a cop, but that didn't last long. I wanted to be my own boss, so I started working for myself as a bodyguard, private investigator, snitch. You name it."

Nick shoved his hands into his denim pockets. It was either that or grab Eve and beg her forgiveness before he even got to the end of his sad, pathetic story.

"Grady and your father had worked together some on training assignments at Quantico."

Eve nodded. "My father went through the academy, but decided he wanted to be a cop instead. I have no idea why."

"Well, when the time came for Roger to work this prostitution thing, there were no girls missing. But we knew the owner, who we now know is Roman, was practically selling girls out of the back room for a ton of money."

Eve finally made a move to sit on the bed. She didn't, however, look him in the eye. Not once since he'd started his story.

"I got a call from Roger telling me he and his partner were going to the club. They thought they could get enough information to bust it. I was on my way, but I got sidetracked."

God, this was the tough part.

Nick leaned against the wall opposite Eve and looked down at her while he spoke. He'd give anything if she'd just look up at him.

"I was getting ready to go into the club when a dancer came out. She approached me, tried to get me to take her somewhere so she could show me a good time. She said I didn't have to pay her so long as her boss didn't find out."

Nick watched as Eve picked at her fingernails.

"She was all over me, and I hate admitting this, but I wasn't exactly turning her away. I knew I was there for a sting, but I thought I could get some information from this girl.

"That's when I heard shots in the back alley."

Eve's hands came up to shield her face. When a sniffle escaped her, it felt as if someone had reached into his chest and squeezed his heart.

"I ran around the side of the building," Nick went on to explain. "The only thing I saw was Roger."

Red-rimmed eyes full of unshed tears looked up. "Was he already dead?"

Shaking his head, he swallowed the lump in his throat. "No. I ran over to him. It was bad and I knew he wouldn't make it. He kept trying to tell me something. Finally he said, 'Rom'."

Eve's brows drew together.

"At the time I didn't get it," Nick went on. "I've been having dreams since then, but it wasn't 'til the other night that it hit me. He was trying to say Roman. He obviously knew who Roman was and he wanted me to know who shot him."

Slowly, Eve stood. "Let me get this straight. You knew my father and were there the night he died, but you got sidetracked by some bimbo who was obviously planted to distract you. Then when you find out the same person who'd been stalking me had also killed my father, you didn't say anything?"

"Eve, I didn't want you in the middle of all this."

"Too damn bad," she screamed. "I *am* in the middle of all this. Do you know how much I wanted to know who killed my father? How I needed to know for sure who pulled that trigger that ended his life? I guess not, since you said nothing about it."

Eve raked her damp hair from around her face. "Oh, wait, let me guess. Grady knows all this shit, too?"

Nick hesitated, but finally nodded.

"You two can just go to hell," she said in a calm, eerie voice. "I don't want or need either of you right now."

"Eve, wait."

"Don't touch me," she commanded when he stepped toward her. "I don't want you to even look at me. I'm finished with you and your lies."

She went to her bag and stuffed what few articles of clothing she had into it. Nick wasn't surprised at her reaction, but he wished to hell she'd stay and let him explain better.

"Eve, you can't leave. It's not safe."

She whirled around on him. "Obviously it's not safe with you, either."

Nothing could have hurt him more—except the fact she'd been right. She wasn't safe with him.

"Please let Grady protect you," he pleaded.

"He can do what he damn well pleases, so long as it doesn't involve me."

Once her things were stuffed into the small bag, Eve jerked up the zipper.

"I'll finish this myself," she told him as she hoisted her bag onto her shoulder and shoved her feet into her flip-flops. "Stay out of my way and my life."

"I love you," he said softly.

Eve laughed. "You don't love me. How can there be love when all we've done is lie? No relationship can be built on that."

More truthful words. They hurt, but not as much as watching her walk out the hotel door.

Nick had a sinking feeling he'd never see her again.

Chapter Fourteen

Eve entered the club through the front door. Even though they didn't open for another couple of hours, Hank would be around.

With a new outlook on life, and a new vendetta, Eve marched around the scarred bar and straight to Hank's office. His door stood ajar a few inches, so she knocked. Without waiting for an answer, she pushed it open.

Hank sat at his desk shuffling through applications. More than likely looking for the next victim to make money off of.

"Do you have a minute?" she asked.

Hank leaned back in his rickety chair, placed his hands behind his head. The gesture only pulled his white button-up shirt even tighter across his protruding belly.

"Eve. I'm surprised to see you. Your boyfriend said you'd quit."

She smiled. "He isn't my boyfriend, nor is he my spokesman. But I would like to speak with Roman. Now."

Hank offered a condescending smile. "Roman isn't coming in this evening. Is there something I can help you with?"

Eve moved farther into the office, placed her hands on the edge of his desk and leaned down. "You can call him and tell him I have a proposition for him. If he's interested, he'll get here in ten minutes."

"Eve—"

"Call. Him."

Hank kept his eyes on her as he picked up his phone with a shaky hand. He relayed her message and hung up.

"He's on his way."

Hank must have seen the anger and murder in her eyes, she mused. He didn't seem so sure of himself. Somehow Eve figured she wasn't the only one making him nervous.

She remained standing in front of the utilitarian-style desk. She crossed her arms under her breasts and looked down.

"Don't let me stop you," she told him, nodding down to his stack of papers.

He cocked his head to the side as if trying to figure her out. Eventually, he began shuffling back through his stack.

Eve glared down at Hank's greasy brown comb-over. "So how much money does Roman give you for finding the perfect women for him to sell as sex slaves?"

Hank's face shot up. "What?"

"You heard me. How much?"

"I-I don't know what you're talking about," he stammered.

"Bullshit. You know as well as I do he's running an illegal prostitution ring out of the club. You probably know where the missing women are."

The nervous man came to his feet. "Now, Eve. Calm down. You're clearly not thinking straight."

"Oh, I'm thinking straight all right," she told him. "I know your ol' buddy Roman is a slithery snake who has taken these women for his own enjoyment. Who knows where the hell they are now."

Beads of sweat broke out onto Hank's wrinkled forehead. "Neither Roman nor I know the whereabouts of those women. The cops have been keeping me informed of my dancers, but so far there's no sign of them."

"You might want to ask your business associate," Eve offered. "I guarantee he knows. If you really don't know, looks like he was screwing you over as well. He owes you some money."

Hank opened his mouth to speak, but before he did, his beady little eyes darted over her shoulder. Just as Eve turned, something sharp stuck her arm.

The room faded to black.

Nick cursed himself for allowing Eve to leave the way she had.

Yeah, right. Like he could've stopped her. Nobody "allowed" that stubborn woman to do anything. The woman prided herself on being independent and determined; two traits Nick feared would just get her into even more trouble. With anger driving her, who knew what she'd end up doing.

Grady came back into the room a few minutes after Eve stormed out.

"She knows," Nick said the second Grady closed the door.

"What?"

He sat on the edge of the bed, rested his elbows on his knees. "That it was my fault Roger died."

"Dammit, Nick," Grady blasted. "It wasn't your fault."

Nick shook his head. "It really doesn't matter whose fault it was, Eve's gone."

"She's not coming back?"

"No."

Grady grabbed Nick by the shoulders, hauled him up. "Would you snap out of your pity party? We don't have time for this shit. Where did she go?"

Nick looked into Grady's angry face. "I don't know."

"The police are getting ready to bust Roman," Grady told him. "If she's gone off half-cocked, we have to find her. She could be in more danger than we first realized."

The image of Eve in any kind of immediate danger snapped him back to reality. Forget she'd left him, he had to find her. His emotional state would have to wait.

"Let's try the club," Nick suggested.

Both Nick and Grady checked the clips on their guns before heading out the door.

Faint voices filtered through her head. She couldn't make out the words, though. Her eyelids felt as if they had cinderblocks on them and she had no idea if she was dead or alive.

Soft. She knew she was lying on something soft. A gentle hand fell across her forehead.

"...she's coming...of it..."

"...who...she..."

Eve forced her lids to work. She couldn't stay like this. Who had taken her? Were they in the room now?

"Shh. You're okay," a woman assured her.

When Eve finally managed to open her eyes all the way, she looked to the man and woman who seemed to be examining her.

A beautiful, pale-faced blond lady with deep blue eyes and a sweet, innocent smile smoothed Eve's hair away from her face.

Another set of beautiful blue eyes watched her. The man had golden skin, like Nick, except this man had softer features. No visible scars, no hard lines to his face.

"Do you know your name?" the man asked.

Eve nodded, winced when her head pounded harder. "My name is Eve."

"Can you tell us how you got here?" the soft spoken lady asked.

Eve tried to sit up. Both strangers slipped an arm around her waist to aid her.

"Do you want some water?" the female asked.

"No. Where am I?"

The two exchanged a look before the man spoke up. "Do you know Roman Burke?"

Even at the risk of splitting her head open, Eve nodded.

"You're at his house," the man said.

"I was drugged," Eve recalled out loud.

"Do you by chance work at The Excalibur?" he asked.

"Yes. Who are you guys?"

"I'm Allison Myers."

Eve whipped her head around, wincing at the burst of pain. "You're okay. I'd heard you were, but I wasn't sure you if were still around or not."

"I'm fine," Allison assured Eve. "Thanks to Max."

Eve glanced back to the man. "You're Max?"

"Yes, ma'am."

"Max Price? The FBI agent?"

"*FBI?*" Allison exclaimed.

"I am an agent," he confirmed. "But if either of you accidentally leak that, we're dead."

Eve nodded. "I'm an agent myself."

The skeptical look Max gave her had her smiling.

"I really am," she said. "I am on suspension, but I work in Quantico. I'm down here trying to find who killed my father last year. He was undercover at the club when he was shot."

"Detective Watts was your father?" Max asked.

Eve nodded. "Roman killed him, and now I'm here to make sure that bastard pays. He must've known I was close because he drugged me."

Allison continued to fiddle with Eve's hair. "I was in here alone when Roman carried you in. He said you were a present for me and that when you awoke, I was to teach you the ropes."

Eve shuddered at Allison's tone. The poor girl sounded so lost, so beaten down. God, how were the other women faring if Allison was so far gone? Were the others even alive anymore? If so, were their lives worth living?

"He told me there was a present for me as well when my shift ended," Max offered. "He said it was double the pleasure because I'd been such an invaluable employee the past week."

"Now what?" Allison asked.

"First of all," Eve started. "I need to see if I can even stand up. I have no idea what he gave me, but I feel like my arms and legs are detached from my body."

With the help of her newfound allies, Eve came to her feet. When the elegant room spun, Max's strong arms came around her.

"Easy now."

"Just give me a minute," Eve told him. "Once I get my bearings, I'll be fine."

After taking some major deep breaths, Eve stood straight up on her own. Her head still didn't feel quite right, but at least she didn't have an overwhelming sense of nausea anymore.

"Where is Roman now?" Eve asked.

Allison looked to Max for the answer.

"When he told me about my little surprise, he was on his way out. He stopped by the front gate and said he had some unfinished business to take care of with his brother."

The nausea came back full force, but Eve wouldn't allow nerves to override common sense.

"Do you have a cell phone?" Eve asked Max.

"Yeah." He dug it from his pocket and handed it to her. "What is it? You've gone pale."

Eve made her way back over to the lush canopy bed and sat down before her legs gave out on her. She punched in Nick's cell number and prayed.

"The brother Roman is referring to is the idiotic man I'm in love with."

ೞ

Nick kicked open Hank's office door. "Where the fuck is Eve?"

The manager of the gentlemen's club stood at his desk, filling boxes with forms, pens, paper clips, a stapler.

"Going somewhere?" Nick asked.

"I don't know where she is," Hank said as he continued to pack. "I swear. I don't know."

Nick pulled his Glock from the holster and aimed it at the lying scum. "Wrong answer. You have three seconds to tell me where she is."

"The back is clear," Grady said, coming in behind Nick. "She's not in the club."

Hank held his hands up. "I tried to tell him I didn't know where she was."

As always, Grady remained calm. "If you don't tell us where Roman and Eve are, I will have you arrested with enough charges that you will not get out of prison until you are at least three hundred years old."

Sweat stained the armpits of Hank's white dress shirt. "All I know is she came in here looking for Roman."

Nick stepped closer, wanting Hank to get a good look at the Glock. His finger itched to have a reason to pull the trigger.

"And?" Grady prompted.

"Um...Roman came in behind her."

Dread filled Nick's gut. His hair stood up on the back of his neck.

"What did that bastard do to her?" Nick demanded.

"He stuck her with some sort of syringe. I don't know what was in it, but she dropped to the floor."

Oh, God.

"Then what?" Grady asked. "Where did Roman take her?"

Hank's hands shook as he shrugged. "I assume to his house. He just picked her up and told me not to say anything until he called me."

Grady moved farther into the room. "Sit down," he ordered Hank.

The slimy creep sat in his creaky leather office chair. Grady whipped out a pair of cuffs from his pocket and slapped them around one of Hank's wrists. The other end went around the arm of the chair.

"The feds are on their way," Grady told him. "You can relay this story to them again. Only next time, you'll need to back up a year or so and tell them what Roman has been up to from the beginning with these dancers."

"I don't know anything," Hank insisted.

"Give me Roman's address," Nick ordered. "Now."

Hank rattled off the directions and the name of the road, but he wasn't quite sure on the house number.

"It has a gate with guards," Hank explained. "You can't get

in without a pass or an invitation."

"I'll get in," Nick promised as he looked to Grady.

"Go," Grady said. "I'll catch up. I want to make sure this guy gets in the proper hands before I leave."

Nick didn't wait for any further instructions. He couldn't get to Eve fast enough.

God, she'd been drugged. How would that affect her mind? Would she remember what had happened to her? If that sick pervert had put his hands on her in any way, Nick prayed she wouldn't remember.

He sped through the streets, not giving a damn how many lights he ran or laws he broke. He had to get to Eve.

Out of the corner of his eye, the red light on his cell phone caught his attention. He'd left it in the console when he'd pulled into the club.

He flipped it open to see he had a message.

"Nick," Eve's sweet voice came through the receiver. "I'm at Roman's estate. Allison Myers is here and so is Max Price. Max is posing as a guard at the gate and I'm on his cell phone. Roman drugged me and he's after you. You have to be careful, Nick. He said he had unfinished business to take care of. I lo—"

His voicemail cut her off...just before she could tell him she loved him. Thank God. She still loved him.

He wasn't afraid of Roman. If Roman wanted to settle the "unfinished business", then so be it. Nick felt like settling the score himself.

At least Eve would be protected with Max, a trained FBI agent. She would be safe until Nick could get to her... She had to be.

Finding the estate was no problem. The large, white two-story was surrounded by a concrete wall and tall, wrought-iron gate.

He pulled up to the gate and waited for a guard. A young man came out of the little guard's station and bent down to Nick's window.

"Can I help you, sir?"

"I'm here to see my brother," Nick said, as if he'd been there a hundred times before.

"Who is your brother?"

"Your boss," Nick gritted between his teeth.

"I'm sorry, sir, I don't have you on any list as a visitor today."

Just then a tall blond guy came jogging down the driveway. "It's okay," he called. "Let him in."

Max Price, Nick presumed.

"Sorry, sir," the young boy said. "Enjoy your visit."

The gate slid open and Nick pulled on up. The tall blond hopped in the passenger side.

"I'm Max," he said.

"I figured. I'm Nick."

"Roman's brother?"

"Stepbrother," Nick corrected. "Where's Eve?"

"I'll show you. Park here."

Nick stopped the car in front of the stone steps that led to the main entrance. A wide porch, bare of any furniture, stretched across the front of the house. The windows were all covered with blinds. The landscaping was cut to precision.

The house seemed cold, sterile.

Nick wanted Eve out of there. Now.

"Follow me," Max said as he stepped from the car.

Nick let Max lead him up the steps, through the impressive entryway equipped with a hanging chandelier that cost more than Nick made in a year.

The large, curved staircase looked like something from a movie set. Unfortunately, real life took place here.

At the top of the steps, the second floor looked like a hotel. Doors lined the long, narrow hallway.

Max went to the end of the hall where a guard stood outside the door. The guard eyed Nick, but Max motioned for the guard to unlock the door.

Nick nearly pushed Max out of the way the second the door opened. In the middle of a bedroom larger than his whole house, stood a leggy blonde with her arms wrapped around the most beautiful sight Nick had ever seen.

"Eve," he said.

She pulled out of the blond woman's arms—he assumed this was Allison.

Nick stepped toward her, thankful when she fell into his arms. Her warm breath on his neck sent comforting shivers all through him.

"Are you all right?" he asked as he buried his face into her mass of red curls.

"I'm fine." She pulled back, placing her small hands on either side of his face. "Are you okay? Have you seen Roman?"

Nick shook his head. "No. I saw Hank, he told me how to get here. He's being arrested as we speak."

Eve closed her eyes. "Where's Roman?"

"Right here."

Max, Allison, Nick and Eve all turned to the doorway. Roman stood with a gun pointed at Nick.

"Sorry to break up this touching moment," Roman said. "But I've got some business with my brother."

Instinctively, Eve stepped in front of Nick. "It's over, Roman. The FBI are on their way and you're going to jail for a long, long time."

His evil laughter filled the room. "Oh, Eve. I don't think so. You see, I'm too smart for them. I always have been. Your old man, though, he was almost as smart as me."

Nick placed his hands on Eve's shoulders, intending to get her out of the way. Unfortunately, she shrugged him off.

"So you killed him?" Eve asked.

Roman shrugged. "What else could I do? He got in the way, just like the four of you are now in my way."

"Roman," Max said, stepping forward. "You won't get away with this. There's four of us and one of you. Besides, do you know the consequences of killing two federal agents?"

Two?

"Ahh, that's right," Roman said, smiling at Nick's surprised look. "You didn't know the girl you were fucking was really a fed, did you?"

"Shut up, Roman," Eve ordered. "It doesn't matter. You're

not going to kill anybody."

"Eve?" Nick asked.

She looked over her shoulder. One glance in her eyes and Nick knew Roman told the truth. She was a fed. He'd been protecting a damn fed.

"You lied," he whispered, shocked.

"I had to."

Eve looked back to Roman. "Put that down before you do something that will only add to your prison time."

"I'm not going to prison, Eve. I'll die first."

"That's fine, too," she said. "Just tell us where the other girls are before you kill yourself."

"I'm not going down without taking you all with me."

Nick heard the shot, saw Eve jerk.

Then she fell to the ground.

Chapter Fifteen

Nick went for his own gun.

"Don't even try it," Roman warned. "Do you want to die, too?"

Nick risked a look at Eve. Blood poured from her shoulder—at least, he hoped the shot had only hit her shoulder. This whole ordeal had turned into a fucking nightmare. A never-ending nightmare that had evolved into reality.

"If she's dead, I'll kill you," Nick promised.

"Cut the hero act, little brother," Roman said. "You won't kill me. You're too worried about your little lying bitch. Threw you for a loop when you found out she was a fed, didn't it?"

Nick still couldn't believe it, but he couldn't dwell on that now. Eve's time dwindled with each passing second.

He glanced back to Max, who had Allison tucked safely behind him. Something Nick should've done when Eve jumped in front of him. She'd saved his life, but at what cost? Her own? It wasn't worth it... Not if he had to live without her.

"Take your weapon out slowly," Roman said.

Nick looked back to him and laughed. "I'm not that stupid."

"Take it out and put it on the floor or join your girlfriend."

He would be of no use with a bullet wound, so he did as Roman asked. He could only pray Grady and his team were on the way.

Relying on others to save the day wasn't quite what he'd had in mind, but at this point he'd do anything to save Eve's life.

"Kick it away from you," Roman said.

Nick smiled as he kicked it back toward Max, who laughed. "Thanks, Nick," Max said. "I wasn't allowed in here with Allison with my gun."

"Now I'm glad that rule was enforced," Roman replied. "Come here, Allison."

"No," Max answered. "She's not moving."

Roman aimed his gun at Max. "If she doesn't want anybody else shot, she will."

"It's okay, Max," Allison said, her voice trembling.

She moved from behind Max and cautiously made her way to Roman. How had this angelic-looking woman gotten mixed up with this mess?

Once she was within reaching distance, Roman grabbed her by the arm and hauled her against him. She winced when he put one arm around her waist and shoved the gun beneath her chin.

"If either one of you guys tries to play hero, I'll kill her, too."

Nick felt so fucking helpless, he didn't know what to do. This was precisely the reason he'd quit after Roger.

"If you kill her, too, you won't have a shield," Nick reminded Roman.

"You may be able to get off one shot, but one of us will get you," Max said. "You might as well turn her loose. I guarantee if you shoot her, you will die."

Roman snaked his hand up to Allison's breasts. A tear slid down her cheek as she looked away.

"I don't want to kill her," he said. "She's been the best. I could get so much money for her. Now I'll have to keep her. But that's okay, we have fun, don't we?"

When Allison didn't answer, Roman squeezed her breast harder. "Y-yes."

"Drop the gun, Burke."

Grady stood directly behind Roman with a gun pointed at his head.

Relief flooded through Nick. Finally, the backup they needed to get Eve the hell out of here.

"Sorry I had to hurt Eve," Roman said. "I was so looking

forward to having her."

Rage poured through Nick. "You tried to blow her up."

Roman's brows lifted. "I did no such thing."

The obvious shock and confusion had Nick believing this criminal, but something about his reaction had him thinking. If Roman hadn't planted the bombs, who had? Someone who knew every move he and Eve had made. Someone who knew where the safe house was. Someone they trusted with their lives.

"It's been bugging me all this time," Nick said. "Why would you try to blow her up, if you wanted to lure her in? It didn't make sense. But no one else knew where we were, except..."

Nick's gaze went to Grady. Suddenly Nick saw his "friend" in a whole new light. Instead of the hard-ass FBI leader, he saw something else. Something sinister.

"You."

The man merely shrugged, still aiming his gun at the back of Roman's head. "Nick, don't be absurd. I'd never try to kill you or Eve."

Nick's blood boiled as he continued to glare at his "friend". "That guy who came after me and stabbed me in the parking lot—that was after I'd just told you where we were. All the time you put us together, played us off each other—and you were trying to kill us both."

Grady's eyes hardened. His grip on the gun tightened. "The two of you were getting too close to the truth."

Nick knew a gunshot didn't hurt as bad as betrayal. "What truth?"

"I like women." He shrugged. "Women I can choose to be mine and they have no choice in the matter."

Roman let out a sinister laugh. "So, you're my secret buyer?"

Grady nodded, sending even more disgust through Nick. How the hell had this happened? And why hadn't he figured everything out before Eve was shot?

"Through a middleman, I bought some of the strippers," Grady said. "Nobody had a clue, not even Roger, but when Eve kept digging, I knew she was too good not to find me out."

Roman stepped to the side, pulling a petrified Allison with him in his grasp, the gun still under her chin. "So you're the one," he muttered. "I knew I had a buyer that wanted to remain anonymous. You got some good ones, I'll give you that."

Disgust rolled through Nick's stomach. He didn't have time for the hurt and anger, not when Eve might be dead. "You're no better than this bastard," he said to Grady. "You'd kill an innocent woman who *trusted* you just so you could continue this sick, twisted game?"

A hint of remorse crossed Grady's face and that's when Nick knew, this wasn't the man he'd gone through the Marines with. This wasn't the same man Eve trusted with her life—ironically, the man who'd tried to end her life.

If Eve did indeed live through this, the realization of Grady's dealings would kill her.

"If you're going to shoot Roman, do it," Max told Grady. "Personally, I'd like for all of us to step out and let the two of you kill each other."

"Nobody's leaving," Roman assured them. "Especially now that I have someone in my corner. After all, Grady wouldn't want anything to happen to me. Where would he get such amazing women who will fulfill his every desire?"

"Actually," Grady piped in. "I have nothing to lose now, so killing you doesn't much matter."

Grady's safety clicked off, then all hell broke loose.

Everything happened so fast, Nick had to react quickly. Roman whirled around, loosing his grip on Allison. Max grabbed for her just as Roman pointed his gun at Grady. Nick lunged for Eve, shielding her with his body.

He didn't want her hit again—dead or not.

Another shot blasted through the room. From the corner of his eye, Nick saw Roman slump to the floor.

"Get help in here. Eve's bleeding to death," Nick yelled to anyone and everyone.

Max pulled his radio from his pocket. "Agent down. Repeat, agent down. Get an ambulance here. Now!"

"Don't move her, Nick."

"Don't you fucking move," Nick shouted over his shoulder.

"Max—"

"I've got him," the other agent assured. "How's she doing?"

"Fine, she's fine." *She has to be.*

Nick heard Grady pleading to Max just to kill him and be done with it. Voices flittered about the room, but Nick felt like he was in a dream. The room seemed so hazy, all the voices jumbled together to make a low, whining noise.

All he saw was Eve lying in a pool of her own blood.

Just like her father.

Nick remained by her side on the floor. He moved her hair away from her face and continued to stroke it until the EMTs came through the door.

"Sir, we need to work on her," one of them said.

Reluctantly, Nick stood up and backed away. He forced his tears to hold on until he knew for sure the outcome. Eve wouldn't want him crying over her.

Max placed a hand on Nick's shoulder. "She's a fighter. She'll be fine."

Nick only nodded. The lump in his throat wouldn't allow him to speak.

"Do you want a ride to the hospital?"

"Yeah," he croaked out.

"Nick," Grady said as a federal agent placed him in handcuffs. "This wasn't personal. It was all about the money. I'm sorry you got caught in the middle."

All the anger, all the emotions from the last two weeks spread through Nick like wildfire and before he thought twice, his fist connected with the side of Grady's jaw.

"I don't give a shit about your pathetic apologies. You make me sick."

Nick took one last look at his brother. Roman's sleek white silk suit, now stained with his blood.

If anything happened to Eve, Roman would never be dead enough and Grady wouldn't serve enough time behind bars. Nick turned away, unable to look at the monster who'd started this whole mess and the monster who'd had a hand in the end.

Fate wouldn't be that cruel. It couldn't be. He'd failed

protecting someone he cared about, again. If something happened to her...

"Give me a second, will you?" Max asked.

"I'll meet you in the car."

Like a zombie, Nick watched the EMTs load Eve onto a stretcher, hook up an IV and take her from the room.

She had to live. They had a life to live. Together.

Oh, God. The baby. What about the fact they might have created a life?

Nick didn't know if his heart could take any more pain. He hadn't realized how much he wanted a baby with Eve. Their baby. A baby they'd made in love.

☙

Allison stood in the center of the room, unable to take in all the activity around her.

Roman had died. Eve might be dying. And this Grady person was not such a good guy after all. Feds were asking questions she didn't know how to answer and all she knew was that she was finally free.

"Allison," Max called from across the room.

She glanced to the female agent who'd been taking her statement. "Excuse me."

Max stood with his arms crossed over his massive chest as Allison made her way to him. Now that the nightmare had come to an end, she wouldn't see him anymore. And as stupid as it sounded, she'd miss his daily visits.

"Are you okay?" he asked.

She nodded. "It's over."

"Yeah. You're free to go outside this room."

Terror filled her. "That's all I've wanted for nearly three months, but now I don't know where I'll go or what I'll do."

"Can you go to your sister's house?"

Allison dropped her eyes to the freshly blood-stained carpet. "I'm ashamed."

"Of what?"

Her eyes snapped back up. "Of everything. Of what I am, what I did, what was done to me."

"It's not your fault," he said with conviction.

"Then whose is it?" she cried. "I take full responsibility for what has happened. I can't go back home. I won't bring that kind of embarrassment to my family."

When Max's stare became too much to take, she looked away. "You'd better get going. Nick's waiting on you."

"Allison."

She looked back to see his face one last time. "Yes?"

"You're an amazing woman. You deserve a good life, and I know your family would help you."

He didn't know her family, obviously. "We'll see. Thank you for saving my life."

Max reached out, cupped the side of her face. "It was my pleasure."

As Allison watched him go, she knew she'd met possibly the most amazing *straight* man ever.

෴

Nick roamed aimlessly through Eve's apartment. Now that he knew her, the real Eve, he looked at the rooms in a whole new light.

The walls were bare because she hadn't planned on staying or getting attached. There were no little knick-knacks sitting around. Plain, simple, straightforward.

Just like Eve.

Nick plopped down on the sofa, grabbed the throw and held it up to his face. With his eyes closed, he imagined Eve wrapped in this afghan as she'd held it as a shield. She'd been so angry, so scared; she'd held her gun on him.

Now he knew better. She never would've shot him.

Shot. Oh, God. Nick buried his head in the throw, inhaled Eve's sweet floral scent and finally lost it.

He cried like he'd never cried before. What if he lost her? Would she ever know how sorry he'd been for lying to her, even if only to protect her?

Right now Eve lay unconscious in surgery. Nick had ridden to the hospital with Max to find that Eve had been taken into emergency surgery. He took a cab to Eve's apartment, needing to feel close to her.

And because he couldn't bear to be at the hospital if the doctor came out with a grim look on his face.

Nick dried his face with the throw Eve had worn over her naked body only weeks ago and tossed it on the back of the couch. On wobbly legs, he made his way down the short, narrow hall to her bedroom.

He stood in the doorway, taking in all the mess. Clothes were strewn about everywhere, the bed was unmade, a corner of the fitted sheet had popped loose and her nightstand drawer was open. A smile formed on his lips.

He'd gotten used to her messes. Her men's boxers lying around, dainty shoes he always seemed to trip over.

Because he needed to do something, he started in the doorway and picked up each article of clothing one at a time. Everything he picked up felt so small, so soft, and smelled like jasmine.

Just like Eve.

"I thought I'd find you here."

Nick turned at Max's voice.

"How did you know where I'd be?" Nick asked.

Max shrugged. "I knew if you weren't pacing the hospital, you'd want to be somewhere you felt equally as close to her. It didn't take long to find her address from some of my co-workers. Grady was arrested, but claimed he wanted to talk to you."

Nick snorted as he continued his trip through Eve's room.

"We found the location of the other women, thanks to him," Max went on. "I suppose he thinks he'll get off easier if he gives up some information."

Nick looked away, went back to picking up one garment at a time. "At least we can get the other ladies back," he mumbled.

"Wasn't one of them your sister?"

"Yeah. I'm waiting on a call when the agents pick her up." Max waited a beat. "Aren't you going to ask about Eve?"

Nick froze with his hand on a gray tank. "I don't want to hear it if it's bad."

"She's out of surgery."

Nick jerked upright and faced Max. "And?"

God, his whole body cringed. He didn't want to hear those words. He didn't want to know her heart would never beat again. He didn't want to live without her beautiful smile and smart mouth.

"She lost a lot of blood, but she pulled through."

Nick sank to the floor, right on a pile of dirty laundry. "Thank you."

Max crossed over to Nick, squatted down to his level. "Now, do you want to tell me why you're picking up her dirty clothes instead of holding a vigil by her bedside?"

"I couldn't be there," Nick choked out.

"Nick, she's fine. Don't you think she'd want you there?"

"It's my fault she's there."

"Bullshit."

He looked into Max's angry face. "If she hadn't been standing in front of me, I would've taken that bullet."

"You're lucky the bullet didn't go on through her, or you would've been hit, too," Max stated.

"Yeah, lucky."

"Get up off your sorry ass and get down there. I don't know Eve well at all, but I'd say she won't put up with a whiny man."

A corner of Nick's mouth twitched. "Yes, sir."

As Nick came to his feet, Max straightened as well. "One more thing."

"What's that?"

"Don't be upset with Eve for not telling you she worked for the feds."

Nick swallowed the lump in his throat. "Right now, I don't care what she does. I'm just glad she's alive."

"Tell her that."

Nick didn't wait for another word, he ran from Eve's apartment. He had to see her, touch her, smell her. He wanted to see for himself she was alive. He wanted to see her smile up at him again.

Just as Nick hailed a cab, Max stepped beside him. "I'll drive you."

⁂

Eve stared at the plain white walls, the plain white blanket on her bed, the plain white floor. Anything to keep from thinking about Nick.

She'd lied to him. Even after she'd berated him for lying to her, she'd still kept the truth from him.

No wonder he wasn't here.

Tears burned in her eyes. Since no one could see, she allowed them to fall.

Max and a whole slew of federal agents from South Carolina had been to visit.

But not Nick.

Eve used one hand to pull the blanket up further. Her shoulder hurt like a bitch and she hated she wouldn't be able to use it for a long time.

Months of therapy, the doctor had said. If she didn't baby it, she would never return to the field again.

Did it matter anymore? Without Nick, did it matter what she did with her life?

Eve closed her eyes as the tears continued to fall. She couldn't control them now if she wanted to. All the memories came flooding back to her.

The first time she'd seen him in the reflection of her vanity mirror. The first time he'd kissed her with such passion and need.

The first time they'd made love.

Would she ever get the feeling of his touch off her? Was she forever dammed?

No one would ever compare to Nick—she wouldn't even try. He'd set the bar so high, she knew she would never find someone like that again. Someone who loved her, who showed her with not just words, but actions.

Her whole body ached and it had nothing to do with getting shot. Nick had touched a part so deep within, she didn't know if the void would ever be filled.

Eve's eyes flew open when someone touched her hand.

No, not someone. Nick.

"Are you hurting?" he said, his voice thick.

Eve nodded, but said nothing.

"Do you want me to get the nurse?"

Eve wiped her tears with her other hand. "She can't do anything for me."

Nick stood silent. Eve wanted to know what went through his mind... At one time she would've known.

"I heard about Grady," she croaked out. "I'm sorry."

"Sorry? Why are you sorry?"

She stared at his strong, solid hand covering her own. "Because he was your friend and you trusted him."

"What about you?" Nick countered. "You trusted him as well."

"Yeah, I did. I can't believe he would get involved in such a heinous crime."

"He'll pay for what he did," Nick promised.

"Will they ever find the other women?" she asked.

"Grady confessed what he knew and the rest of the information was confiscated from Roman's estate. They're being picked up as we speak."

Eve sighed with relief. At least one good thing had come from this.

"I'm sorry," he whispered.

Eve studied his worn face. Red-rimmed eyes, puffy lids, thin lips. He'd been crying.

"Why?" she asked.

He looked to her bandaged shoulder. "You were hurt

because of my negligence."

"I was hurt because Roman shot me," she corrected.

"You never would've run if I hadn't lied to you about your father."

Eve tried to sit up, but a sharp pain pierced her left shoulder. "Dammit."

"Don't move," Nick said. "Please. I don't want you to hurt anymore."

The sincerity of his voice brought more tears to her eyes. "I'm fine. It's going to hurt, but I'll be fine."

"God, Eve." Tears started running down his cheeks. "I thought you were dead."

He practically collapsed onto her. His head rested on her stomach as he broke.

Eve stroked his thick, dark hair and let him cry. Nobody had ever cried for her before. But then, nobody had ever loved her like Nick.

"I'm sorry I didn't protect you," he muttered. "I let you down, just like I let down your father."

"Nick, look at me."

He lifted his head and wiped his face.

"You didn't let me down and you didn't let my father down." Eve cupped his cheek with one hand. "If it weren't for your help, I might have never gotten this far on my own. I needed you and you were there for me."

"You got hurt," he stated.

"Yes, I did, but I've been hurt before and I'm sure I'll get hurt again."

Nick blinked in confusion. "You're going back to work in the field?"

"Is that a problem?" she asked.

"Will your shoulder be okay for that kind of work?"

Eve shrugged her one good shoulder. "In time. I have to go through extensive therapy, but I'm determined to get back to my life."

Nick lifted his body off hers. He stepped back, shoved his hands in his pockets and nodded. "Back in Virginia."

His retreat should have frightened her, but it didn't. If he didn't care for her, he wouldn't have come to her room—wouldn't have broken down.

"Yes, back in Virginia."

"Well, I'm sure the agency will make sure you get the best care."

"What about you?" she asked, heart pounding.

His brows drew together. "Me?"

"What will you do?"

"I guess I'll go home."

"Where's home?"

"Not far from here," he said.

His vague answer didn't give her much to go on. She laughed.

"What's so funny?" he asked.

"After all we've shared and been through, I have no idea where you live."

"I live on the northern coast of North Carolina. It's a small town. Quiet."

"Sounds nice," Eve said honestly. "The doctor suggested I recuperate in a quiet place with no stress."

Nick remained silent—causing Eve's nerves to go on alert. Maybe she'd mistaken his concern for something more. Maybe the love he'd professed had dissolved when he found out her real identity?

"I don't blame you for being angry with me," she whispered. "I don't blame you for wanting to get back home, put this mission behind you. Put me behind you."

Eve picked at the lint balls on the bleached white cotton blanket. She didn't want to see the confirmation in his eyes. By this time tomorrow, he could be gone.

Forever.

"You're right," he said. "I can't wait to put this mission behind me."

The ache in her heart overrode any pain she had in her shoulder. "Well, I hope you're able to do that."

"I want to put every part of this fucked-up op in the past," he added.

Including her, she thought.

Nick sat on the edge of her bed, looked her in the eyes. "I want to forget the point where I screwed up and put you in the direct line of danger. I want to forget I let you down when you trusted me. But most of all, I want to forget how I felt when I thought you'd died right in front of me."

"Nick—"

He took her hands in his. "Wait, let me finish."

With a gentle squeeze to his warm, firm hands, she nodded. "Okay."

"I don't ever want to go through anything like that again. I don't want you to, either. I can't live through another scare like that, Eve."

"I understand," she said softly. "It's okay if you walk away right now. After what happened with my father and with me, I don't blame you for leaving. But I don't want you to leave blaming yourself."

Nick sighed, looking down at their adjoined hands. "I will blame myself until I die, but I don't want to leave right now."

"You don't?" Hope sprang back into her heart.

He shook his head. "I love you, Eve. That may be selfish of me and right now I don't give a shit. I love you more than I've ever loved another human being in my life. If you want me out of your life, then you're going to have to throw me out."

"Kiss me," she said when he'd stopped long enough to take a breath.

"What?"

"You heard me. Shut up and kiss me."

Nick leaned forward, careful of her shoulder, and touched his lips ever so lightly to hers. Eve brought up her other hand, wrapped it around his neck and pulled him closer.

When his mouth opened, Eve took control. She tasted him, savored him. She wanted him to know how she felt.

"I love you, too, Nick," she whispered against his mouth. "I don't want you to leave unless I'm with you."

Their foreheads rested on each others'. Their breathing

came in soft pants. Their eyes expressed nothing but love.

"I wasn't going to go anywhere without you," he told her.

"Really? What if I'd thrown you out of here?"

Nick smiled. "I would have waited out in the lobby. I can't live without you, Eve. I don't even want to try."

"Where do you want to go from here?"

Nick kissed the tip of her nose. "I don't care if we're at my house in North Carolina or yours in Virginia. I just want to be with you."

"I want to stay with the Bureau."

Nick sighed. "Eve, I don't care where you work. If you're happy and you're with me, that's all I ask. But if you're pregnant, will you consider taking a leave of absence for a while?"

Eve nodded. "What will you do? Will you still want to be hired out as a bodyguard?"

"Nah. I don't have to work a day in my life, if I choose not to—and neither do you."

Eve blinked. "Excuse me?"

"I'm loaded. My grandparents passed about five years ago and left me quite a nice sum of money, since I was the only grandchild."

"That explains why you weren't upset when your forty-thousand-dollar car exploded."

Nick laughed. "Actually, I'm still sick about it, but I'm learning there are more important things in life than cars."

"Oh, yeah. Like what?"

Nick leaned down and captured her mouth.

She had all the answer she needed.

About the Author

Sophia Rae has been escaping reality and writing steamy romance for several years. She's thrilled to have found such a rewarding career and attributes all her success to her fans, who she loves to hear from.

When she's not creating yummy heroes and strong heroines, she cares for her children, her husband and her Beagle/St. Bernard mix. Life is never dull in her hectic household.

To learn more about Sophia Rae, please send an email to her at sophiarae@falcon1.net, or snail mail her at PO Box 396, Minford, OH, 45653. She's happy to answer any questions or just chat about books!

*Winning the lottery changes her life forever...
in more ways than one.*

Fortune's Deception
© *2008 Karen Erickson*
Book 1 of the Fortune series.

One minute Brittney Jones is living paycheck to paycheck, and the next she and three friends win a record-breaking lottery jackpot. Sure, she's spent some money on herself—after her rough childhood, she figures she deserves a few indulgences, big and small.

To financial advisor Charlie Manning, his client Brittney is a shallow beauty out to spend all of her money. He thinks she should rein it in. She thinks he should loosen up, and resolves to help him do just that—in a very naughty way.

The passion between them burns hot and fast, and Charlie comes to realize Brittney's heart is as big as her newly fattened bank account. She's not only smart, but beautiful and sexy. And he can't resist her.

Still, Charlie is aware that Brittney's keeping secrets from him. If only she would trust him enough to tell the truth!

Available now in ebook and print from Samhain Publishing.

Enjoy the following excerpt from Fortune's Deception...

Brittney was going to turn him away. She had to.

With a sigh, she threw her brush into the sink and pulled her hair into a high ponytail. No reason getting glammed up if she was going to spend the night alone. She'd realized the minute she walked out of his office she had to do this, sever all sexual ties with her *financial planner*. She should've never done it with him in the first place, and she'd made more than her share of mistakes in her life.

Then he called her at six, his voice so sexy, a little gruff as he spoke. When he asked if he could come over, she didn't even hesitate with her answer. Just hearing him talk made her sex weep with moisture, caused her nipples to stiffen into tight little aching buds.

She'd hung up the phone and known immediately she'd made a mistake. No way could he come over to her house and essentially fuck her brains out. She didn't want to lead him on, didn't want him to think she could offer him something more. Relationships were not a part of her life, they never had been. She didn't do consecutive dating, didn't do any of that stuff. She had no idea *how* to do any of it.

Of course, what she and Charlie had certainly couldn't be called *dating*. That description was downright laughable. No, one illicit encounter in his office did not constitute dating, but she had a feeling he was a serious kind of guy.

She didn't care to stick around long enough to have someone hurt her, because that's what always happened. Nothing could last forever. She'd suffered enough through her entire childhood, taking blow after emotional blow when she'd been young and had no defenses. All of it had been so painful, so heartbreaking. Never, ever again would she put herself through something like that willingly.

Could she recall one serious boyfriend throughout her entire string of so-called relationships? Not really. She was the good-time girl, the one guys liked to hang out with, the one they liked to bang, especially because she was no-strings. No fuss, no muss, just fun.

Mister Number Cruncher Charles Manning probably didn't even know the meaning of no fuss, no muss. He was probably intent on finding a woman ready to settle down with, looking for a relationship. He reeked of commitment. His cologne was probably named Commitment.

That was *so* not her style.

The doorbell rang and she ran her hands down the front of her cotton tank dress, her palms suddenly sweaty. She hated having to turn him away, didn't want to see the disappointment in his eyes, on his face, but it had to be done. One minor encounter with the man and already she was in over her head. She couldn't imagine how an actual sweaty mattress session with him would make her feel.

Be strong. She lifted her chin, straightened her posture and walked with determined steps to the door.

All thoughts of being strong and dumping his sexy ass flew right out the door with her first sight of him on her front porch. Her jaw dropped open in surprise, her mouth going dry. He looked deliciously sexy with his hands stuffed in the front pockets of worn jeans, a black T-shirt stretched tight across his broad chest. He smiled at her, dimples flashing, brown eyes filled with sexual heat behind the wire frames of his glasses. Her heart skipped a beat and her entire body roared to life, eager for his touch.

Just one more time, what can it hurt? She could take it, she thought as she grabbed his hand and yanked him inside, kicking the door shut behind him. She pushed his big body against the door, flattened herself against him and pulled his head down.

"Nice to see you, too," he murmured just before her lips captured his.

They kissed long and slow, wonderful lazy kisses. His tongue traced the outline of her lips and she opened her mouth to him, her tongue dancing with his. His hands slid up and down her sides, dragging her dress up with every pass until they slipped underneath, cupping her panty-clad ass.

She moaned into his mouth and pressed against him, unable to help herself. He got the message, lifting her, and she wrapped her legs around him.

"You're strong," she said, peppering tiny kisses all over his face, darting her tongue out to lick his skin.

"You're light." His dark hair rubbed against her face as he moved down to kiss her neck, nibbling the sensitive flesh.

A shiver consumed her when his teeth hit an extra touchy spot. "You're sweet but I'm not that light."

After they'd won the lottery, she'd been on a non-stop eating binge at the finest restaurants she could find. She had to be packing at least an extra ten pounds since she'd started.

"Mmm, you smell good. Taste good." His lips were soft as they cruised up her neck, skimmed her jaw before finally settling on her mouth. He drank from her, his mouth languid, his tongue teasing and she clutched at him, sank her hands in his hair to keep him there, right where she wanted him.

Oh, the man could kiss. She could do this all night. So slow, so soft, utterly decadent. His tongue searched her mouth, wet and warm and tasting faintly of mint. She tunneled her hands into his silky hair, the dark strands wrapping around her fingers and she undulated against him, wanting more. His erection brushed against her, huge and urgent and her nipples hardened to almost painful points.

"Take me to my bedroom," she whispered against his mouth, licking at his lips.

He lifted his head, glanced around. "Hell, where is it? Your house is huge. How much did you pay for this monstrosity again?"

Brittney tugged on his hair, making him yelp. "You should know and besides, there will be no talk of financial matters tonight, please. You need to focus on the task at hand."

"Which is?" He smiled, dimples flashing again and her tummy fluttered at the sight of them.

She could look at those cute, sexy dimples over and over and never tire of it.

hot stuff

Discover Samhain!

THE HOTTEST NEW PUBLISHER ON THE PLANET

Romance, fantasy, mystery, thriller, mainstream and more—Samhain has more selection, hotter authors, and everything's available in both ebook and print.

Pick your favorite, sit back, and enjoy the ride!
Hot stuff indeed.

Samhain Publishing Ltd

WWW.SAMHAINPUBLISHING.COM

GREAT CHEAP FUN

Discover eBooks!

THE FASTEST WAY TO GET THE HOTTEST NAMES

Get your favorite authors on your favorite reader, long before they're out in print! Ebooks from Samhain go wherever you go, and work with whatever you carry—Palm, PDF, Mobi, and more.

Samhain Publishing Ltd

WWW.SAMHAINPUBLISHING.COM

Printed in the United States
135589LV00004B/32/P